The Margaret Ellen

R.C. Burdick

PublishAmerica
Baltimore

First printing

ISBN: 1-4137-2768-9
PUBLISHED BY PUBLISHAMERICA, LLLP
www.publishamerica.com
Baltimore

Printed in the United States of America

DEDICATION

For my dearest ones for their love and support:
Sharon, Cheryl, Steve, Lindsey, Ken, Ruby,
and Margaret Ellen for her most precious gift.

CHAPTER 1

Anne Murray's voice filled the cabin as I slipped into my deck shoes and ambled to the galley to top off my coffee cup. It was a lovely Monday morning; the torrential rain of the past two days was gone; and, like Anne, I could see clearly now. In fact, the truth in a long-ignored adage was also abundantly clear.

"When you find yourself in a hole, quit digging."

Actually, I was in over my head, so it made good sense to reverse the decisions that had gotten me into a hole in the first place. I'd do it, but another problem loomed, one requiring immediate attention: my lack of money. I finished my coffee, flipped off the CD player, and hurried up the companionway. Yes, it was going to be a bright sunshiny day.

The first stop in my financial quest was the office of World Wide Insurance where I picked up a finder's fee for a stolen yacht I'd located three months earlier. Next, from ten until noon, I worked the counter at Big Al's Pawn and Bond.

The combined compensation, thirty bucks from Al and three hundred from World Wide, wasn't cause for celebration. No. The pittance served only as additional reflection on the mess I'd gotten myself into.

Yes, it was time to quit digging.

The cash from Al went into my purse and the finder's fee into my depleted checking account. Then, before returning to *Bonita*, the thirty-four-foot sloop I called home, I picked up groceries for an overnight cruise. Reversing the decisions that had caused my problems would require some bridge work. One bridge, the one I dearly loved, was past due for repair; the other, quite simply, was past due for burning. Sailing to one of the nearby islands for the night would give me the time and isolation needed to work out a plan.

After boarding *Bonita* I started another pot of coffee and began stowing gear. Then, just minutes before hoisting sail and getting underway, something smacked the starboard hull. A chill swept me as I waited for the next shoe to drop. Moments later I heard fish flopping on the aft deck. My newfound resolve was in trouble.

The Avon lady arrives with the well-known sound of *ding-dong*. With Angus Loman the *ding* of his arrival is his mullet boat, *Mud Flats*, whacking against my sloop. The *dong* is his catch-of-the-day or latest beach-combing treasure hitting the deck. Pretending not to be aboard wasn't an option. I topped off my coffee cup, took a deep breath, and started up the companionway to survey the offering.

At six-four, Angus is tall; with a tan matching his wavy, deep-brown hair, he's dark; but with pothole-size dimples, he's boy-scout cute, not leading-man handsome. Even so he has a captivating aura, one that snared me the first moment I saw him. We've been lovers for a while, despite warnings from family and friends.

Enter the bridge I knew I should burn.

I stepped into the cockpit and sipped coffee as Angus looped his bow line over my sloop's stern bollard. He wore his usual frayed and faded jeans, cutoff to knee length, and a pair of shabby sneakers fitted with orange fishing line as laces. The sea breeze fanned the errant locks at his temples and beads of sweat glistened from within the forest of dark hair covering his expansive chest. More troubling, however, was the sight of him quickened my pulse.

I forced my eyes to the stringer of sheepshead covering most of the stern-locker hatch. Then, while silently studying the offering, the inner voice responsible for the bulk of my woes whispered that a lovely Monday afternoon was not the best time to burn a bridge. Tampa Bay teemed with a variety of fish, but I believed no other one compared with the succulent taste of sheepshead. My smile was part of the payment he sought, but, even so, my words were cool. "Nice fish," I said. "Coffee?"

When he had *Mud Flats* safely tethered, he looked up and grinned. Angus has a sexy grin. He kicked some empty beer cans aside, straddled the boat's bait well for balance, and waved one hand skyward like a salesman pounding home his spiel about a gorgeous product. "Naw," he said, "look at that sky. Let's check out Hangman's Key."

A tingle raced between my shoulder blades. *Hangman's Key? Was he a mind reader? No. No way. He couldn't know I'd planned to anchor there for the night—to devise a plan to end our relationship.*

Hangman's Key, a deserted island located among a scattering of smaller ones near the mouth of Tampa Bay, was a gorgeous, mile-long strip of white sand, sea oats, and Australian pines. Lending to its allure, local rumor spoke to the roving pirate bands that had once used the island as a cache site for plundered booty. And while the thought of buried treasure was captivating,

I'd long loved the island for other reasons, especially its seclusion.

While I was still caught up in thought, he added, "Come on, Seaweed. Grab your gear. Let's have some fun."

The offer was tempting, and I loved the sexy, mellow tone he used when he said my nickname. And there was no time clock waiting to be punched. Even so, with my freshly set goal of reversing some bad decisions, I knew I shouldn't be beachcombing; I should be looking for moneymaking employment, or, preferably, mending the bridge that would get my old job back. After all, it had been my having fun while ignoring responsibility that had gotten me to this unwanted point in my life in the first place. This was my mental argument as I stared at Angus. Unfortunately, I was still weighing duty of life against desires of my soul when he lifted the lid on the ice chest. My eyes widened. "Blue crabs!"

To seal my acceptance of the offer he held up a pair of huge crab claws. "Cooked in Gambino's special crab-boil mix," he said.

I loved crab claws, and Gambino, a bartender at the Rudder Bar and Grill on Gulf Boulevard, made a world-class mix. Despite knowing better, I was softening. "So what's under the ice?"

Turning his eyes away, he mumbled, "Twelve-pack of Bud."

Bad answer. This cost him some points. I tapped the toes of one foot.

He looked up and his sexy grin slid back into place. "And some Diet Pepsi," he added.

That cinched it. Regardless, I wasn't going anywhere in a twenty-two-foot, flat-bottomed, garbage scow. Mullet boats were designed as workboats, not pleasure boats, although one might be used for pleasure in a pinch. Not so with *Mud Flats*. With its array of odds and ends heaped to the gunnels, the vessel looked like a floating flea market. Actually, I'd never been sure how Angus used the boat at all.

This was no problem, however, as I had better transportation available. "Put the ice chest and two of your fuel tanks in *Skipjack*. I'll grab my gear." I started back down the companionway speaking over my shoulder. "And clean those fish while you're at it."

I keep my sloop, *Bonita*, and Dad's Boston Whaler, *Skipjack*, berthed at the Buttonwood Apartments, a seven-story complex fronting the Intracoastal Waterway just north of Tampa Bay. Angus owns the building and lives alone in the penthouse suite. He'd like to change that, the alone part. We've had a few scraps over the subject.

I returned to the cabin, peeled off my street clothes, and slipped into a soft-blue bikini. Blue is Angus's favorite color. I found my backpack under the chart table seat, still holding beach towels, a tube of sun block, and a pair of plastic sandals I'd worn on our last outing. I added a bottle of hot sauce and a box of saltine crackers and zipped the pack shut.

What about the hatches? A frontal system had swept across Tampa Bay over the weekend, and while the first days after such a passage held little chance of rain, predicting Florida weather was a coin toss at best. Gambling was foolish, so I dropped and dogged the hatches, grabbed my sunglasses and wide-brimmed hat, and scooted up the companionway.

With *Mud Flats* back in its slip and Dad's Whaler tied alongside my sloop, Angus was bent over the fish-cleaning table he'd built at the end of the dock. I lowered the backpack into the Whaler and jumped across to where he was standing to lend a hand. While filleting and washing the last piece of fish, I formulated my evening's resolutions. Watching sunset from *Bonita's* cockpit while dining on fried sheepshead and hush puppies would lead the action; then I would kick procrastination's butt and summon the courage to burn a bridge.

Over smooth water it's a thirty-minute run from the Buttonwood Apartments to Hangman's Key. Compliments of a brisk sea breeze still lingering behind the weekend frontal passage, a moderate chop ruled the inland waters. *Skipjack* needed forty minutes to reach our favorite, lee-side anchorage.

In the next hour we decimated the blue crabs, Angus dented the beer supply, and I polished off a Pepsi. It's not that I don't love beer; it's a waistline thing. I watched, disinterested, as he loaded the last morsel of crabmeat onto a cracker and added hot sauce. He popped the top on another can and waved both offerings at me.

"No more," I said. With my backpack in hand, I slipped over the starboard gunnel into the cool, waist-deep water. The sudden plunge took my breath away, and I quickly waded to the beach, a noisy and ungraceful process that displaced a school of minnows and put to flight a pair of gulls intent on a late lunch.

The sea breeze, invigorating and October cool, sang from the pine tops and gave dance to the golden clumps of sea oats clinging to life among the countless dunes. Inland, over the warmer land, patches of cumulus teemed, hinting of an afternoon thunderstorm after all.

Dad had often said, "Only fools and forecasters make weather predictions."

No fool here. I'd closed my sloop's hatches.

When Angus joined me, we set out for the Gulf side of the island. The trip was an easy, thirty-minute stroll we'd made many times, but now we made an hour trip of it, discussing a number of topics as we ambled, or waded, or cuddled on the warm sand. Everything, that is, but the topic I was sure was really on his mind. The one in my opinion we'd beaten to death.

Then he fell silent. We strolled on, hand in hand, veering into and out of the cool, foamy surf. Suddenly, he stopped, turned, and pulled me close to his chest.

I stood on my tiptoes, tilted my head, and met his kiss.

Then he held me at arm's length and flashed that smile of his, the one that'd caught me and reeled me in from that first magic moment. "How long, Seaweed?"

I shivered as his words shattered pleasant memory and snatched me back to the moment at hand. Against countless protestations, he, again, was asking, "How long?"

First, he'd asked me to move in with him. I didn't, but I did move closer by moving my sloop from Dad's charter service to the dock behind the Buttonwood. Next, he proposed marriage with the stipulation of a live-in arrangement of unspecified duration before exchanging vows. Too complicated, so I didn't buy into that one either. Finally, the how-long business began.

Angus was fun to be with until he started badgering me for an answer I wasn't ready to give. This, and other annoying habits, including sleazy friends and drinking to excess, had brought me to the decision of ending our relationship. There was nothing new here. I'd told him so. Many times.

I turned my head and brushed hair from my eyes, stalling to swallow the barbed reply filling my mouth. Repeating it all again would solve no more now than it had in the past. Just getting beyond this for the moment, then, would have to do. "I need time," I said. "I've told you that."

His usual argument was delivered with raised voice and hot words. This time it didn't happen. Instead, his shoulders slumped and his voice softened, barely audible above the hum of the sea breeze coursing through the crowns of the nearby Australian pines. "I know, but you've never said how much time."

Keeping my voice soft was a challenge, but I made the effort. "I'll tell you when it's right," I said. These were safe words, as there wasn't a prayer of our relationship ever being right. Touching my lips to his, I added, "In the meanwhile there's no one else."

"I know … it's just—"

When he didn't continue, I looked into his eyes. They were staring, but not at me. I turned my head, searching for whatever had grabbed his attention. Nothing looked out of the ordinary. A deserted beach stretched before us, lively surf played upon the sand, and above us a gorgeous, cloud-free sky seemed to stretch forever. Looking back to Angus, I said, "What is it?"

Releasing my arms and pointing at the shoreline just ahead of us, he said, "It was right there. Now it's gone."

I looked again at the deserted stretch of beach before us, still seeing nothing unusual. "What's gone?" I said.

"Beats me, but I'm gunna have a look."

Thankful for the distraction, I stepped back and watched as Angus loped into the knee-deep surf. At six-four and two hundred forty pounds, he moved with the grace of a rogue elephant. I was a foot shorter and weighed half as much—extremes that provided challenge at times.

He stopped, looked back at me, and shrugged. While he continued searching, I dropped to a kneeling position at the water's edge. A pair of seagulls peeled from the circling flock and swooped to a landing. When a handout was not forthcoming, they strutted closer, watching with heads cocked as I began digging for coquinas. I'd uncovered a dozen of the miniature clams and was watching them wiggle back into the wet sand when Angus said, "Oh, shit!"

I surrendered my excavation to the gulls and waded into the water. Angus didn't move or speak until I reached his side. The mostly submerged object before us was the size of a small mannequin. It even had the same bleached-bone shading of one, but it was not, nor had it ever been, a mannequin.

"She's dead," he said.

CHAPTER 2

Until he hit the Lottery, Angus had been a career officer with the Florida Marine Patrol. He had nautical savvy. In this case, however, his revelation added nothing to what I could clearly see for myself.

The body was nude and floating face down, but the long silver hair flowing with the movement of the surf, the slender waist, and the wide, well-rounded hips all spoke to the body being female. The legs were lashed together at the ankles; the wrists were secured in a similar manner behind the back. A multitude of abrasions, bites, and bruises covered her legs and torso. When a curl of surf momentarily lifted the body, I noticed a long section of polypropylene line trailed loosely from where it was knotted around the neck. Odd. The line was at least fifty-feet long, but it was a single piece, awkwardly knotted from the ankles to the wrists to the neck.

Angus rolled the body over, revealing more abrasions, bites, and bruises. The face was of a middle-aged woman, one who had been quite attractive before acquiring the half-inch-diameter hole between her eyes. I shuddered. This was a murder victim, not a lady who had accidentally drowned while out for a swim.

Unfazed, it seemed, Angus stooped, cradled the body in his arms, and started for the beach. I coiled the trailing line and followed. He moved inland, past the high-water mark and into the shade of some young pines, where he knelt and placed the body alongside a patch of sea oats. His movements were as gentle as those of a mother returning a sleeping infant to its crib. This sleeping lady, however, would never awaken again. I dropped the line and spun away.

At the age of ten or so, I fell out of the swing set Dad had built for me behind his bait shop. I landed on my stomach. Dad raced to my side, scooped me up, and held me until I could breathe enough to cry. He continued to hold and kiss me until I cried away the hurt.

Just as it had been back then, tears welled in my eyes, and my breath came in gasps, but I knew no amount of tears could cry away the death we'd discovered. I bit my bottom lip and tried to swallow the lump fighting for a place in my throat. Unlike Dad's loving attention after my fall, Angus didn't see or respond to my hurt.

When I could speak without choking, I wiped my eyes and said, "Now what?"

"We have to report it," he said. Then, with a nod at my backpack, he added, "Use the towels to cover the body. I'll go back to *Skipjack* and radio the Coast Guard."

Angus and I had beach-combed and camped Hangman's Key more times than I could remember. And although we'd never discovered buried treasure, we'd found an array of trinkets, cash, clothing, and even a barbecue grill that now dwelled on the dock alongside my sloop. But we'd never found a body. I could handle *TV* dead. But this wasn't TV; this was *real* dead. I didn't like it, nor did I want to remain near it, especially not alone.

I pushed the backpack into his hands. "No," I said. "I can't … I can't stay here with her. I'll go back to the boat."

Without argument Angus accepted the backpack and returned to where he'd placed the body. I hitched up my bikini bottom and set out at a run, retracing our steps to the lee side of the island.

Angus entered my life four years ago, on a day like this day—a day filled with death. I'd just turned eighteen, and while that milestone was memorable for its own reasons, it had been a special summer for a number of other reasons as well: I graduated high school and qualified for my captain's license; Dad gave me *Bonita*, a derelict sloop he'd restored; and, best of all, he promoted me to captain of his charter vessel, the *Margaret Ellen*, running half-day trips to the grouper grounds off Big Tarpon Pass.

I loved it. School was behind me, I had the best job in the world, money in my pocket, and my afternoons were free to do what I loved best: fish for catfish from a small dock just a short cast down the sea wall from Dad's bait tank.

That afternoon I was fishing as usual, but I'd also been admiring two boys as they plugged for speckled trout from an anchored johnboat. Then the roar of a boat's engine filled the air. A Scarab 38 careened into view. The driver had a bottle tipped to his lips. There was no way he would miss the two boys. My scream drowned in the impact.

Two men sharing the dock with me removed their shoes, dove in, and headed for the mess bobbing in the speedboat's wake. Nothing larger than a blue baseball cap and yellow bait bucket remained on the surface. After memorizing every detail of the hit-and-run boat, I ran to the phone at Dad's.

In the next two hours the bodies were recovered. I recited my recollection of the incident to deputies from the Pinellas County Sheriff's Office, officers from the Florida Marine Patrol, and reporters from three of the Bay Area's TV stations. Then, as quickly as they had assembled, the crowd dispersed. With no heart remaining for fishing, I tossed my leftover bait to a brown pelican perched on a nearby piling and was reeling in my line when Angus pulled alongside the dock in his patrol boat. This was when I learned the boat's driver, a prominent attorney, had been apprehended. "Your description," he said, "made the job easy."

I thought about him from time to time, usually when I was sitting alone fishing for cats. He had flashing, hazel-blue eyes, and his first look at me had been one I'd read as assessment and approval. But, he wore a wide-band ring on the third finger of his left hand. He was married. Why did I bother to fantasize?

In the following days my eyes tracked every Florida Marine Patrol boat plying the waters of Big Tarpon Pass. Even so, I didn't see Angus again until the attorney's trial. Several months later the names Angus and Mechele Loman appeared in the divorce column of the *St. Petersburg Times*. The desire to call him was overwhelming, at times, but I didn't give in to it. He knew where to find me—if he wanted to.

Then one afternoon as I was at the bait tank dipping live shrimp for a fishing session, I heard the mellow-tone voice that still invaded my dreams.

"Dip a few more, Seaweed. Let's catch some cats."

That's how it started.

I was living aboard *Bonita*, berthed in a slip behind my dad's place, and Angus was renting an apartment at the Buttonwood. The following month he hit the Lotto, bought the Buttonwood, and moved to the penthouse. He asked, and I considered, but I didn't move in with him. I did accept a berth for my sloop below his picture window.

When I reached the lee side of the island, my lungs ached. Why was I running? No power on earth could help the woman. Even so, after pausing to wipe at the sweat filling and stinging my eyes, I trotted on until reaching a point on the beach abreast of *Skipjack*. The Whaler was riding easy to the ground swell, but there wasn't a chance of reaching it until I rested enough to breathe without gasping.

We'd anchored at slack water on an ebb tide, but now the bay tide was midway into flood. After regaining my wind, I waded in and struggled through the current and extra depth to reach the boat. The gunnel was beyond reach. I jumped for it and fought to hoist myself aboard. Once in the cockpit, however, my first priority was the ice chest, not the radio.

I shrugged off my bikini top, filled one of the bra cups with ice, and held the makeshift arrangement to my forehead. Then, while sprawled in the captain's chair, I worked at deep, evenly spaced breaths until the exploding sunspots behind my closed eyelids diminished.

When I opened my eyes, the spume at the water's edge, the patches of sea oats, and the towering Australian pines all appeared clear. How about speaking? The result wasn't come-hither quality, but I thought the words sounded coherent. I turned on the marine VHF radio, punched in channel sixteen, and opened a Pepsi. Drawing a deep breath, I said, "St. Petersburg Coast Guard, St. Petersburg Coast Guard, the motor vessel *Skipjack*, over."

I tipped the can and took a long pull.

"Vessel calling St. Petersburg Coast Guard, say again."

I swallowed and cleared my throat. "*Skipjack*," I said. "This is the motor vessel *Skipjack*, over."

"Roger, *Skipjack*. Go ahead."

During my years on the water I'd made countless boat-to-boat transmissions on the marine VHF, including a few to the Coast Guard, but none had been for the purpose of reporting the discovery of a body. Should I strain for technical language or just blurt it out? Gripping the mike, I stared at an isolated patch of cumulus far out over the Gulf. Crap! I couldn't think of a technical way of saying it, but I knew how to blurt. "I've found a body on Hangman's Key, over."

In the second or two before the radioman's response, I wondered if he was considering my message a prank call. *A body on Hangman's Key? Sure.*

"Roger, *Skipjack*. Copy buoy ashore on Hangman's Key. Give me a description, over."

This was not beginning well. Even so, I understood his confusion. High winds and seas played havoc with aids to navigation. Each new storm toppled a few day markers from their worm-weakened pilings and ripped a buoy or two from its mooring. When finding such damage, boaters were encouraged to report it to the Coast Guard. Such reports were routine and no doubt accounted for the radioman hearing buoy instead of body. If only it were that way.

Setting the Pepsi can on the cockpit combing, I said, "Negative, St.

Petersburg. Negative. It's not a buoy. It's a body. *B*ravo, *O*scar, *D*elta, *Y*ankee. It's a body, over."

The Coast Guard station was coming in loud and clear, but it still took several exchanges to explain the situation. Maybe my speech wasn't as coherent as I'd first believed. After the radio operator read back the pertinent information, I confirmed it, emphasizing again that *Skipjack* was anchored off the lee side of the island but the body was located on the Gulf side. With this understood, he said he'd notify the Pinellas County Sheriff's Office. I signed off and returned to my Pepsi before realizing he'd given no promise of a response time.

After finishing my drink, I shivered back into my chilled bikini top and pulled a bailing bucket from the locker under the captain's seat. I tossed in two beers for Angus, a Pepsi for me, and covered them with ice. A few crackers remained but I had no means to carry them. With the canvas bucket in hand, I was about to slip over the side and head for the beach when I realized what I was wearing: number fifteen sun block and a string bikini. The sun block was invisible, and the bikini didn't consist of enough material to make a sail for a toy boat. Company would arrive soon. I returned to the locker and selected one of Dad's fishing shirts.

During my return to the Gulf side of the island, images of the dead woman flitted in my mind. The where and when about her were fuzzy, but I was sure I'd seen her face before. I remembered her shimmering silver hair had been up in a French twist and had looked as stunning as the diamond-clustered pin that held it in place. She wore an extravagant amount of makeup, diamond earrings in the shape of interlocking hearts, and a triple-strand diamond necklace. Also memorable was the recklessly low neckline of her black evening dress that had done nothing to enhance her smaller-than-average bosom. Remembering that much about her had been easy, so why couldn't I remember her name? Or, for that matter, where and when I'd seen her before?

Upon reaching Angus I was determined not to look at the spot where he'd placed the body. No contest, as my peripheral vision quickly picked up the red, white, and blue of my huge, Budweiser beach towels. Next, in angst, I was staring at them. Those were my favorite towels, ones Angus and I'd sat on, slept on, and made love on. Now, I never wanted to see them again.

Forcing my gaze from the tree line, I dropped the bucket of drinks between his sprawled legs and sat in the warm sand at his side.

"Any problem?" he asked as he opened two cans and passed one to me.

Accepting the can, and between deep breaths, I also accepted the reality that despite my aerobics sessions, I'd never cut it as a track star. "It's reported," I said.

Before we finished our drinks, I heard a noise like distant thunder. But our sky was still clear, and the noise wasn't an approaching storm; it was the dueling, *whomp-whomp-whomp* of a pair of helicopters. I'd expected a much slower response, one by boat, actually. We sipped and watched the approaching specks grow larger and louder. The first machine, a brown and white belonging to the Pinellas County Sheriff's Office, passed over our position, circled, and landed at a wide spot about one hundred yards down the beach. The second craft, a sickly yellow with Channel Five's black-and-red logo on its sides and undercarriage, made a similar approach and landing a few moments later. I slipped into Dad's shirt.

The rotor on the brown and white was still turning when the doors opened and two individuals jumped out and began their labored approach through the ankle-deep sand. When they were fifty yards away, I nudged Angus. "Looks like Mutt and Jeff," I said.

He drained his beer and chuckled. "Yeah, but they're a great pair." He stood, crushed the empty can, and tossed it into the canvas bucket. "The tall one is Colin Myers," he said. "The other guy's the pilot, Bob Lancaster."

In working the counter at Big Al's Pawn and Bond, an as-needed job I'd taken since my falling out with Dad, I'd met most of the detectives from the St. Petersburg Police Department and the Pinellas County Sheriff's Office. There'd also been a few meetings with patrol officers from both outfits when my white-over-red Camaro and I exceeded the posted speed limits. These two were about the same age as Angus, close to forty and quite handsome, but I didn't recognize either one.

Lancaster was still a dozen steps away when he stopped. Recognition flooded his eyes as he stared at Angus. "Well I'll be damned if it ain't old Easy Bucks. You lost? With your money I'd be on the Riviera."

Angus stepped forward and reached for the man's extended hand. "I should be," he said, "but then who'd find the bodies for you two bums."

While the three men continued their ribbing, handshaking, and backslapping, I turned my attention to the other helicopter. This one held three individuals but only two stepped from the machine and moved our way. One was a lanky young man with unruly red hair and an armload of equipment. The other individual was a woman with blond, shoulder-length hair carrying a black-and-yellow tote bag.

"Seaweed."

I turned to the men. Angus made the introductions. After a reciprocal round of "Pleased to meet you," I cocked a thumb down the beach. "Don't look now," I said, "but I think we're about to be in the movies."

Lancaster jammed his hands into his pockets. "Sometimes I wish our bird was equipped with tail guns."

Myers clapped Lancaster on the shoulder. "You get 'em, I'll use 'em," he said. "For now, keep those two back here out of the way." He turned to Angus and nodded toward my beach towels. "That it?"

CHAPTER 3

I didn't recognize the male half of the approaching duo, but the woman was Gwen O'Dell, one of Channel Five's on-the-scene reporters. She was still twenty yards away, trudging the soft-sand trail blazed by the deputies, when she spotted Angus and Myers heading for the tree line. Intent on her story, I supposed, she gave a this-way nod to the young man behind her and veered to follow the two men.

Lancaster had been standing silently, ignoring my presence while listening to the chatter on his handheld radio, when Gwen's errant move grabbed his attention. "Yo!" he bellowed. "Over here!"

Gwen reined to a halt and fired a look over her shoulder hot enough to grill a backyard burger.

"It's my way or no way," Lancaster said.

Gwen maintained her glare. Lancaster matched it and placed his hands on his hips.

Their steely-eyed exchange reminded me of a Mexican standoff in a spaghetti Western. And while I could glare with the best of them, this was one situation I had no interest in joining.

Leaving them locked in their facedown, I backpedaled to my makeshift ice chest. The ice had long since melted, but one drink remained, wallowing in company with the pair of empty cans. This single drink was a beer, not a Pepsi. Tough. Surely my long run had burned more calories than one beer could replace. I scooped up the can, popped the tab, and ambled down to the water's edge before my inner voice could fault my reasoning. Even so, my respite was short-lived. After a quick exchange I was unable to overhear, Gwen abandoned Lancaster and hurried after me. I shuffled into the water, enjoying the taste of the beer and the feel of the cool surf as it played past my ankles and spilled onto the beach.

"May I speak with you?" she said.

I looked back at the beach. Gwen and the man with the wild red hair were now standing at the water's edge. She held a notepad in the crook of her arm and a pencil poised as if ready to take dictation. The man standing alongside her held a camera balanced on his shoulder. It was aimed at me. With its black, protruding lens, the camera looked like one of the shoulder-held rocket launchers often seen in war movies. And while I loved war movies, I also remembered nothing good ever came from one of these gadgets. I pointed a finger at Red Head, but I was speaking to Gwen. "No. Not with that thing in my face."

She nudged him with her elbow, and he slowly lowered the camera. Dismissing him with a cutting glance, I tugged Dad's shirt as low over my hips as it would go and waded to the beach.

Gwen looked to be my height, a little thicker in spots, and a good ten years older. Her tan was bronze, nearly as dark as mine, but it probably came from a sun lamp, not outdoors exposure. The stiff breeze and heavy humidity had wrecked her hairdo, and loose blonde strands whipped about her face.

She was wearing a white silk blouse with turquoise slacks and matching pumps. Before hitting the beach her outfit had probably been gorgeous. Now the blouse was stained with perspiration, the slacks were water flecked to the knees, and her pumps were filled with sand. On camera, dressed and made-up to perfection, she always looked like a siren. Even now, after buffeting by the elements, she was still attractive enough to turn heads. Would the inevitable aging process treat me as kindly?

When I reached her side, she said, "Thank you. The deputy told me the body is nude. We can't air that, and we won't film it, but foul or fair we have to cover the story."

This was more consideration than I'd expected—certainly more than she'd exhibited the first time we met. I forced myself to smile. "What do you want to know?"

Gwen started with questions about me. When I told her my name, she said, "Karen Cobia? Of course. I was sure I'd met you. Yes. You're Seaweed. The boating deaths at Big Tarpon Pass. Your dad—"

"Cobia's Charter Service," I said.

"Yes, and you're a charter captain."

I didn't want to lie to her, but this was entering murky water, even though it was true I still held a captain's license.

A few months back, in a moment of inattention, I'd placed the *Margaret Ellen* within a hairsbreadth of a catastrophic collision. Dad and I had a tiff. A stupid one made worse because I'd been in the wrong. I could've asked forgiveness—Dad's stern, not unfair—but I didn't. I walked out.

Since then I'd worked on and off at a number of things. But that was about to change. Like the words in Anne Murray's song, I was seeing clearly now. So much so that the thing I now wanted most was my old job back—to once again captain Dad's charter vessel, the *Margaret Ellen*.

To avoid a lie, then, glossing over her statement seemed the easy route. "Yes," I said, "among other things, I'm a charter captain, but many charters are only half-day affairs. That leaves free time to make extra money."

Beginning to scribble on her notepad, she said, "Like what?"

I could've mentioned my work for Big Al, but I chose not to do so. It wasn't work I was proud of, and Big Al went to great length to avoid publicity, so the less said the better. My hit-and-miss work with local insurance companies was another matter.

"Two things, for the most part," I said. "First, because of my time on the water, I've located several stolen vessels. This success prompted a couple of insurers to ask my help in investigating boating accidents."

She shifted her weight to one foot. Interest filled her eyes. "How, exactly," she said, rotating the pencil in her hand as if tracing the outline of a single cloud above us, "do you investigate a boating accident?"

I wasn't ready to add her to my Christmas-card list, but she was becoming easier to like. Even so, how much should I tell her? After I received a boating-accident case, it was my job to interview and obtain statements from witnesses and principals before their memory was contaminated with promises of huge settlements from ambulance-chasing attorneys. That was the *mundane* aspect of the job. Gwen didn't need to know this. I outlined the *exciting* aspect.

"With a vehicle accident," I said, "the physical evidence is scattered about the scene. That's rarely the case with boating accidents. The telling evidence, if it exists, is usually on the bottom. That's my job. Get the evidence. I'm a certified diver."

"I tried it once," she said, before turning her eyes to her sand-filled shoes. "Did everything wrong. Didn't watch the tank gauge. Ran it dry. Scared the be-damned out of me." She looked up and shrugged. "I never tried it again."

I gave her an understanding nod and sipped my beer.

She cocked her head into the wind and brushed a strand of hair from her eyes. "So what's with today?" Gesturing at our surroundings, she said, "Were you out here because you decided to take a day off?"

A fast-moving cold front packing torrential rain had swept through the Tampa Bay area over the weekend, and the hottest beachcombing was always after storm-driven seas pounded the coastline. New islands were formed; old ones disappeared. Best of all, though, during this colossal sand shifting, long-buried objects were sometimes exposed. A for-real beachcomber would have known this. Instead of trying to explain, I gave a silent nod to confirm the guess she'd offered.

"But instead of a pleasant day off, you discovered a body." She hugged herself beneath her breasts and shuddered. "Can you describe how you felt?"

Were her movements no more than an act to put me at ease? Probably, but her voice brimmed with sincerity, and she listened without interrupting as I recapped the emotions I'd felt in the moments after discovering the body. "So, naturally, seeing a body in the surf was startling, but then a chilling numbness set in. You know, a feeling like what's happening cannot be real. After that it was just plain scary."

Looking up from her notepad, she said, "I can understand the first emotions, I'm sure I'd feel the same way too, but why were you scared?"

"Gwen, I don't mean scared as in afraid, just the scary feeling you get when you look at or think about death. It's real. In this case it's worse."

She tipped her head closer. "Oh? How do you mean?"

With a glance toward my beach towels, I said, "Because I'm certain I've seen that woman before." Angus and the two deputies joined us before I could explain why.

Myers ignored Gwen and addressed me. "Unless you have something to add to what Loman told me, you can take off." Not pausing to see if I indeed had something to add, he gestured toward the Gulf and said, "I figure the body was dumped out there somewhere and washed ashore during the rough weather over the weekend."

Being summarily dismissed from our gathering was one thing; Myers's condescending manner was another. I glanced at Gwen, wondering if she'd also caught his tone? Yes. She aimed a smirk at Myers, stepped back, and began speaking with her cameraman.

No one—Myers in particular—was expecting any feedback. Despite his lofty tone, I kept mine light and pleasant. "I don't think so," I said.

CHAPTER 4

My statement cast a moment of silence over our little group. Gwen stopped in mid-sentence. Angus and Lancaster crowded closer. Suddenly, I was the target of everyone's attention. Myers broke the spell when he squinted and spoke through clinched teeth. "You don't think so, eh?" He flipped back a page or two in his notepad, studied a moment, and then looked up and engaged my eyes. "Okay. Karen, is it? Why don't you enlighten us as to why that is."

The stance, the squint, and the speech hissed through clenched teeth all tempted me to ask Myers if he were a Dirty Harry clone. Suppressing the temptation and keeping my response civil, I said, "The polypropylene line."

"The line?" Myers smirked. Glancing at the other men, he added, "Okay, Karen, tell us all about it?"

His voice still held condescension, and now he added a singsong tone when he pronounced my name. KARE—ENN. Friend of Angus be damned, I was quickly getting my fill of this jerk. "Actually, Detective Myers, there are several things you should know about polypropylene line. To begin with, it doesn't hold a knot well, especially the half hitches and granny knots used on the body. This indicates whoever used it didn't know much about line or knots." Pausing to give him a tight-lipped smile, I added, "Your mileage may vary, of course."

"What?"

"Skip it," I said. "The important part is the line is tied to the body in three places, but it's a single piece. The end tying the woman's feet has an eye splice. The other end trailing from her neck is frayed."

Myers took another look in his notepad. "Yeah, Loman said you worked with boats. A charter captain." Looking back to me, he added, "So from your experience you see some meaning in this. That right?"

Ah, his tone was now almost human. "You bet," I said. "You see, that type of line is used as anchor line for small boats: eye splice on one end, the anchor on the other. Large boats use three-strand nylon because it stretches under a heavy strain. Poly doesn't stretch. It breaks."

"Okay, I'm with you so far," he said, "but where're we headed?"

"Let me give you two more points about polypropylene, and then I'll tell you what I think happened."

Myers began taking notes. "Go on."

Gwen had also been taking notes. She looked up and said, "The frayed line, right?"

"Yes," I said, "the proper way to cut polypropylene line is with a hot knife. If you use a regular knife, you have to burn the ends of the line to prevent it from fraying. Second point is, the stuff floats."

Myers gave Gwen a look that silenced further comment. With her shut down he looked back to me. "So from this wisdom about polypropylene line you've developed a theory. That it?"

I winked at Gwen. "One came to mind," I said.

He pursed his lips and blew out his breath, sounding like one of the dolphins at Sea World. "Let's hear it," he said.

Ignoring the sarcasm, I gestured up and down the coast. "Along this stretch of the Gulf, except for the main ship channel, you have to go offshore a mile or so to get into twenty feet of water. I don't think the killer knew that. He brought the body out here in a small boat, used the end of the anchor line normally attached to the boat to tie up the body, and then pushed the body and the anchor overboard."

I dropped to a kneeling position and drew a pair of parallel lines about a foot apart in the sand. "This line down here is the bottom," I said. "This one up here is the surface." I wiggled a finger between the two lines. "Let's assume a water depth of twenty feet and a typical anchor line length of one-hundred feet. The anchor and the body went to the bottom. Here and here." I drew a looping arch from the body to the surface and back to the anchor and then stabbed a finger at the arch-shaped line. "This is the extra line between the body and the anchor. It floated."

"So what?" Myers said.

"So, if the piece of line attached to the body had been cut with a knife, the fibers would be frayed, but they'd be the same length. They're not."

"So what cut it?"

I pointed at my arch in the sand. "I think the slack line was floating on the surface and was snagged and severed by a boat prop. Happens all the time with the float line on crab traps."

A smile replaced his scowl. "Yeah, that would explain the long section trailing from the neck. Then, with nothing holding it in place, the weekend storm pushed the body ashore."

I stood and brushed the sand from my knees. "That's my theory," I said.

"Possible. Just possible." He glanced at the other men.

Lancaster shrugged.

"Sounds good to me," Angus said.

Myers was silent for a moment before his forehead creased like crumpled newspaper. His scowl returned. "Skiers use that line, too," he said. "Maybe the piece with the body was just a scrap with a frayed end. Not only that, it could've been tied to a building block instead of an anchor."

"Maybe," I said, "but skiers prefer lakes and inland waters, not the open Gulf. And a boater, or a skier, would know knots and line. The killer didn't know squat about them. Not only that, if a weight, anchor or building block, had been lashed directly to the body, and knotted properly, the body would still be out there somewhere." With a smile, I added, "Regardless of the weather."

Angus laughed and thumped Myers on the shoulder. "I think she's close, ol' buddy."

"Yeah, maybe." Myers scribbled as he muttered, "It ain't much, but I'll jot it down."

The sound of an outboard engine caught our attention, and Lancaster trotted to the water's edge, waving his badge to ward off an approaching boat. The vessel, a twenty-foot Crestliner with a blue hull and white topsides, held two men and two women, and each gave him the universal, single-finger salute as they turned back toward the open Gulf. It was then I saw a VHF whip antenna on the stern and wondered how many others had overheard my transmission to the Coast Guard and would be arriving to gawk.

Gwen waited until Myers was finished writing before asking to see the body. When it was my turn, I asked if we could leave.

Myers answered her first. "Look but don't touch," he said. "And the camera stays back here." He turned to me. "Yeah, you can shove off. If we need anything, we know where to find you."

He didn't need to say it twice. I scooped up my backpack and bailing bucket, and, despite earlier reservations, I gave fleeting thought to asking for my beach towels. Looking in that direction, I saw Gwen kneeling alongside the body, the corner of one towel in her outstretched hand. A moment later she gasped and jumped away as if the body were a coiled rattler.

"It's Eva!" she said.

I'd never seen a woman get men's attention quicker—with her clothes on, that is. Myers and Lancaster had treated Gwen with contempt, visually and verbally, since her arrival. Now they were rushing her like fans swarming a rock star.

Eva! The name triggered all the emotions I'd first experienced when viewing the body. Now I knew who the woman was and where I'd seen her before. Eva was Eva Marie Park, and I'd heard her name for as long as I could remember. She'd been the Bay Area's best-known and loved philanthropist. Still, it hadn't been until a recent TV special honoring her charitable work that I'd seen the face that went with the name.

"Who's Eva?" Angus said.

I told him, and then added, "But how would a woman like that end up like this?"

He shrugged and took my hand as we hurried to where the others were clustered. Myers was pumping Gwen for information.

"Her name's Eva Marie Park," Gwen said. "Or at least it was."

"Why would she change it?" Lancaster said.

Now it was Gwen's turn to exhibit a measure of contempt.

"Marriage," she said. "If you were up on the social news, you would've heard the rumor that Eva was about to remarry." She arched her eyebrows. "And, before you ask to whom, I've only seen the gentleman, I haven't heard his name."

"That opens a new can of possibilities," Myers said. He studied Gwen's face. "What else do you know about her?"

Despite the hot sun and heavy humidity, Gwen looked as composed as she always did on the late news broadcast. "I have a drawer full of photos and a huge info file on her at the studio," she said. "You're welcome to copies of—"

Myers waved a hand in her face. "Just the big picture for now."

Gwen placed both hands on her hips, drew a deep breath, and exhaled slowly. I expected a verbal barrage, but she continued with a control I was still working to attain. "Her husband died in an automobile accident about five years ago. Eva's sister, Christine Brantley, was with him. She was severely injured and died a few days later."

From his smug smile I figured Myers was about to ask why Christine was out with Eva's husband. Gwen anticipated the question too. "The deaths saved the ugliness of two divorces," she added.

Myers began taking notes, again. "Any kids?" he asked.

"Not by Eva. Christine had one daughter. Amber. She's about twenty-five now and quite beautiful, but, compliments of Eva, she's also an arrogant brat."

"She live around here?"

Gwen paused, as if searching a mental file, and then said, "I believe she has a condo on Tierra Verde. I do know she spends a lot of time in Europe."

Myers chewed on a thumbnail, squinting and staring out over the Gulf. "We may have another body out there," he said.

"Or," Lancaster said, "a Mister Slick on the run with a bundle of new-found wealth."

"Yeah," Myers said, "wouldn't be the first time. Call in. Have a unit check out Eva's home, the niece's condo, and the new-husband angle."

Lancaster moved a few steps away and began speaking into his handheld radio. Myers faced Gwen. "Okay, you know how it works," he said. "Don't leak anything until I release a positive ID on the body and have made notification to the next of kin."

"Whoopee!" she said. "The body of an unidentified woman was discovered—"

"You got it," he said. "And for now absolutely nothing about the rope or bullet wound. Nothing."

"That's not fair," Gwen said. "What if another station scoops me on this?"

Waving his notepad, he said, "Not likely. I have the details. Work with me on this and I'll see you get any developments first."

Further protest from Gwen was silenced when Lancaster rejoined us. "It gets deeper," he said.

"How's that?" Myers said.

Lancaster consulted his notepad. "Stan Avery called the city police to Eva's home at ten this morning. He was her attorney. She lived on Bayway Isles. Avery stated that Eva and her fiancé were out of town, but he'd stopped by her place to pick up some papers she'd left for him. He entered, found the place ransacked, and called it in. City police found sign of forced entry at a patio door. Safe was open. Empty."

"But now we have a body," Myers said. "That could make it robbery, abduction, and murder."

I'd had a thought when Lancaster mentioned where Eva lived: Bayway Isles. That was close. In fact, by using Pass-A-Grille Channel and a boat with *Skipjack's* speed, it was less than a ten-minute run from Eva's home to Hangman's Key. I passed the information to Myers.

Myers nodded. "Very convenient."

Lancaster poked my arm with his notepad. "Maybe you should take up fortune telling, Karen."

"What do you mean?"

Still brandishing his notepad, Lancaster said, "Eva kept a speedboat docked behind her home."

"So?"

"It's missing."

CHAPTER 5

During our silent return to the lee side of the island, I wrestled with thoughts of life and death and the truism that each was the flip side of the other. Accepting the supreme order dictating this was not an option. Quite simply, if we lived ... eventually we died. What I could not accept was a murderer, in one evil moment, had blown away Eva's right to an *eventual* death.

After boarding *Skipjack* Angus opened the last two cans of beer, set one near me, and dropped heavily into one of the portside seats. I remained standing, leaning against the starboard gunnel and staring out across the bay. The wind had clocked to northeast and slacked to under five knots. Once again, Tampa Bay looked as tranquil and inviting as a Chamber-of-Commerce photo. My emotions, however, were still screaming at Force Ten.

I snatched open the seat locker, threw Dad's shirt into it, and slammed the lid with enough force to topple my beer. The can spun wildly, spewing its contents onto the sole carpeting. My mind's eye saw Eva's blood spewing in the same senseless manner. Screaming at the empty can bearing the same colorful logo as my abandoned beach towels, I put enough leg behind kicking it into the aft drain scupper to have made a fifty-yard field goal. The reward for my stupidity was a sharp pain shooting from the big toe to the calf of my right leg. I bit my lips to stifle another scream.

Angus placed his can of beer into a gimbaled holder, stood, and crossed to where I was leaning against the outboard engine. He took me into his arms. "I hate it too," he said.

When I didn't reply, he kissed my overflowing eyes and hugged me close to his chest. "You care, Seaweed, about so many things. I love that in you, but this is one of those times when you have to accept what you can't change."

At times in our relationship I'd reached points where I never wanted to see Angus again. At other times, like this moment, my feelings were the exact opposite, and I couldn't imagine life without him. I blinked and wiped at the corners of my eyes. "I know," I said.

As he hugged me, I tried to think of good things, fun things, anything but the lifeless body we'd left lying like a piece of worthless jetsam on a barren, wind-swept beach.

I'd enjoyed each of our previous trips to Hangman's Key. Even the time we cowered from the lightning strikes and high winds of a flash storm that sent our tent tumbling down the beach. Even the time I packed the food but forgot the cooking utensils. And, yes, even the time a couple with three young children walked up on us as we were making love. Despite all that, I'd always looked forward to the next trip. Could I ever do so again?

An eternity later, it seemed, he rocked me in his arms. "We have fish to fry," he whispered. "Remember?"

Life wasn't always fair, a fact I'd learned as a child, but his assessment of it was correct: Like it or not, I had to accept what I couldn't change. I burrowed my face into his chest and willed the tightness from my throat. When I trusted myself to speak, I said, "Yes, and I promised myself a platter of hush puppies." What I couldn't bring myself to say was that I'd planned to eat alone—for reasons he wouldn't want to hear.

He smacked his lips. "No matter what those fools on TV say, it doesn't get any better than sheepshead and hush puppies. And, hey, I'll even chop the onions and mix the batter. Deal?"

I tried to put some heart into my voice and smile. "You got it." I pushed free of his hug, reversed the power tilt switch, and pumped the primer bulb. "Get the hook up. Let's get outta here."

With the calmer conditions, or maybe spurred on by what she'd left in her wake, *Skipjack* shaved ten minutes from her outbound time. At the Buttonwood I circled wide to kill some speed, nosed her into her slip, and cut the engine. He secured the bow lines and began transferring our gear to the dock. I adjusted the stern lines, giving added slack for spring tide, and then joined him.

I scooped up my gear, kissed his cheek, and started for my sloop. "I'll grab a change of clothes and be up in a minute."

"Bring your nightie."

"I don't wear a nightie."

"You know what I mean."

How could I not know what he meant? Despite having a key to the penthouse, and a standing offer to move in with him, I spent most nights aboard my sloop. Alone. I preferred it that way because it lent an added level of excitement to the times when we shared an *overnighter*. Also, for reasons he could not or would not understand, I cherished my alone time. Marriage, or a permanent live-together arrangement, would ruin that. Tonight, however, no thought was needed to know what I wanted. After a hot shower, a sudsy shampoo, and an unhurried meal, I wanted some warm, up-close companionship—the kind of warmth and closeness only the living with a newfound respect for death could enjoy.

A rush of warm air hit my face when I pushed open the hatch and started down the companionway. In the dim interior the red light on my answering machine blinked like the countdown sequence of a time bomb. I ignored it and opened hatches and ports and turned on my two oscillating fans.

With a flow of cool air coursing through the cabin, I punched the play button on the answering machine and slipped out of my bikini. Al's guttural growl filled the cabin as I rinsed the pieces in the galley sink and hung them from a pair of overhead grab bars.

"Hey, look, doll. Somethin' came up after you left. I'll need you later in the week after all. Wednesday. Thursday. Stay loose, ya hear? Okay? Shit! I don't like talkin' to a machine. I'll get back to ya."

The next two calls were hang-ups. The last one was Dad's.

"I know you're there you little wharf rat, pick up the phone. Don't keep Daddy waiting. De-dum, de-dum, de-dum. Okay, maybe you're not there. Ah … look, baby, I got a problem. A *big* problem. Call me when you get in. Please."

I erased the messages, turned on my VHF, and punched in the NOAA weather channel. The recorded forecast said winds would remain at five knots or less along with the probability of fog setting in by midnight. Tuesday would be clear and cool with winds increasing to ten knots and clocking to south. Seas in the Gulf would run three feet or less. Inland waters would be calm.

A mixed bag, but it was also par for Florida in the fall.

I put on shorts and a T-shirt and began stuffing a change of clothes into an overnight bag. With that chore accomplished, I swung the bag into the cockpit, returned to the phone, and dialed Dad's number.

When I was seven, my mother, Margaret Ellen, died in my dad's arms. We were night fishing in rough seas at Pinnacle Rocks, a submerged reef in the Gulf of Mexico a hundred miles west of Sarasota. Mom was below in the galley fixing a late snack when she lost her balance and fell. She assured Dad that she was fine, but an hour later she went into premature labor. Dad pounded for shore, slamming the wheel and cussing the ancient engine for not having more to give. Despite his efforts, Mom died before we reached the inlet. The baby, a sister I never got to know, was stillborn.

Dad and his sister, Patty, raised me, and, for the most part, I grew up under their feet at the bait shop. I don't remember learning, but Dad said I could swim before I could walk. With patience and guidance, he taught me to rig baits and tackle, read charts and clouds, and to handle and dock small boats. Later, as a teenager, I could run the bait shop and handle Dad's fifty-foot charter boat, the *Margaret Ellen*, as well as he could. Not that he would ever admit that.

"Cobia's."

Clearing my throat and trying for my best imitation of sophisticated, I said, "I'm a woman, not a wharf rat."

He snickered. "And a beautiful one at that, baby, but even so you'll always be *my* little wharf rat."

I warmed, hearing the latent love in his voice, but he continued before I could reply.

"Where ya been all day?"

Telling him about my part in the grisly discovery on Hangman's Key wasn't easy; admitting that I'd tried and failed in my goal of dumping Angus was impossible.

"Eva Park?" Dad said. "Holy Jesus! How in the hell—"

"I have no idea, Dad, but if you have time to catch it, Gwen said she'd cover the story on the early news." I changed tack. "What's the big problem you mentioned?"

"Problems is more like it," he said. "First is Patty. She's down with the flu, and I have six Texans signed up for an early morning charter."

Dad was building to a request for help. Maybe it would also be my foot-in-the-door opportunity to mend the damaged bridge between us. I closed my eyes, bowed my head, and said, "Yeah, okay. No problem. So you want me to help you out in the shop while Cecil and Skip handle the charter party?"

"No, and that's the next problem," he said. "Cecil just had knee surgery. He won't be piloting anything more mechanical than a rocking chair for a few days."

Cecil was a retired tugboat captain and a lifelong friend of Dad's. Ever since I'd gotten my butt on my shoulder and walked out, Cecil had been helping Dad and Patty. "Okay," I said. "So you want me to watch the bait shop and baby-sit Cecil while you and Skip handle the charter. Right?"

"Wrong. Would you believe I'm still fighting with the IRS? I have to be here with my bookkeeper at ten in the morning to answer some more fool questions."

I desperately wanted my old job back, but I knew where this was headed. "Dad, you're not asking me to—"

"Ah, look, baby, it's only a half-day trip."

"And Skip's a wise-ass little shit. All day; every day."

"No argument there," Dad said. "But don't worry about it. I'll talk to him. That's a promise."

He didn't have to promise. If Dad said it, he would do it. "Fine, but you used to let me select my mate."

"And when you're back at the helm of the *Margaret Ellen*, you can do so again. But for now can you find one by six in the morning."

He had me there. "No way," I said.

"Okay. Trip pays a hundred. Wear your bikini. Put 'em on a hot spot. Should be good for another hundred in tips."

"Dad! You want me to feed and fish and provide a floorshow for six guys *and* put up with Skip's crap for a lousy hundred bucks? Get real!"

"That's flapdoodle. You'd wear the bikini anyway. I know that much. Okay. One-fifty. The feed's cold cuts and beer. Skip'll handle that. How 'bout it?"

Skip was Patty's son, my first cousin. We were the same age, within a few days, but we'd been at each other's throats since before we could walk.

"Well?"

"I'm thinking," I said. Hmm. A hundred and fifty from Dad, plus lunch and beer and tips. I'd do that every day of the week, even with Skip along. Still, it never paid to appear eager. "I suppose," I said. "Where am I taking them, and what am I after?"

"The kings haven't shown up yet, so take 'em to Double Sixty for grouper. Should be good after the blow."

The run to Double Sixty was an easy one I'd made a hundred times. The navigation coordinates were in my head as a backup, but usually at the sea buoy I'd put the *Margaret Ellen* on step at twenty-two hundred rpm's and steer a compass heading of due west for sixty minutes. The reef was a mile-long strip of rocks in sixty feet of water. Sixty minutes out plus sixty feet down, hence the Double Sixty name tag Dad had given it. I'd have fun, and if the group of guys did too, maybe there'd be more than an extra hundred in tips. For insurance, as Dad knew I'd do any day the sun was shining, I planned to wear my bikini.

"Okay," I said, "Top off *Skipjack's* tanks and it's a deal."

"That's blackmail!"

I didn't reply.

"Okay." His breath whistled in my ear. "It's a deal."

"You're a dear," I said. "By the way, NOAA said there's a chance of fog after midnight. I'll leave here by five. Have her stocked and fueled, and I'll be there by six." Pausing to gather the courage, I added, "Dad … there's one other thing."

"Yes?"

In my eyes Dad was more than Superman could've ever hoped to be. But Dad wasn't a mind reader. I was sorry for my immature action, but for him to know this, I'd have to be mature enough to say so. "Ah, I've been doing a lot of thinking."

"About—"

"Yeah, about how sorry I am for the trouble my big mouth—"

"Water under the bridge, baby. Let it go and come back home. You belong at the helm of the *Margaret Ellen*."

"Thanks, Dad, that's where I want to be."

"That makes it a done deal."

Hearing those words was better than having received a key to the universe. Now, because Dad's words held double meaning, I could hang tough in resolving my situation with Angus. Dad not only wanted me back at the helm of the *Margaret Ellen*, he also wanted *Bonita* and me back in the slip behind the bait shop. "Thanks, Dad. I won't let you down."

I returned the receiver to its cradle. It would be a short night. In fact, to reach Dad's place before six, I'd have to have *Skipjack* underway by five. Despite my wish to do so, I didn't dare spend the night with Angus. And this time I wasn't any happier than he'd be. I dogged the overhead hatches, grabbed my unneeded overnight bag, and headed for the penthouse.

CHAPTER 6

When Angus purchased the Buttonwood, the entire upper floor was dedicated to the penthouse—half given to a sun deck, half given to living quarters. This was spacious, to be sure, but both areas lacked the appeal of a medieval funeral parlor.

One of his tenants, a foxy interior decorator living in apartment 401, suggested some renovation. I wholeheartedly agreed, but at a point early in the project my woman's intuition nudged me in the ribs, suggesting Ms. Foxy had stronger designs on Angus than she did on the job at hand.

As it turned out, I'd been wrong. Her interest in Angus included nothing deeper than his bank account. And her work was splendid.

She jazzed up the living quarters with light colors and modern furnishings, timesaving appliances, and an entertainment center worthy of centerfold attention. The once barren sun deck became a lanai complete with full kitchen, pool, sauna, Jacuzzi, and wet bar. For added convenience in fetching the drink he loved, Angus modified the poolside fridge to hold a keg of beer and installed an elegant draft handle shaped like a great white shark on the door.

When I stepped from the private elevator, Angus was on the lanai, sprawled in a lounge chair cupping a mug of draft on his lap. Making a quick read of my expression, he said, "Why the long face?"

I curled up in a nearby chair and explained about Dad's request for help. A moment later his deadpan expression gave way to a smile. He jumped up, grabbed a mug, and headed for the draft handle on the fridge.

Drawing the mug of draft, he said, "In that case I suggest a cold beer. Next, we'll enjoy a you-wash-me-and-I'll-wash-you shower. The main course will follow, which will highlight an extended session of Loman's, forget-your-cares therapy."

"That's a lovely prescription," I said, "but how about supper?"

He went on like he hadn't heard me. "Tomorrow night," he said, "you're all mine. Sheepshead, hush puppies, and you. No phone. No friends. No one but you. All mine. All night."

Many evenings with Angus had begun with supper and ended with sex. Even so, I couldn't recall ever having agreed to an advance booking. What the heck. I laughed. "Fine. But how about tonight? I'm starved."

He handed me the frosty mug of draft. "I'll call Pizza Hut. They deliver. For now, drink up and follow me. If I can't take your mind off of food for a while, I'll give up my license."

Oh really? "If you have a lover's license, lover, where've you been hiding it?"

He wiggled his eyebrows and started inside. Okay, actions spoke louder than words, so I'd settle for a demonstration. I set my untouched beer aside and followed.

If Gwen aired the story of Eva's murder on the early news, we missed it. In fact, after our titillating shower, we didn't step outside the master bedroom until the pizza delivery at ten-thirty.

After another shower we took the pizza, a large pepperoni with extra cheese, out to the lanai, but the air was chilly, and the chairs were dripping with condensation. A look from the parapet confirmed the NOAA forecast was dead on. Below us a blanket of fog, looking much like an off-white cake mix, obscured the usually splendid view of the Intracoastal Waterway and my sloop in its slip behind the Buttonwood. We retreated to the comfort and warmth of the living room.

Despite my ravenous appetite of a few hours earlier, two slices of pizza were all I could manage. Maybe the satisfying sex had also satisfied my appetite. He offered, but I declined another beer. I rounded up my overnight bag, returned to his side, and ran my fingers through his wavy brown hair. Each curl snapped back into place. "The fog won't burn off until after daylight," I said, "so I'll have to leave before five."

He took my hand and clicked the remote control at the big-screen TV. "Let's catch the news before you go. Okay?"

A part of me wanted to leave. Another part, probably my morbid curiosity, did not. "Okay," I said, "but not a minute longer." I perched on the edge of the footstool and tapped my toes as Channel Five went through their pre-show hype and claim of being the Bay Area's number-one station for news, sports, and weather. Had anyone other than a car rental company ever admitted to being number two? After the hoopla and a rundown on the stories to follow, Gwen O'Dell's face filled the screen.

She looked stunning. Had she just stepped from a beauty salon? Maybe, as her hair, makeup, and clothes were all now perfect. Obviously, she'd been busy since I'd last seen her. Even so, there was no way she'd had as much fun.

"Since our broadcast at six," she said, "Channel Five has learned the identity of the body discovered on Hangman's Key earlier today .... "

She narrated as she ran footage of the scene at Hangman's Key, the two sheriff's deputies, and of Angus and me. Too much coverage of me. Actually, it was too little coverage, as Dad's fishing shirt had not hidden as much as I would've liked. I hoped he'd missed the broadcast.

" ... Dr. Clayton Muller, along with two of Eva Marie Park's closest friends, made the identification of the body. Later, after a preliminary examination, the Pinellas County Medical Examiner stated Ms. Park's death was caused by a single gunshot to the head. Time of death was estimated to be late Friday or early Saturday. Detective Myers surmised her body was dumped into the Gulf of Mexico somewhere near Hangman's Key where it washed ashore and was discovered earlier today by Karen Cobia and Angus Loman during a beachcombing excursion ... "

Evidently, Myers had OK'd the airing of some details but not the fact that the body had been tied and ineffectively weighted before it was dumped.

" ... and incredibly, just hours before the discovery of Ms. Park's body, her attorney, Stan Avery, called the St. Petersburg police ... their investigation determined that a boat normally docked behind her home was missing. Mr. Avery provided an initial description of the boat, but the Florida Department of Motor Vehicles just released a detailed description."

After flashing the hull registration number on screen, she added, "The boat is a Grady-White 26, white with blue trim, and is equipped with a two-hundred-fifty horsepower Yamaha outboard engine. Anyone seeing this vessel is asked to call the Pinellas County Sheriff's Office or the St. Petersburg Police Department immediately."

The station went to a commercial break, and Angus turned off the TV. He stood and tugged me toward the bedroom. "I have an alarm clock," he said.

I pulled away and grabbed my overnight bag. "I have one too," I said, "and Dad's counting on me."

"Yeah, good old Dad."

"Don't start that!" I pushed past him and stomped out the door. When I reached the elevator, he was at my side. I stepped in, punched the ground-floor button, and spoke without looking at him. "You want me to call when

I'm tucked in, or just cast off and sail out of your life?"

"I want you to call." It was a whisper, but he added, "Please," as the doors closed between us.

At the rear door of the Buttonwood I paused and stared out at the veil of moisture obscuring the dock. My sloop was waiting a hundred feet away—I just couldn't see that far. And while it was no night for sailing, I'd seen enough movies to know it was a perfect night for a killer. Was one lurking in the mist? Poised? Ready to strike? My thoughts were crazy, but, then, weren't all killers crazy? Drawing a deep breath and clutching my overnight bag like a club, I squared my shoulders, pushed through the door, and strode down the dock.

The crosswise planking, now wet with dew, resembled the ash-gray rib bones of an abandoned carcass. The thought triggered a shiver, and I moved quicker, my deck shoes telegraphing each step as they squeaked like frightened mice. Would something sinister manifest at any moment? No. I reached my boat safely, quickly slipped inside, turned on the lights, and secured the hatch. My chest ached. Only then did I realize I'd been holding my breath.

I unpacked my overnight bag and repacked it with items I'd want with me the next day. That done, I set the bag and my thermos bottle near the companionway, peeled off my clothes, and grabbed the cordless phone on my way to the berth. With a reading light on and a pillow folded beneath my head, I punched the speed-dial button for Angus's number. He picked up on the first ring. "I'm tucked in," I said.

In a soft voice, he replied, "And I'm sorry."

We spent a few minutes swapping meaningless banter, trying to smooth feelings. When we finally exchanged goodnights, we still had a few raw edges.

I turned off the light and shut my eyes. Sleep didn't come, however, only tossing and turning, visions of Eva's body, and thoughts of where my relationship with Angus was headed. Long minutes later, and absent a single positive thought, I concluded my relationship was headed nowhere at all. When, then, would I summon the guts to burn the bridge? Tomorrow? Would the new day bring with it the courage to complete what I had failed to do today?

When the phone rang I was still trying to push sleep-robbing thoughts from my mind. I turned and stared at the glowing numerals on my alarm clock. Ten minutes past midnight. It had to be Angus, a heavy breather, or a wrong number.

I picked up the phone and muttered, "Hello."

The voice, a faint whisper, said, "Karen? Karen Cobia?"

I said I was.

"I need help. Desperately."

CHAPTER 7

The voice was female, she knew my name, and, despite my wish for sleep, she'd just made an eye-opening statement. I rolled over and clicked on the bulkhead lamp. "Who is this?" I said.

"Ah, this is Amber. Amber Brantley. I'm sorry to disturb you this late, but I have to speak with you."

After hearing Gwen's assessment of Amber, I'd pictured the woman as overbearing and arrogant. This voice was soft and polite. "Speak to me about what?" I said.

"It's about Reginald Wentworth," she whispered. "He's missing."

"I don't understand. Who is Reginald—?"

"Oh. Sorry," she said. "He's the gentleman Eva was going to marry. He's missing."

Was going to marry? Yes. Gwen had mentioned such a rumor. Until now I'd only thought of Eva's murderer as someone who'd taken her life, but it was so much more. This someone had also destroyed her life's plans and dreams. I tugged my flannel comforter higher. "The police are aware of the man in Eva's life," I said. "They also wish to speak with you. Have they?"

"Ah, no. Not yet. I'll speak with them, soon, but ... ah, this can't wait."

She was still speaking softly and politely, but she wasn't making sense. "What can't wait?"

"The lady on the TV tonight. The one who did the story. She said you were an investigator. I need one to find Reginald."

Me? On a missing-person case? Not likely, especially not after having mended my bridge with Dad. With my old job back, accident investigations and the like were on my burn list. I tried to explain. "What the lady didn't mention, Ms. Brantley, is my niche is nautical investigations. You know, stolen boats and boating accidents, not missing persons and murder. The police can help you. Call them."

"Don't hang up. Please. You can help me. I know it. Just listen a moment."

Dad doesn't waste a heartbeat on unwanted calls. On the other hand, the world of telemarketing would crumble without people like me: I can't hang up on a pitch. Despite not meaning it, I said, "Go on."

"There's a boat missing."

"The police have that information as well," I said. "It's Eva's Grady-White. In fact it was mentioned on the news broadcast. Didn't you catch that part?"

"No, you don't understand. It's not that boat. There's another one. A big one. I want you to find it."

Another boat? "Whoa. First you said a man named Wentworth was missing. Now it's a man *and* a boat? Is that it?"

Her voice dropped to a whisper. "Not over the phone. Meet me. Please."

After midnight? In the fog? Not likely. "I've had a hell of a day, Ms. Brantley, and quite frankly you're not making much sense." I explained about my early-morning charter and my need for a few hours sleep. "I'll be back at Cobia's charter dock by one. If you still wish to speak with me then, fine. I'll be available. For now, call the police."

"But—"

I borrowed Lancaster's line. "No buts. It's my way or no way!"

"Okay ... I will ... I'll be there."

After replacing the receiver, I thought of calling the sheriff's office. What could I tell them? "Hey guys, guess what? Amber's in town."

What would they say? "Thank you very much, Ms. Cobia. Where is she?" No idea. I turned off the light.

When the alarm exploded in my ear, I snapped upright in the berth and cracked my head on one of the hatch knobs. I'd been dreaming.

In my dreams I'm never the beautiful maiden sought by the handsome prince. No. I'm always just me, always fleeing for my life. This time the setting was Hangman's Key. It was midnight and I was there, darting between the dunes. Eva's killer was behind me. I couldn't see him, but he was there—somewhere. A three-quarter moon lit my path. I raced on, zigzagging crazily, and then bolted from the safety of the dunes and onto the beach. *Skipjack* was just ahead, shimmering in the soft moonlight playing upon the quiet water. Only a hundred yards more. Suddenly, the moonlight vanished.

I tripped and sprawled face first in the deep sand. I held my breath, listening for my pursuer. Nothing, just the soft breeze whistling through the tall pines and the far-off calls between a pair of whippoorwills. Reach *Skipjack*, and I was safe.

I started to rise ... then froze as a new sound reached me. Was it just the wild thumping of my heart? No! It was footfalls. Getting louder; getting closer. I peered over my shoulder. It wasn't a cloud obscuring the moon. I screamed.

Damn! It was good to be awake. I rubbed my head, dressed, grabbed my gear, and had *Skipjack* moving north by five.

Fog still blanketed the waterway and obscured the surrounding landscape, but the waterways of the Bay Area were the life's highways I grew up on. A breakdown might stop me. The blind visibility would not. I stopped for a thermos of coffee and a pair of Danish rolls at Blackbeard's Cove, an always-open restaurant fronting the ICW near the Dolphin Village Shopping Center, and still reached Dad's at six.

In addition to the fuel dock, three slips lined the sea wall behind the bait shop. Dad kept the *Margaret Ellen* in the closest one and *Skipjack*, when he could pry her away from me, in the middle one. The outside slip had all the hookups for a live-aboard vessel, but it'd been empty since I moved my sloop to the Buttonwood. Dad said the slip would stay that way until I broke up with Angus and moved back home where I belonged. Yes. With the comfort of having my old job back, returning home would also be a great first step in ending my relationship with Angus.

The throaty murmur of the *Margaret Ellen's* engines was a familiar and welcome sound as I pulled *Skipjack* into her slip. Dad was on the catwalk garbed in his usual deck shoes, cut-off Levi's, polo shirt, and Marlins ball cap. His tanned face, arms, and legs looked a shade lovelier than an old penny. He raised his forearm, dampened with dew, and looked at his wristwatch before taking my bow line.

"A girl'd get to work on time if she lived closer," he said.

I managed a smile but offered no answer. He wasn't expecting one. Glancing around, I saw Skip plodding across the patio with a bucket in each hand, the charter party milling about on the aft deck of the *Margaret Ellen*, and a woman standing under the night light at the rear door of the bait shop. She was slumped against the wall with a two-fisted grip on a macramé purse the size of my backpack.

Dad helped me secure *Skipjack* and then said, "The guys are rearing to go." He nodded toward the bait shop. "I don't know who she is."

Amber Brantley was my guess. After handing Dad my tote bag and thermos bottle, I jumped to the dock but ended up having to grab his arm to keep from falling.

When I was steady on my feet, he said, "Why're you limping?"

Many folks cuss when they're pissed. I do too, but I also kick things. Dad

41

knew this, of course. Regardless, I tried a half lie with a full smile. "Stubbed my toe," I said.

"Sure you did." He swung his leg like a place-kicker. "You booted something. Your boyfriend, perhaps?"

I let it go. He dropped his eyes, muttered something that may have been an apology, and returned to my side. He hugged me for several moments before gesturing to the *Margaret Ellen*. "The fog's heavy, baby, so use the radar. Watch the sounder. Pick up the markers and buoys one at a time until you clear the sea buoy, and—"

"Dad! I'm a licensed captain."

He gave me another squeeze. "Yeah, you can do it," he said. "I just worry. Call me on six-eight when you're in the clear."

This wasn't my first trip out in a fog, and, regardless of the weather, calling him while heading out or back in had always been our standard procedure. But I hadn't been at the helm of the *Margaret Ellen* lately. Maybe he was just nervous. "I'll be fine," I said. "Everything aboard?"

"Skip's getting the bait now."

"And you talked to him. Right?"

"We reached an understanding."

"Oh?"

"You're the captain. He's the mate. 'Screw up,' I told him, 'and you'll be wearing your ass between your shoulder blades.'"

I laughed out loud at the thought. "Thanks."

He scrubbed his knuckles on the top of my head. "You knew I was kidding about the bikini. Right?"

Of course I knew. I'd worked and played on the Gulf Coast all my life and a very conservative, two-piece bikini had been standard attire any day when the temperature was above seventy degrees. Dad knew this. What he hadn't known was my habit of wearing an outrageously skimpy bikini while out beachcombing. And if he'd missed Channel Five's late-news broadcast, in particular the part featuring my backside, he still didn't know. I kissed his cheek, which was answer enough about the bikini. "Let me see what she wants before I cast off."

He took a deep breath, expanding the fabric of his T-shirt to the breaking point, and said, "Okay, and while you check on her I'll step over there and make it perfectly clear to these guys that any hanky-panky could be hazardous to their health."

"Dad! Don't scare 'em. I want that big tip."

He gave me another hug and headed for the boarding ramp. I picked up my gear and walked over to where the woman was standing.

If this were Amber, Gwen's idea of beauty was kinder than mine. Or maybe it was just her clothes. She was wearing white sneakers, loose-fitting black jeans, and a bulky warm-up jacket sporting the Buccaneers' logo. Her nose was slim, like her face, and she had a large birthmark shaped like a crescent moon on her neck. On the plus side her marble-gray eyes and short-cropped auburn hair were attractive. That and lips belonging in a lipstick commercial were the only sensual qualities I believed would rate her a second look. She spoke as I approached.

"Karen?"

"Amber?"

She nodded.

"Have you talked with the police?" I said.

She lowered her eyes and fidgeted with her purse. "Ah, no, not yet."

I rebalanced the gear in my arms and tried to put a stern tone in my voice. "I'm not getting mixed up in this until you do."

"Okay," she said, "I understand, but what I have to talk with you about doesn't have to involve the police."

Her voice was still soft and polite, and I didn't want to be rude, but I'd explained my position to her. Pointing to the *Margaret Ellen*, I said, "Amber, this job comes first, and I'm late now. I have to go."

She clutched her purse and whispered, "Please."

If only I'd hung up on her. Mimicking Detective Myers, I blew out breath between clinched teeth. "Okay," I said. "If you can make sandwiches and open beer, come along. We can talk while we're underway."

Her face perked. "I can make sandwiches and serve beer," she said. "I used to be a waitress."

"A waitress?"

Her eyes narrowed. "Ah, just once," she said. "A long time ago."

I shrugged. "Let's go."

Skip smirked at me and then raked his eyes over Amber as we moved past him to reach the pilothouse. With her settled in, I ignored the question filling Skip's eyes and returned to the aft deck to introduce myself to the charter party. The six men were members of the same Dallas rod and gun club, and like Dad had said, they were rearing to go. Allen, the youngest and best looking member of the group, said they'd hunted blue quail in Mexico the week before. My big tip was looking better all the time.

"This week we're fishing," he added.

I leaned against the gunnel. "So how'd you happen to choose us?"

"Your ad in *Outdoor Life*. I figured anyone named Cobia had to know fishing."

"The name choice wasn't mine," I said, "but I'll prove the fishing expertise shortly."

After pointing out the life vests, the emergency rafts, and reciting the rules they were expected to obey, I panned the faces. Each responded with a nod. "Good," I said. "We're about to get underway, so make yourselves comfortable. There's snacks in the galley and drinks in the big cooler."

Dad tossed the portside lines aboard and headed for the starboard catwalk. I turned to where Skip was leaning against the gunnel. "Close the transom gate, standby for the starboard lines, and stow the fenders when we clear the slip."

He saluted with a middle finger.

I stuck my tongue out at him and headed for the pilothouse.

The fog thinned after we eased under the high-span bridge and entered the Gulf. It continued to thin with the passing of each marker. At the sea buoy the *Margaret Ellen* had nothing ahead of her bow but clear, pre-dawn Gulf. After calling Dad to report position and sea condition, I pushed the throttles forward and set course for Double Sixty. Once the Cummins diesels were throbbing in sync, I engaged the autopilot and turned to Amber.

"Now," I said, "what's this all about?"

At first I thought she hadn't heard me over the drone of the engines. Or, since she was standing stock-still with a fixed gaze, maybe the spray whipping from the bow and snatching a red and green glow from the running lights as it flew past either side of the pilothouse had mesmerized her. I was about to repeat my question when she finally spoke.

"It's a long story," she said.

"Then get started. When we reach the reef, I'll be too busy to talk."

She nodded and edged closer to the helm. "The man I mentioned is Reginald Wentworth. He and Eva met at a charity function a few months ago. They clicked, like a love story, right from the start. It was no time until he proposed. She accepted. Their wedding plan was to purchase a luxury yacht and marry aboard it."

"A luxury yacht?" I said. "Damn! He must be rich."

The *Margaret Ellen* rolled through a rogue swell and Amber latched onto a grab rail for balance. Her eyes widened. "He may or may not be rich," she said, "but it was Eva who put up the money for the yacht. About one-and-a-half-million dollars."

Dad had two hundred thousand dollars tied up in the *Margaret Ellen.* In my book she was the finest vessel afloat. And while one-and-a-half-million-dollar luxury was beyond my imagination, I had no trouble imagining someone committing murder for far less money. I stared at her. "Did Eva give that much money to him to buy a yacht?"

"No, of course not. Eva sent the money to a broker." She paused and swallowed. Twice. "They were supposed to pick up the yacht last week."

"Let's stop right there," I said. "According to what her attorney told the police, Eva and her fiancé, this Reginald, were supposed to be out of town. Together. Maybe to pick up this new yacht. But we know the only trip Eva made was a one-way trip to the Gulf." Rapping my knuckles on the wheel, I added, "Hasn't this suggested anything to you?"

Her narrowed eyes and blank expression said it had not.

"Think about it, Amber. Eva was killed sometime last Friday. Her house was ransacked. Her safe emptied. Angus and I found her body on Hangman's Key yesterday. Reginald was supposed to be with her, but now he's missing. Let's face it. The odds are he's dead too, or he's running because he's the one who killed her."

"No! He couldn't. He wouldn't. The attorney's wrong. Reginald went to pick up the boat. He did. I know it … I just don't know why I haven't heard from him."

Traditionally, men held a dim view of women's logic. In this case I'd side with them, and considering Amber's mindset further argument wasn't going to help. "Okay," I said. "Let's say he didn't kill Eva, and he wasn't killed by whoever did. Where was he going to pick up the yacht?"

"Up north, somewhere … I think."

"In that case," I said, "your worry is premature."

"Why?"

I was a homebody, not a world traveler, but Dad and I drove to Morehead City, North Carolina, once. The trip took two days. I explained this and added, "If Reginald were picking up a yacht anywhere north of there, his return time would be far greater. My guess is he'd need close to a week to make it back."

"I don't care," she said. "I want you to find him."

"Amber, listen to me. He simply hasn't had time to return. He's somewhere en route. On top of that, any search for him would be complicated by not knowing if he's running offshore or running the ditch."

"What ditch?"

"The Intracoastal Waterway. You know, the ICW. Boaters call it the ditch. Regardless, if he's with the yacht, not dead or not running away, he's not overdue. I think it'd be a waste of my time and your money to look for him."

I waited. She didn't reply. What the hell. I had a day, maybe two, before I settled back into the charter routine. And there was no question she had the money. But, money aside, I didn't understand her logic in wanting me to find him. I asked.

"To tell him Eva's been killed," she said.

Could such logic be questioned? I tried. "Shouldn't you spare him that shock until you can speak with him in person?"

We were pushing through three-foot seas and a quartering swell with the movements of a teen's dance step: rise high, dip low, roll right, roll left. Repeat. Repeat. Repeat. I glanced at Amber. "Well?"

She was leaning against the bulkhead, eyes closed, feet spread, hands clutching her stomach. "I don't feel so good," she said.

"Great."

I'd never been seasick, but I'd been around plenty of people who had. They described it as a condition where you prayed to die and were scared you wouldn't. The cure, in most cases, was simply the return of stable ground beneath the afflicted.

She clasped both hands to her mouth. I threw an arm around her waist and rushed her to the head. When her heaves subsided, I showed her how to use the marine toilet and then led her to the pilothouse berth. Stable ground for her was several hours away. So, too, was any chance of hearing the rest of her story.

CHAPTER 8

The sun climbed free of the red haze obscuring the eastern horizon just as I positioned the *Margaret Ellen* over my favorite spot on the reef. "Red sky at night, sailor's delight," was the way I'd learned the first half of the old-timer's rhyme. The second half stated, "Red sky at morn, sailors be warned."

As if lending an additional opinion, in the west, draped high above the still-dark horizon, mare's-tails as orderly as linen on a clothesline were gleaming in the new day's sunshine. Both conditions, the red sky and the distant clouds, were far more than superstition; they were valid signals of a pending change in the weather.

With the anchor set and the *Margaret Ellen* riding easy to the gentle sea, I rolled up my sleeves and pitched in alongside Skip to help with the work. We repaired tackle, rigged bait, and swung fish into the hold. Within an hour a smile replaced his smirk. Not long after that he patted my back as he hustled past. I laughed to myself. Dad wouldn't believe it. If Skip and I could get through an entire day without a screaming match or a slugfest, we'd set a record.

As often as possible, usually while fetching beer or making sandwiches, I checked on Amber. Half the time she was stretched out as still as a corpse in a coffin. During the other half the berth was empty and the door to the head was closed. She was not having a good day.

I'd dressed in layers before leaving my sloop: jeans and long-sleeved shirt over shorts and halter over my most-conservative bikini. The shirt came off at ten, the jeans an hour later. Despite a high, thin overcast, a slight breeze, and a water temperature near seventy degrees, it was hot.

At eleven-thirty, along with a pair of nurse sharks and an eighty-pound stingray, we had a two-hundred-pound assortment of grouper, sea bass, and snapper in the hold. The men were thrilled with the fast action, but they were beginning to move with less animation. Requests for beer outnumbered requests for bait. No one complained when I ordered lines up and gear stowed.

Skip brought the anchor aboard and gave me a respectable salute when he had it locked into the bow roller. I returned his salute with a smile, one I really meant, and then grabbed a Pepsi and a package of crackers and set course for home. A long-fetch swell was still running, but the sea had dropped to under three feet. NOAA got it right, occasionally. Even so, I figured boating conditions would be damned near perfect by the time the next system arrived and stirred it all up again.

I handed the wheel, munching, sipping, and weighing the little I'd learned from Amber against the comments voiced on Hangman's Key. Was Reginald Wentworth also a victim as Myers speculated, or was he a Mister Slick on the run as Lancaster suggested?

Adding my thoughts to the pair of scenarios, I played them start-to-finish in my mind. The exercise was one of futility. More answers were needed from Amber. Myers would want those answers as well. Like it or not, she had to talk with him.

During the morning the barometer dropped slightly and the five-knot breeze clocked to south. Both occurrences were additional signs of a new weather system taking aim at Florida's west coast. I remained at the helm, watching ahead and glancing at Amber. When she jumped from the berth and stumbled to the head, I switched the VHF to channel six-eight and picked up the mike.

"Cobia base, Cobia base, the motor vessel *Margaret Ellen*, over."

Dad answered immediately. "Cobia here. Where're you at, baby?"

"Pointed your way," I said. "Got the sea buoy on the horizon."

"Problem?"

The marine VHF radio provided static-free transmissions over long distances, which made it a great communications tool. Unfortunately, the VHF was also a gigantic party line. And, like any party line, eavesdroppers abounded. I didn't like it, but there was no other choice.

"No, the run was fine. Great catch, unbelievable stingray, but ... ah, Dad, please call Detective Myers at the sheriff's office. Ask him to meet me when we get in. It's about Hangman's Key, over."

"Something to do with your extra baggage this morning?"

I glanced again at the closed door to the head. "You got it," I said.

"Okay, baby, will do and copy this. Fog's lifted, light wind out of the south, but the current's whistling. Lay on the horn when you leave the channel. I'll be there for you."

The current through Big Tarpon Pass became a vicious torrent during the middle hours of each tide change. I'd reach the *Margaret Ellen's* slip at peak flow, and, with her slip lying ninety degrees to the current, docking would be tricky. Tricky, but no problem. Dad would be there—IRS or not.

"Roger. Copy that. *Margaret Ellen* clear on six-eight and switching to one-six."

Amber came to life and sat at the edge of the berth when we hit smooth water inside the pass. I held a no-wake speed up the channel and gave Dad two long blasts on the air horns when I started my approach to the dock. While I was maneuvering into the slip, Amber reeled from the pilothouse. Dad and Skip were still lashing the docking lines when she jumped to the dock. So much for the boarding ramp. I shut down the engines, switched off the electronics, and headed for the beer cooler. I'd earned the indulgence.

From the aft deck I had a clear view of the patio behind the bait shop. Myers wasn't in sight. I snapped the pop-top on a can of Bud, took a long pull, and glanced at Dad. He answered my inquiring look with a shrug. Meaning, I supposed, that Myers hadn't arrived yet. I didn't want to lose Amber, but since she still hadn't fully explained why she desperately needed my service, I couldn't see her leaving. She didn't. With halting gait, she reeled across the patio and sprawled into one of the lounge chairs.

Skip opened the transom gate and Dad set the boarding ramp in place, allowing the charter party to head for the dock. Without counting heads as the men departed, I thought I was alone and was about to sit on the cooler when something nudged my elbow. I spun around.

It was Allen, looking far more worn than he had at daylight. Yet despite his khaki shirt soaked with sweat, his disheveled cinnamon hair, and his sunburned face, he still managed a warm smile as he handed me a wad of bills. "This is for you," he said.

The heft alone told me the amount was well over a hundred dollars. Not a bad tip considering I was still in shorts and a halter, not my bikini. Feeling as foolish as a moonstruck schoolgirl, I said, "I hope you enjoyed your trip."

"Cobia was a good choice. We enjoyed the action. Thank you."

There was more than appreciation in his eyes. Much more. My skin tingled, as I moved to the portside, away from where Dad and Skip were still working. Leaning against the rail, I said, "Where to now?"

"We fly back home in the morning. And, hey, I'd love to show you my town, if you're ever out that way."

"Dallas?" I laughed. "Fat chance."

Most immature guys wasted a lot of time with chitchat. He didn't. "I still have tonight," he said. "How about dinner?"

This wasn't the first time a customer had asked me for a date. And unlike women in other professions, I had no policy against accepting. In fact, I'd found after watching a man fish for a few hours I could make a good call as to his character. Allen was first-class material. The only real obstacle, then, was my unburned bridge with Angus. Reluctantly, I said, "I'd love to but I have a date for dinner."

Instead of a look of rejection, his expression brightened. "All right! So you're not married?"

Despite myself, I laughed. "No," I said. "Just dating for now."

His eyes locked with mine. "Okay," he said, "I was stupid to think otherwise. But may I call you if I get back this way?"

This required no thinking. "Of course. I'd love to take you fishing again."

He raised his hands in surrender. "No, what I meant—"

I touched a fingertip to his lips. "You don't have to explain, Allen." At another time, a right time, I would've said yes. To avoid any hurt feelings for now, though, I gave him a wink and said, "You get back this way, this is where you'll find me."

He returned my wink as he headed for the ramp. "I'll remember that."

With a warm roll of cash in one hand and a cold beer in the other, I ambled toward a deck chair, intent on a few moments of relaxation. Dad called out to me first.

"Myers should be here in twenty minutes. Said to keep her busy."

I glanced at the patio. Amber was slumped in her patio chair, apparently still lethargic from her bout with Neptune's revenge. "She's not going anywhere," I said.

CHAPTER 9

Seasickness would have killed all thought of food for Amber, but not for me. I was starved. The *Margaret Ellen* was well stocked with food and drink, of course, but since daylight I'd been busy serving others, not myself. That was about to change. I slipped the roll of cash into my pocket, finished my beer, and headed for the patio.

Amber opened her eyes and spoke as I reached her side. "I've never been on a boat before," she said. "I should've known better. God knows I get sick just watching a merry-go-round."

I waved off her apology. "It can happen to anyone," I said.

"Thank you." Then, as if we hadn't had a several-hours gap in our conversation, she added, "Will you find Reginald for me?"

Rubbing my stomach, I said, "There's a few items to cover first. Let's talk over lunch."

Places to eat are plentiful along the beach, but most are the fast-food variety. Shanley's is the rare exception, which makes it my favorite for a number of reasons. First, like the bait shop, it occupies a weathered, clapboard building serving its owners as business site and residence. Next, in addition to a seafood platter few are able to finish, they make the tastiest steak-and-onion hoagies in the county. Best of all, though, Shanley's is just two doors up the street from the bait shop.

Speaking with an added decibel for emphasis, I caught Dad's attention and told him where we were headed. If there'd be a wait for Myers, I'd choose the location. With a follow-me gesture, I led Amber through the bait shop, out the street-side door, and past our next-door neighbor, Danny's Outboard Service.

The aroma of grilled steak and onions met us halfway up Shanley's oyster-shell walk. As usual, my mouth watered in anticipation, but Amber's lifeless expression deepened as we climbed the sand-covered steps. Would the sight of food trigger a relapse? We'd soon know.

The spacious dining room was sprinkled with paddle fans, picnic tables, and a row of booths along one wall. Roxie, Steve Shanley's wife, met us just inside the door. She planted her feet about shoulder-width apart, closed her eyes, and placed a fingertip to her temple. "I see a patio table, a steak hoagie, extra onion, a tall draft, and a side order of onion rings." She opened one eye. "How'd I do?"

I slapped my thighs. "I don't know how you do it, Roxie."

She swiveled her rotund torso and pointed to Amber.

"I don't think I want anything."

Roxie glanced at me. I sucked in my cheeks and crossed my eyes.

Taking Amber's hand, Roxie said, "Don't worry, honey, I'll bring ya something that'll perk ya up."

In Florida if you have waterfront it's a safe bet you also have a patio. Shanley's has a huge, awning-covered one, and a portion of it supported by wood pilings extends over the water. On a hot day it's a cool place to be. I led Amber to my favorite table and selected a chair that would allow me to watch for Myers.

She dumped her purse and warm-up jacket onto the deck and dropped into a seat. I watched as she used the tail of her Disney World T-shirt to blot sweat from her face and neck. In the jacket she'd looked boyish. In the damp T-shirt, she didn't.

Within seconds of sitting Amber jumped up and headed for the restroom. While she was gone I thought on how to talk myself out of the job she wanted me to perform. Ideas came to mind, but I wasn't a liar. The truth would have to do. Dad wanted me back at the helm of the *Margaret Ellen*. This, above all else, was also what I wanted. Amber would have to understand I couldn't afford to let her problem stand in the way.

When she returned to the table, I explained my position. Nothing. If anything, her pained expression deepened. My next step was to explain the insurance angle in the recovery of a stolen vessel. "In this case," I said, "with a vessel of that value, my finder's fee would be huge. But the vessel hasn't been stolen. Eva purchased it and it's headed this way. I'd earn zilch for locating it."

She reached for her purse. "I'll pay you."

Roxie arrived at our table before I could reply. She set a frosty mug of draft and a sizzling platter of onion rings in front of me and a glass of Gatorade and a saucer of saltines before Amber. "This'll fix ya up, hon." She winked at me. "Hoagie'll be up in a jiff."

I squirted ketchup over the rings and snaked one free of the goo with my little finger. "No hurry," I said. "This'll keep me busy for a moment."

When Roxie was out of earshot, Amber said, "How much?"

"Amber, do you understand if Reginald picked up a boat late last week, up north somewhere as you've said, and if he ran day and night, which no one traveling alone could do, he couldn't possibly get here before the end of this week?"

With a deadpan expression she repeated, "How much?"

And Dad thought I was hardheaded. Okay. How much? First I'd have to find out where the boat had been built and, if in a different location, the yard where it'd been commissioned. In most cases this would also be the same yard where Reginald would take possession of the yacht. No problem. I knew ways to do this.

Then I'd have to learn when Reginald got underway. With this information I could make an educated guess as to where he might be. The next step would be to call marinas and fuel facilities either side of that area and ask each of them to attempt a radio contact on channel sixteen. That sounded easy enough, but did Reginald know boaters were required to monitor the emergency channel while underway? Maybe. Maybe not.

The initial search for Reginald would only involve the phone and the radio. Doing this wouldn't jeopardize my position with Dad. I wiped my fingers on a napkin and then folded it neatly as I formulated my reply. "Okay, Amber, I'll give you three days, billing time and expenses against a fifteen-hundred-dollar advance."

Bingo. She stiffened and dropped her gaze to the untouched drink in her hands. Her knuckles whitened. "I don't carry that kind of cash," she whispered.

"Then make it a check," I said.

For a moment I thought she'd changed her mind. She bit her lower lip and studied her purse. "I don't like doing this," she said. I watched and waited while she mentally wrestled with whatever it was she didn't like doing. When she pinned it, she pulled a leather pouch from her purse and opened it on her lap.

I reached for my beer but leaned forward enough to look into the pouch at the same time. It contained jewelry. Lots of jewelry, and right on top were a pair of diamond earrings shaped like interlocking hearts. My mouth was on autopilot. "Eva had earrings like those," I said.

Amber's head snapped up. "Ah ... yes, some of this is hers. I was taking it with mine to be cleaned."

After considering several pieces, she selected a ring and pushed it across the table. "This will more than cover your fee," she said. "Hock it for fifteen hundred and give me the ticket. I'll redeem it when I get the cash."

Every item in the pouch was elegant, and with its cluster of diamonds atop an engraved gold band, the ring was no exception. "Okay, I'll get started, but this would go much easier if you could tell me where Reginald was picking up the boat."

She closed the pouch of jewelry and returned it to her purse. "New Jersey," she said. "Yes, I remember now. Eva had the money wired to a broker in New Jersey."

In response to the same question earlier, she'd said, "Up north, somewhere." Why was she suddenly able to narrow it down? Better yet, why hadn't she told me the truth in the first place? Something about her wasn't ringing true. Maybe it was the way she avoided my eyes when she spoke. Maybe it was her slow, thought-out replies. Maybe it was because I detested those evasive characteristics in anyone I spoke with. Crap! Maybe she was just still groggy from her bout of Neptune's revenge.

I shrugged it off and was forming another question when Roxie approached with my hoagie. Myers was right behind her. She set the sandwich down, and he slid into the seat alongside Amber. Pointing to my sandwich, he said, "How about one of those and a small draft."

"Coming up," Roxie said.

When Roxie turned away from the table, I introduced Myers. Amber stiffened, pushed back in her chair, and started to stand. I grabbed her arm. "Let's get this over with," I said.

She glared at me. "I don't have to talk with the police."

"Yes, you do," Myers said. He poked a finger at her seat. She hesitated for a moment before slumping back into her chair.

He stuck his face close to hers. "Yesterday," he said, "your lawyer told the St. Petersburg police you were in Paris. What gives?"

She squirmed in her seat. "I ... I don't tell him every move I make."

"Fine," Myers said. "So when you learned of your aunt's death, Ms. Brantley, why didn't you come to us first?"

She didn't answer.

"Tell him," I said, "or I will."

She dropped her eyes and sat with her hands clasped on her lap. After relating what little I knew, Myers fished a notepad and pencil from his shirt pocket.

"Ms. Brantley," he said, "our primary interest in finding you was to notify you of your aunt's death. It's standard procedure. We'd also like your help in clearing up a few minor details. You have nothing to fear by speaking with me."

His gentle manner and soft, reassuring voice surprised me. On Hangman's Key most of his dialogue and mannerisms had been quite the opposite.

Amber sat as if she hadn't heard a word he said. Only her eyes moved as she tracked a gleaming white Bertram equipped with outriggers and tuna tower pulling away from Dad's fuel dock. I watched the big, beautiful sucker, too.

Dad said the kings were still a few days away, but these guys were decked out and rigged for a serious try at the few that always preceded the main school. From experience I knew once the king mackerel reached our stretch of coastline, Dad's bait and charter business would become a seven-day-a-week madhouse.

"What do you want to know?" she said.

The Bertram passed close behind the patio, its twin exhaust tubes emitting a low rumble like distant thunder. A moment later the first ripple from its wake collided with the pilings under the patio. The deck began a subtle, back-and-forth motion. The table followed. I steadied a vase full of hibiscus blooms before it could topple onto the salt-and-pepper shakers.

In my opinion, one shared with Steve and Roxie, the patio's demise would occur when the next real storm hit the area, or when the barnacles and woodworms quit holding hands. Whichever came first.

Myers gave Amber his thoughts on Reginald, much as I had, but she still, passionately, rejected both possibilities. He didn't push it. "Okay," he said, "you told Karen that Reginald and Eva were picking up a new boat last week. We know Eva made a trip to the Gulf instead. If Reginald had nothing to do with that, and his body is not still out there somewhere, when and how would he have left to pick up the boat?"

Her eyes danced across empty space as if reading from a cue card invisible to all but her. "Friday," she said. "He left at noon on Friday."

"Okay," Myers said. "That takes care of the *when*. Now tell me *how* he left."

"From Tampa," she said. "From the big airport. TPA. He flew."

After butting in and giving my estimate of a yacht's run time from New Jersey, I had a thought. She'd said Reginald and Eva planned to marry aboard the yacht, but she hadn't said the ceremony was planned for St. Petersburg. If it were, where had he planned to berth the vessel? It certainly wouldn't have been in the canal behind Eva's estate, as I was sure that narrow waterway could accommodate only shallow-draft vessels. The next best choice was Maximo Marina. It was close to her place by land or sea. I asked about this.

Amber gestured east, toward downtown. "Somewhere near the yacht club, I think. That's where the reception was planned."

In that case the St. Petersburg Municipal Marina was Reginald's most likely destination. It had an easy, deep-water approach from the Gulf by way of Southwest Channel or the main ship channel, and, in my estimation, the best yachting facilities on Tampa Bay. If Reginald had enough sea-savvy to single-hand from New Jersey, I was sure he had enough to reserve a berth prior to his arrival. I planned to check.

Myers picked it up, speaking to no one in particular. "If he really did leave here that early on Friday, it kicks my worry about a double homicide out the window."

"Lancaster's thought, too," I said.

"Yeah. Considering her time of death, it's unlikely he could've killed her."

Amber bristled. "Reginald? Don't be stupid. Of course he didn't kill her."

"I can't rule out anything or anyone, Ms. Brantley. Even you. Where were you last Friday?"

"Me? Surely you don't think—"

"This is a murder investigation," he said. "I have to know."

While waiting for her reply, I ate the last onion ring and drained my beer. My wait was for naught. Amber remained silent. I wrapped my hoagie in napkins, slid Amber's ring back across the table, and stood. "Have a nice day," I said.

Amber snapped upright in her chair. "Wait! What do you mean?"

"Exactly what you heard me say this morning. Until you talk with the police, I will not get mixed up in this." More silence. This was Myers's problem, not mine. I waved goodbye to him and turned to leave.

"Just a sec," Myers said. Turning back to Amber, he added, "Ms. Brantley, it's your call. Talk with me here or we'll do it at the sheriff's office."

Her acidic glare looked potent enough to melt boilerplate. She held it for a ten-count. Myers didn't soften. She did when he stood and reached for the handcuffs on his belt.

"Okay," he said, "let's have it."

As she squirmed in her seat, pulling and twisting the tail of her T-shirt, I wondered if he actually would've used the handcuffs.

"I was at Disney World," she said.

CHAPTER 10

With the facedown resolved, I dropped back into the deck chair and unwrapped my hoagie. Myers dug into Amber; I dug into my sandwich.

"When did you leave for Disney World?" he said.

Her eyes darted between Myers and me, and then she sipped at her drink before answering. "Friday morning."

He asked questions and scribbled in his notepad as she replied. I worked on my sandwich, switching attention, at times, between their exchanges and the tail fin flipping of a school of mullet working among the pilings under the patio.

At this time of year mullet began to school. In a few weeks they would begin to spawn. Judging by their early numbers it would be a good year for those who earned a living plying the waters with small boats and huge nets.

"And you returned Sunday night?" he said.

She nodded.

He leaned forward and drummed an index finger on the chrome top of the napkin dispenser. "Ms. Brantley, this isn't adding up. I've called your condo. You haven't answered. What gives?"

After another long pause and some squirming in her seat, she said, "It's my boyfriend. He's been bothering me, so I'm not staying there now."

"When do you plan to return?"

Another pause as she stared at her nails. I looked them over too. They were dirty, devoid of polish, and chewed to the quick. So much for her socialite image.

"There's been a management change," she said. "I'm not sure I'll stay there any longer."

"So where *have* you been staying?"

"With my girlfriend."

Myers tapped his pencil against the notepad. "This Jean Hampton, the girlfriend you were with at Disney World?"

"Yes."

"So I can reach you at her place?"

"For a while, yes, but I'm looking for another apartment."

Myers leaned back as Roxie served his order and set another mug of draft in front of me. Balancing her serving tray on one finger, she gave me her famous double-dimple grin, and said, "You didn't order it, kiddo, but I saw it in the cards."

I scooped it up. "You're a world-class psychic, Roxie."

Roxie strolled around the table, humming "El Paso" as she wiped at the condensation rings. Once satisfied with the clean result, she flipped the towel over her shoulder and waltzed back to the main dining room. When I returned my attention to Amber, she was staring at Myers. "Am I in trouble for not calling you first?" she said.

He shook his head. "No, you're not in trouble."

Her eyes moistened. She sniffed and wiped her nose. In a whisper I almost missed, she said, "Is that all?"

"Relax," he said, "we're getting there." He bit into his sandwich and gestured to her with his pencil. His mouth was full when he continued. "We'd like to determine what's missing from Ms. Park's home. How familiar are you with her possessions?"

"I've spent very little time in her home. I don't think I'd be much help."

"Maybe; maybe not," he said. "What do you know about her safe? It was open and empty, but it hadn't been cracked. You have the combination?"

"Of course not! I didn't even know she had a safe."

Myers hurried on. "She owned a lot of jewelry. Do you have it?"

I'd told him of the piece of jewelry Amber offered as a retainer, but I hadn't mentioned she had a pouch full of the stuff.

She gestured to the ring. "Only that piece and a couple of others. I was taking them with mine to be cleaned."

"Did she keep her jewelry in the safe?"

His question brought her head up. He was studying her face. Columbo used to do that: rephrase the same question and study the response.

Amber bristled. "I just told you, I didn't know she had a safe."

Maybe she used to watch Columbo.

"Skip it," he said. "The neighbor across the canal said Eva kept a boat docked behind her home. What do you know about it?"

"I remember seeing it. Blue and white, I think. Nothing more." Glancing at me, she added, "I'm sorry, but I don't like boats."

After finishing my sandwich, I swept up the crumbs and studied a pair of pigeons pecking at scraps under a nearby table. Like Roxie, they looked well fed. I tossed the crumbs over the railing. A school of sand perch swarmed to the surface and attacked the floating particles like slashing piranhas.

Myers pulled a card from his shirt pocket and waved it in her face like a vendor hawking programs at a ball game. "Call me as soon as you settle into a new place." His emotionless expression hardened a notch when he pressed the card into her hand. He added, "I mean that, Ms. Brantley."

She bobbed her head like that long-necked turkey in the luncheon meat commercial and then leaned over and tucked the card into her purse. When she straightened, her eyes fell on the ring. She studied it for several moments before picking it up with the tip of her little finger and extending it to me.

Her eyes held the question I put to Myers. "You have any problem with me trying to locate Reginald and the new yacht?"

"No," he said, "not if we agree on the ground rules first."

"What do you mean?"

"This boat business is also a part of my investigation. I need to know how you plan to operate so I don't bump into you."

In other words, he didn't want me screwing something up. Fine. I'd fill him in later. Turning from him and taking the ring, I said, "I'll get to work on this, Amber, but you'll also need to give me a way to contact you."

She grabbed her purse and jacket and stood. Most of her drink and crackers were untouched, and she still looked greenish and unsteady as she shifted her weight from one foot to the other. "Don't worry. I'll call you both," she said. "Promise."

We watched as she scurried across the patio, brushing tables and chairs with her hips and purse before stumbling through the dining room door. When she was out of sight, Myers shook his head and returned to his sandwich.

As he ate my attention shifted to the antics of a flock of seagulls and an albino pelican, darting and diving after the offerings tossed by a deck hand on a passing shrimp boat. When Myers pushed his plate away, I turned back to the table, intent on explaining my plan to track Reginald. Myers spoke first.

"Let me explain some things before we go on." He reached for his beer and engaged my eyes. "I can't discuss some aspects of the case with you, nor can I knowingly allow you to do anything on Ms. Brantley's behalf that would jeopardize my investigation."

I shrugged my eyebrows but kept my mouth shut as he sipped his beer. The man had the tact and personality level of pond scum, so I braced for more onslaught as he set his beer aside.

"I'm sorry if that sounded hard-assed," he said, "but it's the law. I didn't make it and I can't change it." He rolled his beer glass between his palms. "The good news is there's no law against my accepting your help. In fact, you've already been a big help. I appreciate it."

"You mean my calling you about Amber?"

"That and your input out on Hangman's Key. You've been straight from the get-go. I like that."

A compliment from Myers? "Glad to help," I said.

"All that said, I can tell you this much. The first thing I need to learn is if Reginald is another victim, Eva's killer, or if he's doing exactly what Amber believes he's doing."

That sounded like logical procedure to me. He hadn't asked for my blessing, but I nodded confirmation anyway.

"I'll start by checking out her story," he said. "Then I'll see what I can dig up at the airlines. How about you? Will you begin an immediate search for the boat?"

He was beginning to sound like Dad and his interrogation of me before I was allowed out on my first date. Big deal. I'd handled Dad. I could handle Myers. "Of course," I said.

"Okay. If you don't mind, I'd like to hear how you plan to do it."

I saw his polite request for what it really was: an order. Fine. I began by explaining why the Municipal Marina would most likely be Reginald's destination. "If he reserved a berth there," I said, "chances are the dock master also has an ETA for him."

"Good start," he said, "if it works out that way. But you could strike out. Then what?"

"The obvious," I said. "I'll call every marina in the area."

"And if you still strike out?"

I was tiring of his questions. "You pumping me here because you're planning to switch to marine investigation?"

He grinned. "No, just professional interest in your methods."

"There's nothing profound to it," I said. "If I don't get lucky on this end, I'll start on the other end."

In addition to his Dirty Harry stuff, Myers had a great scowl. He gave me one. "And just how would you know where to start?" he said.

I explained about my contacts with local insurance companies. "It's likely Eva was insured by one of them. When I know which one, I'll ask where the binder was sent for the new yacht. With that information one phone call should get me the yacht's make, size, name, and most likely the time of Reginald's departure."

"Slick, but that won't help you find Reginald if he's en route."

"Sure it will," I said. "In two ways, actually."

"Such as?"

"First, many boaters are also ham radio operators. They use a forty-meter frequency where they meet daily. Typical coverage includes the entire East Coast, the Bahamas, and a good portion of the Caribbean. They call their meetings rag chewing, but get a yacht's name and description to this group and someone will spot the missing vessel in short order."

"Impressive," he said. "And you can do this because you're a ham operator?"

"Yes, I hold a General-Class license, but I'm not as active with it as Dad. He has a rig in the bait shop and another aboard his charter vessel."

Myers leaned forward and placed both elbows on the table. "You said 'two ways.' What else do you have?"

"The other way," I said, "would have to come after obtaining the yacht's name. I'd contact the Coast Guard, pass on the vessel's name, and tell them I was holding an emergency message for Reginald. They'd relay the call up the East Coast, and if he was monitoring channel sixteen as he should be while underway, I'd have him."

"And I thought Seaweed Investigations was a joke." His scowl eased to a grin, as he tipped back in his chair. "You're okay," he said, "but I have a question."

I knew it was coming. Always. I aped Roxie's routine by closing my eyes and placing a fingertip to my temple. "Let me guess what your question is, sir. Yes, it's becoming clear now. Your question is, 'How did a nice girl like you—?'"

Myers laughed. A for-real, out-loud laugh. "Please give me credit for wording it a little better than that, but yeah. How did you get into investigations?"

"The B.A.L. method," I said. "Pure and simple."

"Never heard of it." His brow wrinkled. "That a correspondence school, or something?"

"No," I said, "not even close. B.A.L. simply means, Blind Assed Luck. Like in the right place at the right time."

He crossed his legs at the ankles and said, "This I have to hear."

I fussed with the salt-and-pepper shakers while glossing over the details that led to my tiff with Dad. "That afternoon I had to get away so I drove out to the tidal flats off the mouth of Grassy Creek. It's desolate there. Good place to sulk. I parked, got out of my car, slammed the door, and began wandering among the buttonwood and sea grape thickets. I kicked sand, fiddler crabs, and anything else in my path. I'd been at it for an hour or so, and I was about a quarter-of-a-mile north of the creek, when I spotted something tucked into a pocket of mangrove. I ambled closer and studied it. It looked familiar. When I realized why, I dropped my pouting and got out of there."

Myers leaned closer and said, "What the hell was it?"

"It was a stolen vessel," I said. "A houseboat, actually. The owner had left photos of it at every nautical-related facility in the county. Dad had one copy of the photo by the cash register and another pinned to his Notices-to-Mariners board on the fuel dock."

"What'd you do?"

"Hotfooted it to a phone and called the good guys," I said. "What else?"

"Okay, good citizen, but how would that lead to investigation work?"

"That's part of the blind assed luck," I said. "The owner's insurance company paid me a reward for my recovery tip. It was the easiest money I'd ever made, and since I'd just quit my job with Dad, I began looking for other stolen vessels. Next thing I knew, World Wide hired me to investigate boating accidents. Now I work for several insurers."

"You said it was part of the luck."

I laughed. "You don't remember Scott Mason?"

Myers drummed the fingers of one hand against his forehead. "He the rapist?"

"Serial rapist," I said. "Final count's still unknown, but local women screamed when he was allowed out on bond."

"I didn't work the case," he said, "but what about him?"

"Just what the women feared. Mason skipped out on his bond. Didn't show for trial. But," I gave Myers a thumbs-up, "he was aboard the houseboat when the deputies arrived. A real two-for-one special."

Myers nodded and said, "Neat wrap-up."

"There's more."

"Oh?"

"You bet," I said. "Big Al had posted Mason's bond, and since my tip led to Mason's capture, Al gave me a two-thousand-dollar reward and a part-time job at his pawn shop."

"So you lost one job and picked up a couple of others."

He made it sound like progress. I knew better.

His smile faded. "Let's back up to your insurance contacts," he said. "I might have something that'll save some time."

"What is it?"

"Eva's attorney. In his statement he said Global insured the runabout."

I thanked him for the tip and mentioned I'd worked several jobs for Global. "I'll start with them," I said. "Maybe they covered the new yacht, too. If so, I'll let you know."

"Good. That'll save me a few steps." He clasped his hands on his lap and studied them for a moment before returning his attention to me. "Look," he said, "I use a what-if approach on most cases. If you have any thoughts you'd like to toss in the pot, do it."

His tone was heavy with sincerity. I studied his eyes. His expression. Same reading. Liking the guy wasn't within grasp, but my not liking of him had dwindled a tad. "Thoughts?" I said. "You bet I have thoughts, but I don't want to step on your toes."

"If I couldn't take it, I wouldn't ask."

"Fair enough." No one was close enough to eavesdrop, but I hunched over the table anyway. "To begin with, Amber seems less concerned about her aunt's murder then she does about Reginald's welfare. It's as if she cannot or will not accept the fact he might well have killed Eva or have been killed at the same time she was."

"Maybe it's a denial thing," he said. "If she keeps her mind on him, she doesn't have to cope with thoughts of Eva's death. Something like that. Psychiatrists probably have a forty-dollar word for it."

"That could be," I said, "but when she called me, she said she was worried because he hadn't contacted her. Just now she told you she'd been at Disney World for three days. How could he, or anyone else for that matter, have contacted her?"

"Good point." He tipped his beer glass in a salute. "And her answering machine, if she has one, wasn't on when I called her condo."

Answering machine? Surely they'd checked Eva's. I asked.

"The TV cops always leave that for the PI," he said, "but yeah, it was checked. Several messages. Nothing from Reginald."

That seemed strange. I told him why. "By the time the police entered her home, she'd been dead for nearly three days. Right?"

"That's close," he said. "What of it?"

"Because, among other things, lovers talk when they're together. When they're separated, they call each other. If he's alive and well, why hasn't he called?"

He spread his hands in a don't-ask-me fashion. "You got something else?"

"You're the detective," I said, "but from what I've gleaned from reading mystery novels, the motive for murder boils down to one of four things."

"Same in the real world," he said. "Greed, revenge, power, or sex."

"In this case," I said, "greed tops my list. And if that's true, Reginald and Amber seem to have the most to gain from Eva's death."

"Agreed, but unless I can prove differently, it appears they were out of town at the time of Eva's death?"

"You only have Amber's word for that," I said. "In fact, if she left for Disney World Friday morning, as she said, how can she be sure Reginald caught a plane at noon?"

"I didn't call her on that, but it didn't slide by. I'll check the airlines. The girlfriend, too. When it comes to an alibi," he added, "I don't take anyone's word. I check."

"Good. I have the feeling she wasn't telling us all she knew, but, in town or not, I don't think she or Reginald killed Eva."

When his scowl was firmly in place, he said, "Why's that?"

After explaining about her seasickness aboard the *Margaret Ellen*, I said, "The front moved ashore late Friday afternoon. By dark the Gulf and inland waters were a mess. If Amber had been a party in dumping Eva's body, she wouldn't have been a minute's use. She would've been flat on her back."

"Interesting. So what's your thoughts on Reginald?"

"Just that if Eva had agreed to marry him, why would he kill her, or have her killed, before he was in position to inherit her estate?"

He laughed. "I can't believe he would."

"What's so funny?"

"Think about it," he said. "First you named two people who had the most to gain by Eva's death. Then you built a case against their involvement."

"You asked for my thoughts. They may not make sense, but you got 'em. Now it's my turn. Give me your feeling for the case?"

"At the moment," he said, "that's all I have. Just a feeling. Even so, I have to ask that you keep a lid on it."

I nodded.

Myers started to speak but paused as a busboy began clearing an adjacent table. When he moved on, Myers said, "I believe Eva knew her killer and she admitted that person into her home sometime on Friday. She had bruises on her body that occurred before death, so I believe she was forcibly restrained while the house was searched and the safe emptied."

"Bruises, like in—"

"Yeah," he said. "The medical examiner said the bruises on Eva's body were consistent with those from a beating. Maybe even torture."

There'd been several ugly marks on her body, but I never dreamed she'd been beaten ... or tortured. Crap! I shuddered and changed direction by saying, "The press said her home had been ransacked."

"They erroneously implied a destructive nature in their use of the word," he said. "It wasn't that way at all. The house was in a mess, but it was the result of a very meticulous search."

"Wouldn't she have kept anything of value in the safe?"

"You'd think so," he said, "but with the safe open and the house searched as well, there's no way to know if the killer found what he was looking for. Regardless, I believe sometime on Friday the killer forced her into the runabout, took her to some point offshore, killed her, and then dumped her body."

That was also my belief, but I had one additional thought. "If the killer arrived at Eva's by car," I said, "he probably abandoned the boat within a reasonable walking distance of her place when he returned."

Myers nodded agreement. "That's my guess," he said. "We're canvassing all of the homes and condos on the water within a mile of her place. If it's still floating, we'll turn it up." He pulled another card from his pocket, wrote something on the back, and pushed it across to me. "You can reach me at one of those numbers: office, beeper, and home. Use them in that order if you uncover something. Big or little; day or night."

"Count on it," I said.

He drained his beer and stood. "I better shove off. I want to see if we have anything on Reginald in our files." A few steps from the table, he stopped and looked back. "You got a good head on ya, Seaweed. Thanks for the help."

I don't blush. If I did, I would have. I waved the card at him. "I'll stay in touch."

He headed out through the dining room. I finished what was left of my beer, scooted my chair out of the sun, and tipped back against the patio railing. Priorities. I had to line up my priorities.

Al wanted me to fill in at the pawnshop later in the week. No way, now that I had my old job back. I'd break the news to him when he appraised Amber's ring.

Finding Reginald would go well or it wouldn't go at all. And, one way or the other, it wouldn't take the three days I'd promised to give to the job. I'd make some calls, pass along the results to Amber and Myers, and then bow out of the situation.

Dad was the sticky wicket. On one hand I was grateful he wanted me back at the helm of the *Margaret Ellen*; on the other I also knew nothing would please him more than my breaking up with Angus. Before finding Eva's body, I'd been ready to do just that. Since then my feelings had vacillated, even though in my heart I knew the best course was to burn the bridge. When would I muster the guts to do so?

I was still leaned back, thinking with eyes closed, when I heard Roxie's voice.

"You asleep?"

I opened my eyes and tipped forward in my chair. "Naw, just daydreaming."

"That cute guy you were with picked up the check." She set another mug of draft on the table. "Including this," she said.

I wiggled my eyebrows. Myers was full of surprises.

She grinned and hugged her serving tray to her bosom. "New boyfriend?"

"No way," I said. Her enthusiasm waned as I explained who Myers was and why he'd been there.

"That reminds me," she said. She turned to a nearby table and picked up a newspaper. "There's a big article in here about you and that lady you found."

"No pictures, I hope."

"Just your front side," Roxie said.

"Meaning you saw my backside on TV. Right?"

She giggled. "Seaweed, honey, if I had a can like yours, I'd take it out that door and make a fortune with it before the next high tide."

She scooted for the dining room before I could swat her with the newspaper.

Ignoring the unwanted beer, I browsed through the front-page portion of the story, but it contained nothing I hadn't learned firsthand. The story continued on page A-twelve. Still nothing new, but a quote from Stan Avery expressing his grief over Eva's death gave me an idea.

Avery had handled Eva's business affairs, so if I ran into a snag with my insurance contacts, he'd be a prime source to pry.

CHAPTER 11

It was three-thirty when I left Shanley's and began ambling back to the bait shop. What a difference in the comfort level. The patio side of Shanley's was cooled by ample exposure to the nearly constant sea breeze. The street side of the same building was another matter. Despite abundant shade provided by the canopy of Australian pines covering Charter Drive, the air was still and uncomfortably warm.

The palm-size bells, tethered to the screen door at the entrance to the bait shop, tinkled in welcome as I pulled the door open. But the place was empty— silent, except for the hum of the large-face clock on the wall behind the counter. This was not unusual for a weekday. After all, fishing was a leisure sport, which made weekend business a madhouse. Dad loved it, the selling of bait and tackle and the opportunity for shooting the breeze with customers. As for me, I preferred being on the open Gulf at the helm of the *Margaret Ellen*, weekday or weekend.

Like Shanley's, this first room facing the street had once served its owners as a spacious living room. Now the room was crowded with shelves and product display racks and served as a sales area complete with homey flair.

Well, it had been homey at one time. Now I saw an overflowing ashtray sitting alongside the cash register, an empty beer can perched among the trout lures, an oil-stained rag draped on a shelf of net-making supplies, and a liberal layer of sand and fine bits of oyster shell covering the once-lovely hardwood floor. Maybe Dad's mostly male clientele didn't see this as a mess, but when I returned as captain of the *Margaret Ellen*, I also planned to return a healthy measure of neatness and cleanliness to Cobia's Bait Tackle and Charter.

While still surveying the room's deplorable condition, I heard Cecil's voice, a stirring bass that never failed to put dance to the hair at the base of my neck. Then the succulent aroma of smoked mackerel drifted into the room. I loved both, Cecil's voice and smoked fish, and both were coming from the patio behind the bait shop. Vowing to clean up the unsightly mess later, I moseyed to the rear door of the shop.

The sight of Cecil, looking like he'd come in second in a brawl with a bear, set off a shudder between my shoulder blades. I hated any kind of hurt—mine *or* anyone else's. His left leg was bandaged from mid-calf to the mid-thigh length of his khaki shorts. But, even though he looked like he belonged in a hospital bed, he was smiling, rotating racks on the smoker, and spinning a yarn for a young, pale-skinned couple garbed in souvenir caps and T-shirts.

This was the Cecil I knew, the Cecil I couldn't remember not knowing. He was in his mid-seventies, but he was still lean and handsome, still topped with a head of silky-white hair that now fluttered before the sea breeze sweeping across the pass. I'd often wondered if he were ageless, as even after a lifetime spent in the sun, his complexion rivaled the tone of hand-oiled teak. My hope and prayer was I'd fair as well.

Just outside the rear door I paused and listened for a moment. The tale Cecil was unfolding for the tourists featured him and Dad, a small boat on a big ocean, and their hours-long battle with a hammerhead shark. The story was a nail-biter, especially the part when the shark rammed and nearly capsized their boat, but the story was also one I'd heard a hundred times. After exchanging a knowing smile with Cecil, I crossed to where Dad was sitting at a metal-topped table building trolling rigs.

Skip was supposed to be at work washing down the *Margaret Ellen's* decks, but he wasn't in sight. "Where's Skip?"

Dad nodded toward Danny's Outboard Service, our neighbor to the west. "He's over at Danny's."

Why would he be there instead of doing what I'd asked him to do? "He's taken an interest in outboard engine repair?"

Dad laughed. "No, I'd say his current interest is in short skirts."

"Sheila?"

He nodded.

Sheila was Danny's daughter, and in the last year she'd blossomed into an attractive and well-built young lady. The problem for Skip was that Sheila was also a sixteen-year-old senior at Bayside High School. On top of that, her father was an AAA Wrestling champion. Danny had been working in his shop when I left Shanley's, so I didn't see Skip getting beyond the window-shopping stage on this visit.

To make myself useful I swept the completed rigs onto a tray and carted them to the freezer. Speaking loud enough to be heard over the hum of the refrigeration equipment, I said, "How'd the IRS session go?"

I winced as Dad slammed the wire cutters onto the tabletop hard enough to make it ring. "You're gunna love this," he said. "The bastards are hot and bothered because they think I'm not reporting all of my income."

As I separated the rigs for quick freezing, I said, "Well, you don't report the bait business."

Dad cut a glance at Cecil and then hissed at me. "Why don't you jump on a box and tell the world, child."

"Sorry."

He scooped up the cutters, measured a piece of leader wire against the width of the table, clipped it, and began attaching a swivel to one end. "Anyway, that's the part that's bothering 'em. The bait. I opened the tanks for 'em. 'Look at all the dead ones,' I said. 'Loss. Total loss.'"

"Not really," I said. "You sell all the dead stuff for crab bait."

"Like I said, jump on a box—"

"Sorry." I fished more mullet from a blue-plastic milk crate in the cooler and carried them to the table. I leaned close to Dad and whispered, "What're you going to do?"

Dad didn't whisper. He bellowed. "Nothing! Not one damned thing. I ain't gunna count minnows for them mud suckers." He raised his voice another notch. "They want records, they can park their ass here and keep 'em. Bunch of bottom feeders. That's all they are. They don't worry me." He straightened his back and said, "Bring me another spool of leader wire."

I knew the answer but asked anyway as I headed for the back door of the bait shop. "Eighty pound? Right?"

"Yeah."

The bells on the screen door tinkled as I pulled a spool of leader wire from the rack. It was Skip. I batted my eyes. "Five'll get you ten, Skippy, baby."

Skip leaned against the counter and stuck his face close to mine. "What the hell's that supposed to mean?"

I spun away from his glare. "Sheila, you dumb muck. She's jailbait. Five minutes in the sack will get ya ten years in the slammer."

"Screw you."

"Only in your wildest dreams, butt breath." I put a swishy-tail movement in my stride and returned to the patio. Our getting through a full day without a confrontation was the Impossible Dream.

As I placed the leader wire on the table, Dad looked up and said, "How'd it go with Myers?"

I sat facing Dad, measuring and cutting leader wire while explaining the events of that morning's charter and the outcome of Myers's visit with Amber.

"All in all," he said, "it sounds like you have another job? That it?"

His concerned tone was unmistakable. I couldn't let him continue with such a thought, so I quickly outlined what little I'd agreed to do for Amber. "Dad, I *will not* let anything stand in the way of my coming back. That's a promise." I bent over, rinsed my hands in a bucket alongside the table, and looked for a towel as I stood. "In fact, if I'm lucky, maybe I can clean this job up with a couple of phone calls."

"That sounds good to me," he said, "but gimme a minute before you get started."

I began to ease back into my chair, but he nodded to the one alongside his. As he did so, I noticed the gap between his bushy eyebrows and his head full of thick black hair narrow by a full inch. This phenomenon, as I'd learned early in life, meant what followed would be serious. I stepped around the table, sat, and dried my hands on my shorts. "What is it?"

"Just a little somethin' between us," he said.

Between us? I searched his eyes but saw no clue to what was coming. I hadn't dinked up the *Margaret Ellen's* props by running aground or marred her hull by scraping a piling while getting underway or docking. Damn. It had to be my pushing too hard about my pay for the charter. Or was it my bribing him to top off *Skipjack's* tanks? I squirmed, waited, and worried.

"A few weeks ago," he said, "Patty told me she was ready to hang it up. Now Cecil's banged up. I doubt he'll be striding up a boarding ramp any time soon." He glanced across the patio before shaking his head and adding, "Maybe he never will."

The thought of any diminished capacity for Cecil was as painful as the real pain I'd felt after falling from the swing set. I looked to where it still sat just off the edge of the patio, now surrounded by a patch of sandspurs. The swing's seat, made from half of an automobile tire, was rotted and hanging in shreds; the once brightly painted metal frame was now pitted from corrosion, streaked with rust, and dotted with seagull poop. I looked away, uncomfortable with the toll time extracted from all things. Swing sets were one thing, but men like Dad and Cecil and John Wayne were supposed to live forever. They didn't, I knew, but they should.

"Anyway," he continued, "I've got to make some changes. I'd like you to be part of them."

Before I was born, Mom and Dad, along with my Aunt Patty and Uncle

Bill, started the bait and tackle business. A year later, while Patty and Mom were pregnant with Skip and me, Bill packed up and pulled out. Then, after Mom died, Dad and Patty kept the business running, even expanded it, and still managed to raise Skip and me. Dad had handled the hard work and the passing years well. Patty had not. I'd known the day was fast approaching when she'd have to give in and give it up.

I leaned closer. "What kind of changes?"

"I'm going to buy Patty's interest in the business."

"When?"

"Next Monday," he said. "In the meanwhile the *Margaret Ellen* goes into dry dock Friday for a bottom job. She'll re-float a week from today. The following day, that's a Wednesday, I have a party booked for her. That's also the day I'll need a new captain and a new partner. Two positions, but I want it to be one person. One I can count on." He squeezed my hand and added, "I'd like it to be you."

Me? My mind raced. When I could speak, I said, "How about Skip?"

"No way," Dad said. "He's flunked the captain's exam a dozen times."

It was four times, but I didn't argue.

"Florida Power didn't want him," Dad continued. "Same with the telephone company and that outfit up in the north end of the county. You know, the one that makes those electronic gadgets."

I supplied the name.

"Yeah," Dad said. "That's it. Honeywell. Now the kid's trying to get in the Air Force."

"Oh?"

"Yeah. He won't hang around five minutes after Patty leaves. I wouldn't want him to. We're blood, but it's not thick enough." Dad shook his head and added, "It just wouldn't work."

I'd known that before asking.

"Well," he said, "what do you think?"

I grinned and said, "Dad, how do you figure I can afford to be your partner when I can't even afford to keep fuel in *Skipjack's* tanks?"

Dad played with the pair of pliers, pushing them back and forth across the metal tabletop. When he looked up, he said, "You let me worry about that."

Thinking about our tiff always made me uneasy, but I had to ask. "You're not worried about my dumb ... you know?"

"Like I said yesterday. As far as I'm concerned the issue is dead and buried at sea. You're a good skipper, baby, but you made a mistake. I hope you learned something from it."

Learned? Had I ever. I wanted to tell him how much, but my throat tightened. I couldn't speak. Instead, I turned and leaned into his arms.

When I sat up, he kissed my cheek and pointed toward the sea wall. "You see that?"

I sighted along his gaze. "The *Margaret Ellen*?"

"Yes," he said. "The *Margaret Ellen*. She's just a boat, but her name was your mother's name. That makes her special. Just like your mother was." He took my hands and held them tightly in his. "Here's the rest of my offer. Pitch in with me, take over the charter business, and she's yours."

"Mine! Dad! I couldn't—"

"No," he said. "You have a week. Think on it. We'll talk later." He released my hands and patted my knee. "Right now you have a job to finish. Get to it."

He shifted back to the table, picked up a mullet, and reached for a trolling wire. I stood, and then paused a moment to quiet my quivering legs before crossing the patio and entering the rear door of the shop. Skip was demonstrating a spinning rod for a customer, but he paused long enough to send an icy stare my way. This was nothing new, as at this point after a fight we'd ignore each other for a few days; then we'd launch into a new squabble.

I hurried down the narrow hall to Dad's office, a room that had been my room from birth until the day I moved aboard my sloop. My America's Cup posters still covered the walls, and the shelves of the room still held my adolescent seashell collection, the miscellaneous trinkets I'd won at the Pinellas County Fair, and a black-and-white photo of Mom, Dad, Patty, and Bill standing arm-in-arm in front of their just-opened bait shop. I dropped into the swivel chair behind Dad's desk and shivered as I thought of his words and the possibilities they presented.

I'd be captain, permanent captain, of the big, beautiful *Margaret Ellen*. I'd have the lucrative charter business with the certainty of making more in a week than I now made in a month. But, most of all, I'd be Dad's partner. This thought was too precious to hang a price on.

Amber's ring was in my pocket, a ring representing payment for a job I'd given my word to do. I grabbed the phone book. The sooner I located Reginald and his *luxury* yacht, the sooner I could get back to doing what I loved best.

The dock master at the St. Petersburg Municipal Marina was courteous and patient during the several minutes I spoke with him, but he was not holding a slip in the name of Reginald Wentworth or Eva Marie Park. He even checked the waiting list for permanent berthing, but there was no listing in either name.

I thanked him for his time, replaced the receiver, and returned my attention to the marina listings in the Yellow Pages. The Bay Area had marinas. Lots of marinas. I was about to start calling from the top of the list when I remembered the first question the dock master at the Municipal Marina had asked me: "What's the name of the vessel?" I didn't know its name, its make, its size, or its color. The other end seemed like a better place to start. I had Global's number in my head. I dialed.

"Global Insurance. This is Melanie. How may I help you?"

"Hi, Melanie. Seaweed."

"You're fast," she said. "I just left a message on your machine five minutes ago."

Hmm. Should I admit not having checked for messages or just gloss over it? I chose the gloss. "So what's up?"

"Weldon. He's looking for you. Hold on."

If Global had insured the new yacht, Weldon would know about it. I held until he came on the line, and after an exchange of greetings, I said, "What've you got?"

"A humongous headache, thanks to your beachcombing."

"Huh?"

"The Eva Park thing," he said.

I listened and made sympathetic noises as he explained what Eva's death was going to cost Global. The big-ticket was her ten-million-dollar life insurance policy and its double indemnity clause. Next, in order of value, was her missing jewelry insured at three million dollars, and last, but by no means least by my financial benchmark, was the missing Grady-White 26 insured at sixty thousand dollars. "So you were calling me about the Grady-White?" I said.

"Why not?

"Because the detective on the case told me the police were searching for it."

"So what?" he said. "At this point I want to clear this mess up so I'll take all the help I can get. Five percent on the finder's fee. You want a shot at it?"

Hmm. A three-thousand-dollar reward wasn't bad, but if the boat hadn't been scuttled, which was unlikely since the Grady-White was foam filled and self bailing, the police would find it in a matter of hours by snooping the canals near Eva's home. Of course I could do the same, and *Skipjack's* shallow draft would be ideal for the job. The problem was I already had one job standing between Dad's offer and me and I didn't want another one. Even so, alienating Weldon made no sense. Without committing, I asked, "You have a picture of it?"

"The police picked up a stack of 'em earlier, but I still have several. Swing by."

Global's office was in Pinellas County, but it was on the east end of Gandy Boulevard, which made it impossible for me to reach before five. I told him so.

"No problem," he said. "I'll leave a photo and spec sheet with security. Pick 'em up when it's convenient. And good luck."

"Hold a sec, I need something." I told him about my meeting with Amber Brantley and the job she'd hired me to do.

"Good God!" he said, "don't tell me that one's missing too."

"Relax," I said. "It's only overdue in her mind, but she's paying me to look for it. Where was the insurance binder sent?"

"Hold on a moment. I have her files right here."

I heard muttering and paper shuffling. "Got it," he said. "The boat's a sixty-seven-foot Hatteras, white with mahogany trim."

Yep, that was a luxury yacht. "Did they give you a name?" I said.

"Yeah. A real beaut. *Fifth Amendment.* Anyway, the binder, in the amount of one-and-a-half-million, went to Northeast Yacht Brokers in Margate, New Jersey. Eva paid cash for the boat, but it's Northeast's policy that nothing leaves their dock without proof of coverage."

I scribbled as he recited their address and phone number.

"If you find something amiss," he said, "get back to me ASAP."

With this info on the yacht, the search for Reginald would go quickly. Even so, after telling him not to worry about my locating the yacht, I was still curious. "Weldon, this is none of my business, but rumor has it that Amber is Eva's only heir. Was she the beneficiary on any of this?"

"Any? Shit! She gets it all. A year ago Eva's attorney advised her to retitle her worldly goods. It was a life estate setup to get around the inheritance tax. As it now stands, it all goes to Amber sans probate. Freely translated that means she's about to be one rich princess."

Rich, maybe, but I doubted even Gwen's makeup artist could make Amber look like a princess. "So, if Amber gets it all," I said, "the man Eva was about to marry wouldn't benefit from her death?"

"Not a penny."

This revelation was worth passing along to Myers. "Okay," I said, "let's go back to the jewelry for a moment."

"What about it?"

"You said the insured value was three million. Right?"

"On the button. The one-and-only, pompous, Stan Avery, Esquire, filed a claim this morning."

"I take it he's not a drinking buddy of yours," I said, "but maybe this'll make your day. Do you have individual descriptions of the pieces?"

"You bet."

"See if you can find one for a pair of diamond earrings shaped like interlocking hearts."

"I don't need the list for those," he said. "They're part of a million-dollar set."

I pulled the ring from my pocket and studied it under Dad's desk lamp. After describing it to him, I said, "There's also an inscription on either side of the band. A coat-of-arms, or something."

"You see it! Good God! Like you're holding the damned thing?"

"Right here in my hot little hand." After explaining how I'd obtained the ring, I added, "She had a pouch full of the stuff, Weldon, including those earrings."

"Guess whose chain I'm about to jerk. Thanks, Seaweed; I owe you one. A big one."

Yes, and if I ever needed the favor I'd remind him of what he'd just said. "Ah, one more thing before you go. What's this ring worth?"

"Seventy-five-thousand dollars."

CHAPTER 12

Paying such a sum for a trinket and then sequestering it to a safe deposit box for most of its life was beyond my imagination. No way. Given such a sum of money my purchase would be something visible and practical, like a new outboard engine for *Skipjack* and updated electronics for the *Margaret Ellen*.

I replaced the receiver and stared at my watch. Half past four. At this point, with the vessel's name and a quasi-legitimate reason for doing so, no one could fault me for contacting the Coast Guard and requesting a radio search for Reginald. But was this a wise move in the face of my belief he'd never arrived to pick up the boat?

And even if he had made it there, what if there'd been a last-minute snafu in the commissioning of the vessel? Such glitches were common and would've delayed his return. Taken a step further, what if the problem still hadn't been corrected? Simple. He hadn't started back yet. This possibility suggested that determining Reginald's status, still there or on the way, was the proper move before involving the Coast Guard. And a single phone call would probably provide the answer.

Margate, New Jersey, and St. Petersburg, Florida, were both in the Eastern Time Zone; however, a phone call to Northeast Yachts this late in the day was probably a waste of time. I was thinking happy hour and the propensity of yachtsmen for elbow bending. The better plan, then, would be to call in the morning after another check with the dock master at the Municipal Marina.

The number for the Pinellas County Sheriff's Office was on the card Myers had given me. I placed the call, intent on passing along my progress report, but Myers wasn't in. With a voice sounding more like a yawn than intelligent speech, the dispatcher asked if I wished to leave a message. What the heck. It was a warm afternoon; maybe my call had disturbed her nap.

My information was interesting, but was it important enough to hound him by calling his pager or home number? No. I opted to leave a message.

"Anything else?" she said.

"No, that's it. Unless he tells me otherwise, I'll follow up on the delivery status of the yacht in the morning."

"Got it."

With my call on record, Myers couldn't say his new recruit wasn't playing ball. I returned my thoughts to Reginald.

Before talking with Weldon, I'd been half-sure if Reginald was alive, and he wasn't Eva's killer, he would show up without my assistance. Now, knowing he had no financial motive in Eva's death, I was certain of it. In all likelihood he was somewhere en route to St. Petersburg with thoughts of Eva and marriage on his mind. But if so, why hadn't he called her? Myers had checked Eva's answering machine and said there were no messages from Reginald. Could it be Reginald didn't like talking to answering machines any more than Big Al?

I slipped the scrap of paper with Northeast's address and phone number into my pocket and gazed at my poster of Dennis Conner at the helm of *Stars and Stripes* while I mentally ticked off things to do. First, I'd see Al and get an advance on Amber's ring. She may have been comfortable toting a fortune in jewelry in her purse, but I wasn't. The sooner the ring was out of my pocket and into Al's safe the better I'd feel. Then, of course, there'd be the uncomfortable task of telling Al I could no longer work for him.

That done, I'd pick up a photo of the Grady-White. This was window dressing for Weldon's benefit, as I had no intention of competing with the police in the search for the vessel. Even so, while at that end of the county I'd stop and ask Gwen if she had a shot of Reginald in her photo file. Myers might see this as meddling, not assistance, but I'd long wanted to see a TV studio. Now I had a reason.

These were the things I wanted to do, but to do them all would put a crimp on the evening I'd planned with Angus. I picked up the phone and dialed his number. At this time in the afternoon he was usually sprawled in a lounge chair on the lanai or floating on an air mattress in the pool. Either way, he'd have a mug of draft in his hand.

After four rings his answering machine picked up. The first sound was the theme song from *Apocalypse Now* playing softly and then Angus's overriding voice saying, "Hi, I'm not able to answer the phone at the moment. I'm out back in the lagoon wrestling with Old Jim, my twelve-foot alligator. At the beep please leave your message. After I whip that big sucker, I'll return your call. Of course if I don't return your call ... BEEP." Last month's message contained the theme song from the movie *Jaws* and had Angus pitted against a great white shark.

After the beep I gave the electronic ear an edited account of my new job and wrapped up the message with, "Keep the fish on ice. I'll bunk on the *Margaret Ellen* tonight."

I broke the connection but held the receiver. Al's Pawn Shop was on Second Avenue, a few blocks west of the waterfront in downtown St. Petersburg. Considering the rush-hour traffic, I'd have to push it to get there by closing time—if I could borrow Dad's pickup. My Camaro was at the Buttonwood. Would Al wait for me? I dialed his number.

"Al's Bail Bond and Pawn."

"It's me, Seaweed."

"Ho! Ho! Ho!"

I grimaced. Al's chuckle sounded like a juice blender chewing carrots. "Ho! Ho! What?"

"I saw your face on the front page and your fanny on TV, kid. That's what."

"Al!"

"Hey, there ain't no problem with that, doll. Most dames don't look good coming *and* going. You do."

To describe Al was to describe decadence. I rarely agreed with his choice of words, but I was never at a loss as to his meaning. I tried to flow with it. "Thanks, I guess." I explained a little about my new job and what Eva's death was costing Global. "Stan Avery's already filed a claim. He handled Eva's affairs."

"He does now," Al said, "but his old man, Mack, did until he retired last year."

"Wow! You knew Eva?"

"No such luck. What I know about her came from Mack. We go back away. Whiskey parties, poker games, 'n' other stuff."

Anyone who read the local papers knew about Al's parties. I changed the subject and told him what Gwen had mentioned.

"Yeah, that's close," he said. "Christine was Eva's twin sister. They were moneyed people but complete opposites. Eva had brains, led a respectable life, and made good investments. Stuff like that. Christine, pure and simple, was an airhead with hot pants. She was knocked up but still single when she and Eva went to Mack in the first place."

A safe bet said Al would never be a guest speaker at a feminist convention. I let it go and asked, "Why did they go to Mack?"

"Financial advice," he said. "Mack had been the family's tax lawyer for years, and Eva and Christine had just come into their inheritance. Twenty-five million dollars each, or thereabouts, was what I heard. Anyway, a few years before he retired, Mack said Eva's net worth was close to a hundred million."

Amazing. With such a net worth Eva must have considered the three million she'd spent on jewelry as just so much pocket lint. I asked how Christine had fared.

"Complete opposites again," Al said. "Christine couldn't touch the principal amount of her inheritance because it was protected by some legal clause, but Mack said she pissed away the interest as fast as it came in."

What would be the yearly interest on twenty-five million dollars? My mental math powers couldn't handle it. "So what happened to her money when she was killed?"

"Eva became executor of Christine's estate, but it all goes into Amber's hands on her thirtieth birthday."

"Damn! That's some birthday gift: twenty-five million from her mother's estate and another one hundred million from Eva's. I should have such troubles."

"Whatcha bitchin' about? Marry that boyfriend of yours and you're set."

This wasn't the first time Al had offered the same advice. Others had as well. "Sure," I said, before taking a deep breath and wondering how to phrase the unpleasant task of telling Al I couldn't work for him any longer. "Ah ... Al, you wanted me to work Wednesday or Thursday, but—"

"No problem," he said. "The dealing's changed. Besides, you working with the cops, I don't want you hanging around here."

One problem solved, but I tried to sound disappointed. "Thanks a lot." That taken care of I mentioned the ring and the cash advance I needed. "Would you look at it?"

"Sure," he said, "bring it by."

"That's a problem, Al. I'm at Dad's and I can't get to your place before five."

"No problem," he said. "Some of the boys are coming by later. I'll be here. Come up the alley. You remember the knock?"

If he hadn't changed it I did. "Still your Lucky-Three numbers?" I said. "Yeah."

I hung up and headed out to the patio. Cecil was restocking the racks on the smoker, and Skip was finally at work hosing down the aft deck of the *Margaret Ellen*. As I strolled toward where Dad was working, I exchanged a smile with Cecil and a scowl with Skip. Dad was pushing back from the table after having finished the last trolling rig. To save him the trip, I scooped up the tray full of rigs and carted them to the freezer.

As he began cleaning the tabletop with an old T-shirt, he said, "Make your calls?"

I spread the rigs on a shelf for fast freezing and closed the lid before turning and giving him a curtsy. Then with a loving-daughter's smile and the sweetest voice I could muster, I said, "Yes, sir, I've made my calls."

His eyes narrowed. "What's got into you?"

My smile blossomed to a grin. "Well, sir, since you asked, I need to borrow your pickup for a couple of hours."

He threw his head back and his hands high into the air. Shaking both, as if having an epileptic fit, he said, "My boat. My truck. Dammit all, if you were a boy, you'd want my clothes."

With my grin still firmly in place, I hooked my thumbs under my halter straps and said, "Actually, I'd like to borrow your blue polo shirt too."

He muttered something I didn't catch, wiped his hands on the T-shirt, and fished the keys from a side pocket of his khaki shorts.

I gave him a hug. "Dad, think about it. If I were your partner and moved back here, you'd have to put up with me every day."

He stared at *Bonita's* empty slip before pushing the keys into my hand. "Let's give it a try," he said. "Maybe I could learn to live with it."

I pocketed the keys and kissed his cheek. "Thanks. I know where you keep your shirt."

It was five-thirty when I pulled Dad's black-and-gray Silverado into one of the visitor-parking slots at the St. Petersburg Municipal Marina. Parking here made it a six-block walk to Al's, but, with the marina's around-the-clock security, it was a safer spot to park. In Al's neighborhood the definition of a suspicious vehicle was one that had been parked for thirty minutes and still had all its parts.

I checked that Amber's ring was still in my pocket before locking the truck and crossing Bayshore Drive. Vehicle traffic was still heavy but only a few pedestrians dotted the wide, downtown sidewalks as I hurried toward Second Avenue.

The taverns flanking Al's place were doing a thriving business. His front door, however, was closed and covered by a heavy set of roll-down bars. Looking through the grimy front window I could make out a pair of nightlights behind the counter and clearly see the interior was deserted. I continued around the block and entered the narrow alley. A pair of scruffy cats perched on the lid of a dumpster stood their ground as I hurried past. At the gray-steel door behind Al's, I rapped out four-two-three, the numbers Al had once used to win a few bucks in the weekly Lucky-Three drawing.

No response. Suddenly, I sensed movement behind me. I spun around, heart pounding, but the only thing in sight was the cats locked in combat over something in a grease-stained bag. I turned back to the door and was about to knock again when I heard Al's voice.

"Yeah?"

"It's me. Seaweed. Open up."

I heard movement deep within the room and then the bone-snapping noise of the locking bolts as they were slammed back. Al pulled open the door. He had a cigar stub clenched in his teeth and some playing cards in his hand.

"Come on in before someone spots you. And lock it back." He waved the cards. "Wait in the office," he said. "I'll be with you after this hand."

Doing as he said, I quickly stepped inside, closed the door, and pushed the locking bolts closed before pausing to look around. In all the time I'd worked for Al the back room had simply mirrored the unkempt appearance of the other rooms in the building. Now the room was smoke filled, dimly lit, and resembled a scene from a forties gangster movie. Four men, each holding cards, were hunched over a round, blacktopped table. In unison they turned their not smiling faces my way. I pretended not to see them or the pile of cash in the center of the table as I hurried through the room, my steps in time with the clunk, clunk, clunk of the wall air conditioner. Live, money-on-the-table poker was legal in some states. Florida was not one of them. Such knowledge could be dangerous, so I decided to keep it to myself.

Al's office reeked of cigar smoke, stale beer, and other obnoxious odors I couldn't place. A pair of overflowing ashtrays, a half-dozen Miller bottles, and several well-worn magazines obscured most of his desktop. As bad as it was, it looked like he'd cleaned a little since my last workday.

After poking through copies of *Penthouse* and *Playboy*, I found a *Sports Illustrated*. Great. It was the swimsuit issue with a sexily posed twit on the cover. Curiosity made me flip through the pages and study the models. What was for sale here? Swimsuits or sex? Could I do this sultry pose bit if I wanted to? My tan was just as dark, my bikini covered no more, and I had the same stuff they had. The problem, of course, was I had a little more stuff in some places and a little less in others. Maybe if I lessened my beer intake and increased my aerobics workouts, I could .... Nah, wouldn't work. I dropped the magazine and reached for the phone.

I dialed my number and pressed in my message-replay code. There'd been two calls. The first was Melanie asking me to call Weldon. The second, although the caller never said a word, was probably from Angus. I replayed the messages three times, concentrating on the second call: jukebox playing, laughter, and "Two more over here."

In my opinion Angus had two major faults: pressing our relationship and getting drunk when things didn't go his way. I was sure he'd been at the Rudder Bar and Grill on Gulf Boulevard when he placed the call. The Rudder had long been his favorite home away from home, most likely because it was within stumble-home distance of the Buttonwood.

I hung up and was reaching for the phone book to get the Rudder's number when Al entered the office. He rubbed his palms together and said, "I'm hot tonight, doll. Let's make this quick."

The quicker the better, actually. I handed him the ring.

He carried it to his desk and snapped on a high intensity lamp. Al had appraised jewelry for cash-hungry customers many times while I'd been in the shop, but this was the first time I'd known the value of the item before he did. After a few grunts and growls during his inspection, he looked up with a pained expression.

"How much?" I said.

He tossed the ring onto the stack of magazines. "You might trade it for a bus ticket to Jacksonville."

"A bus ticket?" I stared at him and then grabbed the ring. "You mean—"

"I mean it's fake." He snapped off the lamp and stood. "This week's off but try to be free next week. I got dealings in Tampa."

Fake? The ring couldn't be a fake. Eva had been a rich woman. There'd been nothing fake about her.

Al grabbed my shoulder. "You hear me?"

I looked up. "Hear what?"

"I said I got dealings in Tampa next week. Be loose."

Dealings? Dealings meant a card game, not some underworld activity? "Al! You mean all the times I've covered the shop for your remote dealings, you've been in a poker game?"

"What the hell'd you think *dealings* meant? No. Don't tell me. Get outta here."

CHAPTER 13

I got outta there.

My reluctance in taking Amber's job had been because it stood in the way of the job I desperately wanted back. Now there was an honest way out. No retainer; no job. When she contacted me, my message would be brief: "Kiss off!" At the end of the alley I headed for Second Avenue, where I caught a break in traffic, jaywalked to the south side of the street, and then marched toward the waterfront.

The downtown's newest condo, Bay View Towers, blocked the late afternoon sun and shaded the oak-lined sidewalk, but the temperature and humidity still hovered on the redline side of my comfort zone. So did my thoughts of Amber. Just how dumb did she think I was? I marched on, kicking acorns and bouncing her ring in my palm.

With an earnest expression and a voice devoid of deceit, she'd looked me in the eye and said, "Hock it and give me the ticket." Was she a world-class actress? Maybe. Even so, if she had the walk-around sense of a windup toy, she would've known a pawnbroker would appraise the ring before advancing a dime on it. Why, then, knowing the real value, had she asked me to pawn it?

A block later it hit me. Crap! Maybe she didn't know what I'd just found out: the ring was only an inexpensive copy of the very-expensive original. And since Weldon hadn't brought up the possibility of Eva having a copycat set of jewelry, maybe Amber hadn't known either. Quite possible, I supposed, if her statement denying knowledge of Eva's safe was true.

A recent movie had featured a wealthy matron and her two sets of jewelry. Normally, she kept the real set in a safe-deposit box and wore the imitation set to all but the more glamorous outings. Her ploy fooled everyone but a slick conman. That was another story, but what if, as the ring suggested, Eva also had an imitation set of jewelry, a set Amber hadn't been aware of? If so, she hadn't tried to con me—she just hadn't known.

I slowed my pace and pocketed the ring, all the while listening to the persistent little voice of my conscience whispering something about benefit of doubt. Okay. Until proven otherwise, I'd give her the benefit of doubt. Even so, this concession didn't extend to running up any expenses until she produced my retainer in cash.

It was now nearly seven, and making the trip to Global was unnecessary, as even with a photo of the missing Grady-White in hand, I had no intention of searching for it. On the flipside, I was hungry, and Global's sprawling office complex was within shouting distance of Casey's, a great eating spot on Gandy Boulevard.

At Bayshore Drive, adjacent to where Dad's truck was parked, I ducked into a curbside phone booth and probed my pockets for change and Myers's card. A security-patrol officer in a green-and-white golf cart hummed past. Despite his austere manner and rigid posture, the officer waved. I returned the gesture. My tan, Bermuda shorts, deck shoes, and loose, sun-bleached hair all painted me as a member of the boating community. In his eyes, then, I belonged, and he didn't give me a second look. I fed coins into the phone and dialed the Pinellas County Sheriff's Office.

The fact that Amber had given me a ring worth less than the cost of a day at Disney World wouldn't mean much to Myers's investigation, but, big or little, he'd said to pass it on. This was my second pass in a game I was eager to exit.

Unlike my first call, this dispatcher's voice was vibrantly alive. Unfortunately, her answer to my question was the same: "No, he's not in at the moment," she said. "May I take a message?" Great. My pocket was full of bills but no more change in which to try the other pair of numbers on his card. I explained my plight to the woman, along with the iffy nature of my information and where I'd be in the next hour if Myers had any questions. She promised to track him down and relay the information.

I unlocked the truck, jumped in, and slammed the door. Taking I-275 could cut half the time and some of the distance from the Municipal Marina to Global's office. Doing so, however, wasn't a wise choice. Until now I'd only kicked acorns, but my anger was still roiling, and in a pissed off state of mind, Florida's notorious white-knuckle super slab was no place to be. Especially so since there was also a much calmer route to my destination— one that would allow me time to simmer down.

I started the engine and threaded my way to Gandy Boulevard the old-fashioned way, the way it was traversed before the peninsula was crisscrossed with multilane streets, expressways, and the Interstate Highway System. The old, two-lane route was once desolate and lined with stands of buttonwood, thickets of sea grape, and pockets of mangrove; now, because the pristine area was a magnet for deep-pocket developers, the route was lined with wall-to-wall homes.

Even so, the self-prescribed therapy worked. By the time I reached Coffee Pot Bayou, my not-so-nice thoughts of Amber had given way to thoughts of the fun times I'd had right here in the not-so-distant past. I drove slowly, rubbernecking the new homes on the inland side of the road and picking out the familiar spots on the bay side where as a kid I'd handed the wheel of Dad's mullet boat while he worked the net. We caught mullet, drum, and perch. On the way home, I always maneuvered the boat across every grass-flat I could spot, all the while shouting encouragement to Dad as he worked his shrimp net. We rarely returned without enough to have, enough to share, and enough to sell. Back then the bayou was a fisherman's Eden. Now, it was catch as catch can.

At Gandy Boulevard I turned right and began moving through the numbers of the truck's five-speed gearbox. Ahead, and off to the left across the divided highway, I saw Channel Five's giant logo atop their broadcast studio and the blinking strobe lights on their sky-scraping transmission tower. Before dropping the shift lever into fifth gear, I was at Global's palm-lined entry drive.

The Grady-White photo and spec sheet were waiting for me. A minute later I had them on the seat beside me and was headed for Casey's, the one-of-a-kind spot my granddaddy introduced me to. It was his favorite watering hole when he worked at the Tampa Ship Yard during the war, and it was still his favorite home away from home when he died a year ago.

The oyster shell parking lot was scattered with cars, and a half-dozen heavily chromed motorcycles were parked near the door. Not a bad crowd for a weekday evening. I parked alongside a Mazda the color of ripe sugarcane, locked the truck, and started for the door. The smooth sounds of Eddie Arnold singing "The Tennessee Stud" met me at the entrance.

Stepping inside, I exchanged a warm smile with a familiar couple locked in a slow-dance embrace near the jukebox and headed for an empty booth near the wall phone. A blonde barmaid wearing a fixed smile, tight black jeans, and a white cowgirl shirt two sizes too small waltzed up to the table before I settled into my seat.

"Hi, your name Seaweed?"

I said it was.

With fluttering eyelashes, she said, "Some dude just called for you. Milo or Myron or something like that. Nice voice, kinda sexy, if you know what I mean. Said to tell you he'd be right here."

I nodded even though it was a tough stretch to tag Myers's voice as sexy. But, then, Dad said it took all kinds. "Thanks," I said.

"My pleasure." She batted her lashes in time with the pencil stub she tapped against her bottom lip. "Anyway," she said, "I'm Penny, what'll ya have?"

No thought needed here. Shanley's was my favorite for hoagies; Casey's was my favorite for chilidogs. After ordering one with extra onion and a small draft, I handed Penny a dollar bill and said, "I need some quarters."

"Neat!" She fished my change from her apron. "Garth's latest is on G-7."

Returning one of the quarters to her, I said, "Play it. I have to use the phone."

Penny stroll-danced toward the jukebox. I dropped a quarter into the phone, punched in my number, and interrogated my answering machine. Three hang-ups. No messages. Bracing for a hassle, I fed another coin into the black box and called Dad to tell him I'd need his truck a little longer.

"No problem," he said. "I don't have to go anywhere."

It'd been fifteen years since Mom died, but Dad hadn't remarried. Early on, for reasons I wasn't mature enough to understand, this worried me. Later, when I did understand, his infrequent female companions brought me discomfort. Not worry; blatant jealousy. But now he had a lady friend, a real estate broker with an office on Indian Rocks Beach, who I both admired and approved of. They got together during the week and, at times, had been known to disappear for a weekend.

He also attended the Wednesday night wrestling matches, bowled in a mixed-doubles league on Friday nights, and hit Tampa Stadium when the Bucs had a home game. He stayed busier than I.

"So what are you doing, spending a quiet evening alone?"

"Oh, it's quiet enough," he said, "but I'm not alone. Cecil's here. We're sitting around having a cool one. You know, talking old times."

Yes, I knew. For him, talking old times often meant reliving Mom's death. Then, as now, Dad had twice the strength of most men, but it hadn't been enough to save her. I never blamed him. I was there, and no one but God Himself could've done more. The problem was, Dad never accepted that. And each time he dwelled on those old times it meant he'd be depressed for days. I hated that and hoped Cecil would steer the conversation in another direction. For safety I tossed him a diversion.

"Talk later, Dad! Y'all get out your snake beaters and wet a line. Last I heard speckled trout were hitting mirror lures and live shrimp. Go get 'em."

His voice lifted a notch. "Yeah, I heard that. And the tide's 'bout right. Maybe we'll take a crack at it." I listened to his breathing for a moment before he gave me the one line he'd been dishing out since the day I got my driver's license: "Get back in one piece, baby."

I promised I would.

With my last quarter I called Gwen. Running up expenses on Amber's behalf was still on hold until she came through with my retainer, but I could start snooping.

After my call was transferred and I'd endured a music-filled session on hold, Gwen came on the line with a cheery, "What's up?"

"Amber called me last night," I said.

"You're kidding!" When I didn't confirm her statement, she added, "Okay, you're not, but why in the world would she call *you*?"

I explained that Eva and Reginald's marriage plans had included a new yacht. "Amber won't accept the thought he could be dead too, and she also rejects the possibility he could've killed Eva. In her mind he went to pick up the yacht and he's overdue. She wants me to find him." I didn't mention the ring or Al's appraisal of it.

"Find him?" she said. "Oh, sure. Seaweed Investigation. I mentioned that in the broadcast."

"I'd thank you for the plug, but Amber has no chance of making my favorite-client list. In fact she can't get it into her head that the only investigating I've ever done has been boating accidents."

"Yeah," Gwen said, "she's squirrelly to say the least. And, look, I'm sorry for not being more clear in my report."

I borrowed one of Dad's lines. "Water under the bridge."

"So, are you going to do it?"

"I've already started," I said, "but I need some help."

"From me?"

"Yes, if possible. At Hangman's Key you said you had a photo file on Eva. Is there a chance you have a shot of Reginald as well?"

"I think so."

"You're not sure?"

"Let me put it this way," she said. "If the gentleman with Eva at the last charity ball was Reginald, I have a photo of him. Like in one. He avoided the camera all evening. Blatantly. In fact, when the event was over, I still didn't have his name."

"That event was recent enough to believe if she was about to remarry, the man with her was probably Reginald."

"That's what Myers thought. He had a deputy pick up a copy of the photo."

Hmm. Unlike TV detectives, Myers seemed to be touching all the bases. "Any problem giving me a copy?"

"No, of course not," she said. "When I found out Reginald was so popular, I asked our photo department to make extra prints. Where are you?"

"Close. I'm at Casey's."

"Yum! Love their chilidogs. Sit tight. I'll grab the photo file and be right there."

"Thanks, I—"

"Wait!"

"What is it?"

I heard a hurried exchange, but the words weren't directed at me. A moment later she said, "Got to cancel. Big pileup west of the hump on Franklin Bridge."

Franklin Bridge was one of the major links between Tampa and St. Petersburg. It was also a notorious accident corridor. "When can I—"

"Call me early in the morning," she said. "I'm listed in the Tampa exchange as Wendell O'Dell."

"Wendell?"

"Gwen gets kook calls," she said, "Wendell doesn't. Got to go."

I hung up the receiver and returned to my booth. Wendell? Interesting. I was listed as K. Cobia, and I still got a raft of kook calls. Would changing the listing to Bubba Cobia cure the problem?

My first draft was history and I was working on a second chilidog when Myers walked through the door. The bikers froze, their game of eight ball forgotten as they watched him pause and survey the room before heading my way. He was wearing dark slacks, matching sport jacket, and a white shirt open at the collar. I thought he looked like any other civilian. The bikers didn't. They *made* him two steps inside the door. The clacking of pool balls didn't continue until he reached the booth.

"What brings you out this way?" he said.

When he slid onto the seat across from me I told him of my attempt to obtain a photo of Reginald. "At the last second, Gwen was called out. Another pileup on the Franklin." I gave him a pitiful shrug. "Can I peek at the one she sent to you?"

He shook his head.

I narrowed my eyes. "Look, I've been playing ball with you, so I don't see why you can't—"

He waved his hands in my face and said, "I mean you could look at the photo, but I left it at the department. I didn't recognize him, but he and Amber made my most-wanted list an hour ago."

"Why?"

"We'll go through it in a moment," he said. After adjusting the placement of the napkin dispenser, the menu holder, and lining up the salt-and-pepper shakers, he added, "Let me hear what you have first."

I started with the information from Weldon about Reginald's inheritance status and the new yacht, items touched on in the first message I'd left for him. Myers's tired expression said my information was old news. I moved on. There was no way he could know about Al's appraisal of the ring. I explained and said, "It might not mean much, but I thought you should know."

He slouched in his seat, hands clasped behind his head. I eyeballed the last chunk of chilidog, decided not to tackle it, and pushed my plate away. He was nodding with a slow mechanical rhythm. After watching a dozen reps, I asked, "What're you thinking?"

He improved his posture and transferred his gaze to me. "Just that your information is beginning to mesh with a scenario I've been shaping."

"Scenario?"

He waved his palm at me like the Mickey Mouse greeter at Disney World. "We'll get to it," he said. "What else ya got?"

"That's it," I said. "Until she comes up with some cash, I won't be looking for the *Fifth Amendment*. That's the name of the yacht Reginald would be picking up if he were actually doing what Amber believes. I explained all that in the message I left for you."

"I used it," he said. "Thanks. Anything else?"

Used it how? I wondered. "Only that Global asked me to search for the Grady-White. I have no plan to do so, but to appease Weldon I picked up a photo of it a few minutes ago."

"Then we haven't picked your pocket," he said.

"What do you mean?"

"A search team found the boat a couple of hours ago."

The finder's fee would have been easy money, but finding the boat was more important to Myers's investigation than it was to my pocket book. "Where was it?"

"Drifting off Frenchman Creek," he said. "Damned near in sight of Eva's home."

"Any clues?"

He didn't answer. Maybe he hadn't heard me. Penny was standing close to his shoulder and his trance-like attention was on her.

"What'll ya have?" she said. The melody in her voice suggested choices not mentioned on the menu.

"Ah, a small draft'll do it," he said.

Without taking her smoldering eyes off him, she asked if I wanted a refill. Myers had either not heard of a gentleman ordering for a lady or he had a temporary case of lockjaw. After an uncomfortable moment of silence, I said, "Sure, top it off."

She picked up my glass and gave him a smile, one of those I-get-off-at-two jobs, and then spun away, hips swinging and blonde locks flying.

I was about to repeat my question when he spoke. "Where were we? Clues? Yeah, they picked up a couple."

He swiped at a few crumbs, sending them flying across the table and onto the floor. The crumbs were remnants of my first chilidog. Casey toasts the bun, brushes melted butter into the fold, inserts an oversize wiener cooked to succulent perfection on a gas-fired rotisserie, and then ladles on a mountain of chili hot enough to put the squeak back into ten-year-old sneakers. There's just no civilized way to eat one; no one who would patronize Casey's twice would try.

I ignored his attempt at neatness and stared into his eyes.

"I can't tell you much," he said.

I continued the stare and screwed a pout onto my lips.

"I don't know much … yet … really."

I kept a lock on the expression. When that didn't work, I said, "What if I run out to the truck and get my good-guys hat? It's white. Snakeskin band. Got a little blue jay feather tucked right—"

"Jeez! All right." He swiped at another lode of crumbs. "But keep a lid on it."

I dropped the pout and leaned closer. With my so-so cleavage hidden by Dad's shirt, there was little chance Myers would fall into another trance. I flashed him my coconspirator's smile and said, "Sure."

The closest customers to our back-wall booth were two couples slow dancing near the pool tables. Even so, Myers glanced around for eavesdroppers before answering. "I haven't inspected the boat yet," he said, "but I was told it contained an empty .45 caliber cartridge case."

I raised an eyebrow.

"And ... some bloodstains," he added.

"Then the boat *was* used in her murder."

"Yeah," he said, "and before you ask if the anchor was missing, it was."

My thoughts weren't on the anchor; they were on the awful act that had caused the bloodstains. The thought of her bleeding and dying still gripped me when he added, "Have you heard from Amber?"

"No," I said, "and that includes my answering machine. How about you?"

"Not a peep." He clasped his hands and flexed them backwards, cracking one knuckle at a time. I flinched. He continued. "Right now I wish I had my hands around her throat."

Her throat? "Why?"

"Everything she told me was bullshit, that's why!"

My thought had been that Amber was withholding something when she first talked with me. Same thing when she spoke with Myers. And I'd mentioned as much to him. But, crap, I'd never dreamed she was outright lying. "Like what?" I said.

His expression took the set of tombstone marble as he straightened the first finger of his left hand and pointed it at me as if he were sighting a pistol. "She said there'd been a management change at her condo! I talked with the super! He said the damned building's been under the same management for ten years! And, on top of—"

Wondering what Penny thought of his voice now, I framed my hands in the traditional time-out signal and waved them in his face.

"What?"

I leaned closer and whispered, "You said to keep a lid on it."

He glanced around the room. The dancing couples were cocooned in their own world, but Penny, the bikers, and several others at the bar were looking our way. "Yeah. Thanks." He lowered his voice and straightened another finger. "Okay. She said she wasn't sure she wanted to stay at her condo any longer. The super said she redecorated last month and prepaid her lease through next year."

Damn. He hadn't exaggerated when he said Amber dished up nothing but bullshit. *But why would she lie?* I asked.

"At this point," he said, wagging a finger with the enthusiastic rhythm of a puppy's tail at feeding time, "all I have is a good guess. But don't change the dial, we're getting to the good part."

CHAPTER 14

Good part? My God, what else had she lied about? My mouth was open, so I reached for the chunk of chilidog I'd pushed away earlier. Penny arrived at our booth before I could chomp into it or ask him to explain.

She flipped a pair of coasters onto the table and then placed both glasses of draft onto them without spilling a drop. Myers reached for his wallet.

Waving off his offer, I pulled the roll of bills from my pocket. "My treat this time."

She winked at Myers, counted out my change, and whispered, "Lucky guy," as she turned and flowed toward a biker whistling and waving an empty mug.

I studied Myers as his eyes tracked Penny's swaying hips until they were hidden from view behind the pool table. What was on his mind? Love or lust? Their meanings were worlds apart, but they were both four-letter words. To shatter his spell, I reached for my beer and said, "Tell me about the good part."

When his attention returned to me, he began waving another finger, the fourth occurrence in his recitation if I'd kept an accurate count. "Fasten your seat belt," he said.

I nodded and sipped.

"Amber said she'd been staying with Jean Hampton. I called on her. She's staying at the Bamboo. You know it?"

The Bamboo Lounge, Package Store, and Motor Lodge was located far out on Fourth Street North in St. Petersburg. The joint's major drawing cards were room rates by the hour, mirrored ceilings, and triple-X movies. Local newspapers and TV stations featured the establishment from time to time. Police raids mostly. It wasn't a place I'd be caught dead in, and it certainly wasn't one where I would've expected to find Amber. Avoiding Myers's eyes, I muttered, "By its nickname."

"Yeah, the Whore's Haven," he said. "Anyway, it only took thirty seconds for sweet little Jean Hampton to recite Amber's alibi—word for word."

"Recite? You think she lied?"

"Think? I know damned well she did."

I waited to hear how.

"Amber said Reginald left TPA at noon last Friday? I checked. There were three departures during the few minutes either side of high noon. Delta's twelve-oh-five p.m. flight was one of them. His name was on their passenger list. Seat twenty-seven-A."

Damn! Leaning forward I said, "My money was on Reginald as crab bait at the bottom of the Gulf."

"I had him as Eva's killer. I still do."

Still? "Look," I said, "Amber's first statement to me was that Reginald and Eva were supposed to have traveled together to pick up the yacht. We know they didn't. We also know at or near the time he was catching a plane Friday, someone was dropping her body into the Gulf." I fashioned a smug smile and added, "No doubt he's involved somehow, but he couldn't be the one who dumped Eva's body."

Myers made a wait-signal with the finger he'd been wagging. "Don't get ahead of me," he said. "There's more goodies in the box."

I waited.

"Finding Reginald's name on the passenger list was the first thing in Amber's story that appeared to be true."

"Appeared to be? Look, if he was on their passenger list, he had to be on—"

"Hold on," he said.

"Sorry."

"Reginald *was* on the plane. The surprise was the name of the passenger listed for seat twenty-seven-B."

"You recognized the name?"

Tom Selleck's eyebrow wiggle was sexy. Myers tried it. He looked ridiculous. "The name," he said, "was Eva Park."

With a mouthful of chilidog, I would've choked. "Eva? I don't get it. There's no way she could've been on that plane."

He replaced the eyebrow wiggle with an all-knowing smile. "She wasn't."

My interest in the last scrap of chilidog was forgotten. I dropped it back into the wicker basket and pulled a napkin from the dispenser to wipe the goo from my fingers. "Well, I asked for the good part. You delivered."

"Not quite," he said, "but we're getting there."

Several questions churned in my mind, but he continued before I could voice the big one: Who flew in Eva's place?

"Two of the other passengers seated in row twenty-seven were local people, a doctor and his wife. They flew out Friday and were back Sunday night. I talked with them separately, he at his office, she at their home. What they gave me as description for the man sitting in twenty-seven-A matched the man in Gwen's photo."

"So he really was on the plane. How about the person in twenty-seven-B?"

"That's the good part," he said. "The doc said the person sitting in that seat was female, mid twenties, narrow features, and auburn hair. The doc's wife gave me the same description with one important addition."

I took his pause for an eyebrow wiggle as my cue to ask, "What was it?"

"She said the young woman had a birthmark on her neck."

"Amber?"

"Amber."

"But why?"

Myers scooped up his glass, sipped, licked his lips, and said, "Simple. Eva's killer never meant for the body to be found."

Let's see. Her body had been tied, weighted, and dumped offshore. Yes, even as a non-detective I could've come up with that conclusion. Raising my glass of draft and tipping it in a salute, I said, "Nothing gets by you, I like that."

He almost grinned. "What I mean is, Eva told two of her closest friends she and Reginald were leaving town on Friday."

Now I saw his logic. "So," I said, "if the body hadn't turned up—"

"Right. Sometime down the line, next week, next month, or whenever someone got around to reporting Eva missing, all an investigation would turn up is she and Reginald flew out of town together last Friday."

"What about the break-in to her home?" I said.

"The detectives would've believed the break-in was a crime of opportunity. Unoccupied residence. Happens all the time."

"And the boat?"

"Same thing," he said. "By the time someone reported it missing, there wouldn't have been an all-out effort to find it."

"Just another missing boat," I said.

"Right. And without suspecting foul play when the boat *was* recovered, the cartridge case wouldn't have meant much. Same thing with the blood. Could have been fish blood, or all sign of blood could have been washed away."

"Okay," I said. "If Amber left town with Reginald on Friday, I'm sure they have some explaining to do, but they couldn't have had anything to do with the break-in or Eva's murder."

"They could have everything to do with it," he said. "Amber posed as Eva on the flight. At the least she's an accomplice."

"But why would she do it? Flying in Eva's place doesn't make any sense."

"Maybe it does," he said. "Let's play some what-if."

"Your scenario?"

"Yeah. First, let's back up to the two you believed to have the most to gain by Eva's death."

I filled in the blanks. "Amber and Reginald."

"Right. Let's take him first. He's about to marry Eva, but he finds out what you found out: he inherits nothing in the event of her death."

"If so," I said, "he had no motive for killing her."

"Sit on it a sec and let's move on to Amber."

I sipped beer.

"She's on an allowance, probably generous by our standards, but she wants more, and she wants it now. Her mother's estate is sizeable, but she doesn't inherit it for another five years. She knows, or finds out, there's no such time provision in Eva's will. She sees the answer to her money problem and makes a move on Reginald."

"You think she paid him to kill Eva?"

"It might be that simple," he said. "More likely, since he was about to marry Eva, Amber offered him a chunk of the estate he wouldn't get otherwise."

"Considering Eva's time of death," I said, "I don't see how they could've killed her and still have been on time to catch the plane?"

"That worried me too," he said, "until I ran it by the medical examiner. He based his preliminary time-of-death estimate on the bay water temperature."

"That was a mistake," I said. "The Gulf water is colder."

"Right. And time of death in a case like this is a wild-ass guess at best. Her body started out in colder water and then washed into the warmer water along the beach. How long had it been there before you and Angus came along? No way to tell. Anyway, the ME said her body could've been dumped as early as Friday morning."

I did some mental arithmetic. "That," I said, "would've given them time."

"Yeah, and they already had the motive."

I chewed on his scenario. Some points made sense. Too many others did not. I spelled out the biggest one. "Let's assume that Amber and Reginald conspired and killed Eva. Somehow they caused a couple of Eva's friends to believe she and Reginald were out of town. Together. Later, when someone reported them missing, a casual look at Delta's passenger list would've shown they left TPA last Friday. By that time no one would remember the faces of the passengers sitting in row twenty-seven."

"So far so good," he said. "Go on."

"So at that point, Eva and Reginald are missing. More specific, she's dead and he's in hiding, but Amber cannot collect a cent until Eva is declared dead. That could take some time."

"You've met her," he said. "She's a classic airhead. It's my bet she never thought about that."

"Maybe so, but there's something else very wrong."

"Like what?"

"Eva's body," I said. "It popped up. When it did, the smartest thing Amber could've done was keep her mouth shut and let everyone believe Reginald's body was out there, too. But she didn't stay quiet. She asked me to find him. Why? And if they were in this together, I think they would know how to contact each other."

He made raisin skin with his forehead and a silly whistling noise through his pursed lips. "I think she came to you first thinking you could find him without involving the police. As to his not contacting her, I don't know, unless the ring has something to do with it."

"Like what?"

"Like maybe you were right about Eva having two sets of jewelry. Reginald stuck her with the phony set. She's pissed, but she can't call the police. She hoped you could find him."

That didn't float well, but I set it aside and moved to another point before it slipped my mind. "Okay," I said, "let's take the bit about the airline. Eva's friends said she was out of town. They didn't mention how she'd left. Amber did. Why would someone trying to get away with murder do that?"

When he didn't answer, I took it to mean he didn't have a clue. Fine. I didn't either. I stretched back into the vinyl seat and sipped beer. Amber was a liar, and, in her behalf, so was Jean Hampton. Amber was also involved, directly or indirectly, in Eva's death. I just didn't feel her involvement was the way Myers believed. I sat forward and set my glass aside. "I don't know why she lied to you," I said, "and I don't know why she was on that plane, but I do know the bucket holding our little scenario has a few holes in it."

"How so?"

"The ring, for one thing," I said. "If she'd had the cash for my retainer, she wouldn't have given up the ring because I'm convinced she believed it to be real. For another thing, I talked with her in a way you never could."

Myers smirked. "The woman-to-woman thing, right?"

After being hit with that line, a feminist would've spit in his eye. Instead, I fed him some of his own venom. "Call it the man-to-man thing, if it'll help you grasp my meaning. If that doesn't work for you, call it any damned thing that comes to mind. I don't care. I'm just telling you her feelings for Reginald were full of concern. Real concern."

His expression and tone softened. "I'm sorry," he said. "That wasn't called for. It's just that *I know* she's involved in this—"

"I couldn't agree more," I said, "but *I know* it's for a reason you haven't uncovered yet."

CHAPTER 15

Myers slumped in the booth, silent and motionless, staring at the graffiti-rich section of wall beyond my shoulder. I would've turned and helped him stare, but no study time was needed, as I could recite the lewd listings with my eyes closed—even the triple-X poetry, Wanda's pager number, and the declared length of Doug's dangling participle.

Gazing at Myers, I wondered what my outburst had earned. Was it a front-page slot on his shit list? If so, I could live with it, but that hadn't been my goal. All I'd wanted was for him to rethink his scenario. So which was it? A better question was, did I even care? No! I'd now reached a point beyond caring. With Amber and Reginald holding place on Myers's wanted list, I had every right to flush further commitment to her. In fact, considering Myers's worry that my involvement might botch his investigation, it was the right thing to do. And once free of this mess, I'd waste no time in running back to Dad and the waiting *Margaret Ellen*—the best charter boat on Florida's Gulf Coast. "Captain Karen reporting for duty, sir!" Yeah. That was a scenario worth embracing. And the first step was simple: take the ring from my pocket and hand it to Myers, wish him luck, and head for the door. Why, then, did I ask, "What now?"

My voice broke his trance and his eyes swung back to mine. "I'm not sure," he said. "Right now I have a hard time believing a young woman of her means, even an airhead, could allow herself to become a part of this."

"Men don't have the only key to stupidity," I said.

"So I'm learning." He squirmed in his seat before continuing. "There's something else I'd better tell you about the *Fifth Amendment*."

"What's that?"

"When I learned Reginald really flew out of here, I used the info you left for me and inquired about the boat. By the time I called, Northeast was closed, so I asked for help from the Margate police. I told them Reginald was wanted for questioning in Eva's death and that I was sending them a copy of his photo. They said they'd watch for him. They also contacted Northeast's manager, Steven Binkey. He was home with the flu but he called me back."

I could've tried the same tactic, but would my effort have obtained the same results? Doubtful. "What'd you find out?" I said.

"For one thing, Northeast does not sell boats. They sell yachts. Binkey was adamant about that. What's the difference?"

I laughed. "Some say it's a matter of size. Others say it's a matter of price. One of those, if-you-have-to-ask-you-can't-afford-it kind of things."

Myers shrugged. "Whatever. Anyway, Binkey said Stan Avery completed all paperwork on the yacht by mail early last week. Avery also instructed Binkey to comply with Reginald's instructions for delivery. And get this. The boat, er, the yacht, was not only titled in Amber's name, she also signed the transfer-of-title document."

I leaned forward. "You mean to tell me she's known all along where the yacht was located?"

"Yep. The woman's a first-class bullshit artist."

Quite obvious, but I couldn't understand why. If she'd really wanted me to find Reginald why would she have withheld the truth? "So where is the yacht now?"

"On the way here."

"All right!" I said. "Amber hired me to find Reginald, but you did the job. When you find her, hit her up for my fee. You've earned it."

"Not really," he said. "Reginald's not with the yacht."

"Not with it! So where is he?"

"Good question," Myers said. "Binkey said Reginald showed up at Northeast's office Saturday morning and spoke to the assistant manager about arranging delivery for the yacht. They were happy to do so, but during sea trials they found the autopilot to be erratic."

I read the question in his eyes. "A sea trial is a short shakedown cruise where you look for problems," I said. "Like a test drive in a car. What I don't understand is why they'd release the yacht if the autopilot wasn't working."

"Reginald insisted. Still, the assistant manager didn't agree to the delivery until he called Binkey. Since the yacht could be steered manually, and the delivery captain was willing to do so, Binkey gave his okay."

I pulled the ring from my pocket and dropped it into his hand. "Amber gave me this to cover my fee for finding Reginald," I said. "The job sounded simple, but with them both on your wanted list, it's now police business, not mine." Brushing my hands together, I said, "I'm out of a job."

"Only a paying job," he said. He studied the ring a moment and then put it into his pants pocket. "Right now Amber and Reginald look good for Eva's murder. They left together on Friday. Saturday morning he made delivery arrangements for the yacht and dropped out of sight. Early Tuesday, Amber showed up at your place wanting help finding him." He lowered his voice and leaned closer. "They were in this together, but something went wrong. So, I'd still like your help. If you're willing."

Knowing better, I asked, "How?"

"Amber wants to locate Reginald, but by now she should know I know she lied to me."

"No argument there," I said.

"Okay, Seaweed, this is a long shot, but if she doesn't find him on her own, I believe it'll be you she returns to for help." He studied my eyes to see if I was paying attention. I was. He continued. "Here's what I'd like you to do. If she calls, don't mention the ring or me. Tell her you're close to a break on Reginald's whereabouts but insist on a way you can contact her. Once you get that, call me. I'll take it from there."

When he was sure I understood my role, he stood, wished me a pleasant evening, and headed for the door. I stifled a yawn and glanced at my watch. Ten. I'd been awake for eighteen hours, and my bunk on the *Margaret Ellen* was still two hours away. The only way I could get there quicker was to forgo a stop at my sloop for a shower and a change of clothes. A scratch-and-sniff test wasn't needed to know that idea wasn't an option.

I swapped Penny a five for a fistful of quarters and used one of them to check my answering machine. Another hang-up. On the way to the door, I fired a Girl Scout salute at the bikers. The fat one with the bushy red beard grinned. A little. I think.

There were a number of routes from Casey's to the Buttonwood. All of them were twenty-mile runs, minimum, and all of them, with one exception, were infested with stoplights. That lone exception was the Interstate. It wouldn't shave a mile of driving distance, but it would shave half the time. I accessed it two miles west of Casey's and headed south for the Pinellas Bayway.

Unlike the bumper-to-bumper flow of rush hour, the super corridor of white concrete stretching before me was nearly deserted. I kept Dad's truck at the speed limit, a feat I hadn't mastered with my Camaro, and began some serious thinking about how I'd handle the three uppermost things on my mind: Dad, the Amber-Myers combo, and Angus.

Actually, the Amber-Myers situation was simple. I'd promised my cooperation to Myers for seven days. Not a minute longer. As for Angus, I was ready to spell it out for him. "Back off on the demands or I'm shipping out." The trouble was, even if he backed off, I was shipping out anyway, at least back to Dad's. Angus would try to talk me out of doing so, but chartering was an early-morning business, and Dad's comment, "A girl could get to work on time if she lived closer," was true. The long commute from the Buttonwood would get old in a hurry.

When I reached St. Petersburg Beach, I'd also concluded my thinking. Dad's partnership offer meant the world to me. Despite the wants of Angus, Myers, Amber, or the devil himself, I *was* going to be at the helm of the *Margaret Ellen* next Wednesday.

At Gulf Boulevard I turned north and kept my speed low until reaching a spot where the upper floor of the Buttonwood was visible. The lanai was dark. I continued north to the Rudder Bar and Grill. Angus's canary-yellow Eldorado was parked near the front door. A short-box Ford pickup, too dirty to distinguish color, and a maroon MG convertible were the only other vehicles on the lot. I made a U-turn on the boulevard and headed for my sloop.

The Buttonwood sits in the middle of a large rectangular lot, three times deeper than it is wide. The area in front and to both sides of the building, except for walks and flowerbeds, is blacktopped and striped for parking. Royal palms, spaced at consistent intervals, line the street and both side-property lines. The area behind the building hosts a pool and patio for tenants and guests and a hundred-foot-long T-shaped dock with berthing for sixteen vessels. Mine is the outer-most slip. It's also the only one fitted with live-aboard amenities.

I hurried through my shower and change of clothes in the hope I could reach my bunk on the *Margaret Ellen* before midnight. After bounding up the companionway, I remembered my answering machine. A quick check revealed there'd been two more calls. Both of them were hang-ups. I locked up and headed for the truck.

At the front of the Buttonwood I saw Angus's car in its penthouse-parking slot. Next to it was a maroon MG convertible. The top was now up, but I was sure it was the same one I'd seen at the Rudder. A beer can, drink glass, and an empty cigarette package were scattered on the pavement behind the two vehicles. Easy read: a drinking buddy he'd brought home to continue partying on the lanai. I had no desire to join the festivities, but I did want to tell him my new job fizzled and that I'd be there by six with the trimmings for our sheepshead and hush puppies supper.

I grabbed the first empty parking slot and started for the entrance. The scene in the entry alcove stopped me before I'd pushed the front door halfway open.

Angus was facing the penthouse elevator. So was the woman at his side. They were holding hands. Laughing. She was about my height, with washed-out red hair hanging several inches below her shoulders, and was wearing spike heels, white short-shorts, and a navy-blue tube top. Her thighs belonged in a holiday-ham commercial.

They stepped into the elevator and turned to face the open door. She pulled the tube top below her breasts and thrust them at him. He hesitated a moment and then touched them like someone selecting tomatoes at a produce stand. I stood, staring in unbelief. Her age was an impossible call, but she was the poster child of ugly. Just as the elevator doors slid shut his eyes found mine. His face blanched and he jerked his hands away from her breasts. Clutching my churning stomach, I turned and ran for the parking lot.

The engine in Dad's truck was a 454-cubic-inch V-8. I peeled rubber to Gulf Boulevard, careened into the northbound lane, and floored the throttle, not easing up until nearly rear-ending a minivan with Michigan plates. Keeping the truck in my lane by aiming more than driving, I screamed my repertoire of profanity over and over until I was hoarse. What in the hell did he think he was doing? Stupid question, Karen. Drunk or not, Angus *knew* what he was doing.

The slow-moving van kept me from speeding, and the flow of oncoming traffic kept me from passing. Still tailgating the van when I crossed the Big Tarpon Pass Bridge, I made the first right onto Charter Drive. The narrow, two-block-long street was dark and deserted except for a few late customers parked in front of Shanley's. A pair of spotlights in the front window of Danny's beamed at the latest and greatest Mercury outboard engine. The bait shop was dark. Cecil's vintage Impala was gone.

I swung into the two-rut driveway on the east side of the shop, eased through a gap in the hibiscus hedge, and pulled into Dad's parking place alongside the patio. In the late evening silence, I stared out over the pass. Black water ebbed toward the Gulf, moonlight shimmering on its surface. At dawn this same water would return, renewed and rinsed to emerald green by the light of a new day. My feelings for Angus would not. The bridge I'd wanted to burn was now blown to smithereens. It was over.

With my tears under control, I locked the truck and ambled toward my bunk on the *Margaret Ellen*. At the boarding ramp I paused, sensing another presence. It was Dad, slumped in a deck chair and holding a long-stemmed rose on his lap. It looked soft yellow in the moonlight slanting over the gunnel.

As I crossed the aft deck, he said, "This is for you."

I dropped into the chair alongside him and accepted the rose without replying.

He studied my face. "Bad evening?"

Looking at the rose instead of him, I said, "What do you mean?"

"You've been crying."

Suddenly, I was crying again. He put one arm across my shoulders and hugged me until I had it all out. Then, I told him.

His hands balled into fists as I spoke, but he listened without interrupting. When I'd recounted the experience, I expected him to say, "I told you so." Without doubt I'd earned a harsh reply, but instead he asked, "What are you going to do?"

I kissed his cheek. "Try to fix something I shouldn't have broken in the first place. You made an offer this afternoon and asked me to think about it. No thinking was needed, Dad. There's nothing in this world I want more than to be your partner." Turning in my seat and looking at the empty slip beyond *Skipjack*, I added, "If you still want us, *Bonita* and I are ready to come home."

He brushed the back of his hands across his eyes and nodded.

No other answer was needed. I waved the rose at him. "What about this? I didn't know I had a secret admirer."

"Secret? It was written all over the poor fellow's face."

"A fellow? Who?"

"Allen. He was one of the guys on the charter party this morning. He sat out here with Cecil and me for most of the evening, so we never did get to do any fishing. They left ten minutes before you pulled up."

When I'd shopped for flowers for Granddaddy's funeral, the florist handed me a sheet titled "Language and Sentiment of Flowers." The information made my unwanted chore easier. I chose zinnias because they meant, "I mourn your absence," and red roses because they meant, "I love you."

A yellow rose, I remembered, meant "Friendship." Maybe that was all Allen had on his mind, but at the moment I didn't care one way or the other. He was a very handsome man, but so was Angus and all it had led to was a kick in the gut. I wasn't looking for another. I tossed the rose over the side and took Dad's hand. "I'm not ready for roses," I said.

Dad grinned, slapped my knee, and stood. "Good. Get some sleep. I'm moving you back home tomorrow."

CHAPTER 16

D ad nudged me awake at seven. He was carrying a large cup of coffee and a napkin stacked with cinnamon-raisin toast. Seeing the logo on the Styrofoam cup wasn't necessary to know it came from Shanley's. For years, at five each morning, Dad and Cecil had met there for breakfast. I used to join them on mornings when I had an early charter, but the great breakfast whipped up by Roxie was only part of the reason why. The main reason was twofold. Dad and Cecil were not only great men, they were also nautical legends. On the other hand I was still a neophyte captain eager to acquire their knowledge through association. Being in their company, then, came with a feeling of acceptance, a gratifying one I was looking forward to embracing again.

It'd been well after midnight when Dad returned to the bait shop and I'd finally crawled into the bunk, knowing a good night's sleep was out of the question. In fact for a while I didn't believe I'd sleep at all. Regardless of whether my eyes were open or closed, the image filling my mind's eye was the penthouse elevator and Angus with his hands on the breasts of his house-call whore. Thankfully, sometime before dawn exhaustion took over, and I slept the sleep of the dead. No dreams, just deep sleep.

I fluffed my pillow for a backrest before sitting up and accepting the coffee. Dad set the toast on the nightstand next to the bunk. I sipped, smiled, and said, "If this is part of the welcome home, I like it."

"Actually," Dad said, gesturing to the coffee and toast, "it's bait from Roxie. She told me to get you up and send you over for a real breakfast."

"Real breakfast?" I pointed at the toast. "That stack will hold me all day."

"Good." He palmed a piece and started for the companionway stairs. "Call me when you're ready," he said. "Patty and Cecil will watch the shop while we fetch things."

He was up the steps before I could argue.

After finishing the toast and coffee, I washed my face, dressed, and combed my hair. I was ready to go, but I sat on the edge of the bunk instead of calling Dad.

Last night he'd said, "I'm moving you back home tomorrow."

This was a simple and direct statement had it not been for the declarative tone and hammering cadence of his delivery. That, and what he hadn't said, gave me good reason for worry.

In a four-point comparison of Angus and Dad, Angus was the younger, the taller, and the heavier. But the fourth point meant more than the other three combined: Dad was the stronger. Angus would learn this the hard way if an altercation between them got out of hand. And, no matter how much Dad would love that, or how much I now despised Angus, I didn't want it to happen.

I grabbed my hat and sunglasses and started for the topside. Aunt Patty was sitting on the patio. Her back was to me, and a box of Kleenex and a cup of coffee were on the table beside her. Dad wasn't in sight. I crept across the aft deck to the *Margaret Ellen's* starboard gunnel, crawled over the mahogany rail, and dropped quietly to the catwalk. After another peek at the patio to insure my movements hadn't been detected, I began loosing *Skipjack's* docking lines. When she was free, I stepped aboard and pushed off. Anyone on the patio could see me now, so I drifted with the current, waiting for sufficient separation so I'd not hear Dad's scream when I started the engine.

Once underway I made good time down the ICW until slowing at a point a half-mile north of the Buttonwood. The thought of a confrontation with Angus fueled my caution. Continuing my slow approach while carefully watching the penthouse was my plan. Then I saw movement on the lanai. Pressing my hip against the wheel to steady my course, I reached for the binoculars. No problem. The movement wasn't human, just seagulls fighting for position on the parapet. I swept the glasses past the upper windows. The draperies were drawn. Would they remain that way and allow me to get *Bonita* underway without being seen?

My berth's location at the end of the dock had a number of advantages. Getting underway was simple; it provided a measure of privacy from the prying eyes of the dock-walkers; and it was not visible from the usually crowded pool or patio. The big disadvantage was everything I did above deck was visible from the upper floors of the Buttonwood. Especially the penthouse, if the draperies were open.

Nosing up to the stern of my sloop, I cut and tilted the Whaler's engine and used one of the docking lines to tie off short. I lashed one end of a fifty-foot line to the Whaler's bow cleat, the other end to the sloop's stern bollard, and tossed the remainder of the line into the aft cockpit. *Skipjack* was ready for towing. In five minutes, or less, my sloop and I would be ready too. I glanced up at the penthouse. So far so good. The draperies were still drawn.

After boarding my plan was to start the engine and stow all loose gear. Then, while the engine warmed up, I'd disconnect the lines for water, power, phone, and TV. Next, I'd get the eight docking lines aboard—two at the bow, two at the stern, and the pair of spring lines at her beam, port and starboard. The last move would be to pull clear of the slip, throw off the line holding *Skipjack's* bow close to the sloop's stern, and pay out the tow painter as I headed for the channel.

That was my plan, and it might have worked if I had ignored the blinking light on my answering machine when I entered the cabin.

I listened through a series of hang-ups until the tape reached a real message.

"I've been trying to reach you ... "

The voice was Amber's, still soft and polite, but this time fear rode heavy on her words.

"I don't know what's going on. No. I ... know. I do. I'll know for ... I'll call back at four. Please be there."

I let the tape run. There were two more calls. Both were hang-ups. Despite her promise to do so, she hadn't given any information on how to reach her, and four p.m. was over seven hours away. I'd promised Myers my cooperation. Waiting around for the phone to ring hadn't been part of the agreement— especially not under the current circumstances. I started the engine and began stowing loose gear.

When the below deck area was shipshape, I headed for the companionway. Before I reached it, however, I stopped and stared at the phone. It wouldn't hurt to call Myers and tell him Amber had called. I'd do that much. Nothing more. The phone rang as I reached for it. The voice was female, but it wasn't Amber's.

"You were supposed to call me this morning. Remember?"

"Gwen?"

"Who else? You forget?"

"No," I said, "but I no longer need the photo."

"Reginald turned up?"

"Not exactly." I didn't want to lie, but I'd promised to keep a lid on the information Myers shared with me. "I pulled out," I said. "My activities might have jeopardized Myers's case."

"Bullshit! I bet Grim Lips told you to butt out. Right?"

Grim Lips. Accurate. I liked that. "No, that's not it at all. I start another

106

job next week." I touched on the high points. "I can't do both, so I'm going with the one I love."

"I'm happy for you," she said. "I also want to hear all about it."

I couldn't imagine why, but I said, "Thanks."

After a few moments of silence, she said, "What is it you're holding back?"

Was I that easy to read? Even over the phone? "It's Angus!" I said.

She made sympathetic noises as I gave her the story.

"You've been busy," she said. "Catching your man like that is a bummer. I know. Something very similar trashed my marriage."

She didn't offer details, and I wasn't interested enough to ask.

"Look," she said, "I have an idea. Eva's file is here. You don't need it now, but it's full of lovely photos of her. How about coming out about eleven. We'll have a beer, browse through the photos, try out the hot tub, and then have lunch by the lake. It'll take your mind off things. What do you say?"

"It sounds wonderful, Gwen, but I'm about to castoff and move my sloop back to my dad's place."

"Pooh," she said. "You have all day to do that. I have to be at the studio by four. Come on."

I thought it over. If I towed the Whaler back to Dad's now, I'd still have to have someone bring me back to pick up the Camaro. On the other hand, if I visited with Gwen and then picked up Aunt Patty on the way back, I could move the boats and she could handle my car. That would work. "Where do you live?" I said.

"Lake Como."

"That's the ... "

"Yes," she said, "it's the nudist resort. But you'll love it. Promise."

When I visited Hangman's Key, more times than not, I sunbathed in the nude. I'd also skinny-dipped with a boyfriend or two. But, I'd never been nude in a crowd. "I don't know if I can, you know."

"You don't have to," she said. "Honest. On Hangman's Key you told me you live in your bikini. Bring it."

What the hell. If nothing else, I was curious. Where did nudists carry pocket change? How did they—

"Well?"

"I'll be there about eleven."

I broke the connection, but held the receiver. I still needed to leave a message for Myers, and, like it or not, I knew I'd better call Dad and explain why I'd sneaked away earlier. He was *not* going to be happy. I drew a deep breath, held it as I muttered a short prayer, and dialed.

"Cobia's."

Prayer works. The voice was Patty's. "It's me," I said.

At first I thought she hadn't heard me. Finally, she said, "You *are* on your way to Canada, right?"

Now I understood her pause. "It's that bad, huh?"

This time her response was immediate. "I'd say it's as bad as anything you can remember."

I hated that, but to her credit Aunt Patty listened, clucking at times, as I explained why I'd wanted to avoid a confrontation between Dad and Angus. When I'd made my best argument, she said, "That's mature thinking, young lady. And you're right. Your dad would pound Angus to powder. I don't want that any more than you do."

"Thanks for understanding," I said, "but now I'm in trouble with Dad for trying to avoid trouble with Angus."

"You won't be for long. I'll handle your dad."

More than once it'd crossed my mind that the real reason Dad hadn't remarried was his fear of getting a woman as strong willed as Patty. If she said she'd handle Dad, it was a done deal. "Thanks," I said, "I'll pick you up at three."

After dodging that bullet I felt a surge of confidence. I squared my shoulders and dialed the Pinellas County Sheriff's Office. I'd leave a message for Myers, lock up the boat, and head for my car.

A crisp, female voice answered. I started my spiel. "Save your breath," she said, "Myers just walked in."

Crap! He'd never been there when I'd wanted him to be. Why now? I held until he picked up the line.

He didn't say, "Good-morning." He didn't ask, "How are you?" No. All I got was a terse, "She call?"

Fine. If Grim Lips could skip the pleasantries, so could I. "Yeah, one message." I repeated her words. "And she sounded scared."

"Hmm. You're docked at Loman's place. Right?"

"Not for long," I said

"Why? You moving?"

"Bet on it," I said. With few words I told him part of the reason why.

"Shit! I thought he had his stuff together."

I'd never thought Angus had it all together, but I'd thought he would.

Someday. Myers didn't need to know that.

"Look," he said, "I'm sorry as hell, and I know you want to leave, but I need you there to take her call. In the meanwhile I have time enough to put a trap on your line."

Those "trap" gadgets always worked with TV movies, but this wasn't TV. "What if she's using a phone booth in the boonies?" I said.

"Always possible," he said, "but it's more than we have now."

It wasn't much more, in my opinion, but I kept it to myself. "Okay," I said, "my phone line is plugged into a terminal alongside the boat. It's easy to see. Do what you want with it. I won't be here. I'm meeting Gwen for lunch."

"Seaweed, I can't order you to stay, but I can beg. Please sit still. Just till she calls. Okay?"

"I told you I'd help," I said. "I will, up to a point, but I am *not* going to sit here all day in Angus's backyard waiting for the phone to ring."

"I'm not asking you to do that. Just be back there by four. If you're afraid of Loman, I'll tell him to keep his ass off the dock until we're finished and you're on your way. Okay?"

I wasn't afraid of Angus. At times during our relationship he'd been aggravating, even a pain in my lower backside, but he'd never been physically abusive. For that reason, and the Colt .357 I kept under my pillow, I wasn't afraid. I just didn't want to see him again.

"Please!"

"All right!" I said, "But you better have a new game plan in place when you get here. She calls at four; I'm outta here five minutes later. We *do* agree on that. Right?"

"I'll have it set up by four," he said. "Be there." He broke the connection without saying good-bye. What should I have expected? He had never really said hello.

I returned the receiver to its cradle and stepped to the companionway. With the exception of a few more seagulls crowding the parapet, the top floor of the Buttonwood looked as quiet as it had when I first arrived. Funny, I'd never noticed the crazy lines of dung streaks on the wall before. Some were impressive, reaching as low as the third-floor windows. I figured it had to do with the fish oil in their diet.

I shut down the engine and rummaged through the clothes locker for my flesh-tone bikini. Angus hated it. I stuffed the bikini and a clean towel into my tote bag, locked the companionway hatch, and hopped across the narrow gap between my sloop and the dock. As I stood there making a safety survey of *Bonita's* docking lines and the towline I had in place holding *Skipjack*, I heard the grumble of far-off thunder. Thus far I'd had a shitty day. The increasing overcast, along with the sooty-gray clouds hugging the horizon, indicated it was also going to be a wet one. I hoisted my tote bag and headed for my parking space on the far side of the Buttonwood.

CHAPTER 17

As I hurried to my Camaro, I thought of my childish display of temper the previous evening. Compounding this immature action, I'd been driving Dad's truck as I flew from the parking lot, engine screaming and rubber peeling. But that was last night. This morning, with a tight rein on my faculties, I'd exit the parking lot safely and quietly.

I put on my sunglasses and unlocked the car. Noon was three hours away, but the interior of the vehicle was already Fourth-of-July hot. Musty too. Probably a combination of sitting exposed to the elements for the last five days and the wet towels I'd forgotten to remove from the back seat. I started the engine, put the windows down, and flipped the a/c selector to high. It was then I noticed a note on a cocktail napkin pinned beneath the wiper blade. The napkin bore the logo of the Rudder Bar and Grill and the note's handwriting belonged to Angus.

It was NOT anything like what you're thinking!

Really? Dad's creed was simple: Until something was proven to his satisfaction, he didn't believe anything he heard and half of what he saw. And he'd preached the same caution to me. In most cases I'd found his words to be good advice. This case was not one of them. There was no *thinking* about what I'd seen.

For me there were only two occasions when I'd allow a man's hands on my breasts: when I was sharing his love, or when I was sharing his lust. I'd done both with Angus. He had no business doing either with the hippo-hips I'd seen him with.

I glared at the note. My first impulse was to roar from the parking lot. I didn't give in to the temptation. Just as Dad loved his truck, I loved my car. She had a dazzling white top and a gorgeous, candy-apple-red bottom. On our first day together, I pet-named her Ridin' Hood. To wreck her in anger would solve nothing. I repeated these words over and over as if rehearsing a single-line part in a play. When the words finally made sense instead of noise, I eased from the parking lot.

At Gulf Boulevard I slipped into a gap in the northbound flow of tourist-heavy traffic. When I reached thirty-five miles per hour, the napkin fluttered like a kid's kite, but it didn't dislodge. Conditions wouldn't allow me to go faster, so I endured my unwanted hitchhiker until I reached Treasure Island Causeway. While waiting for the light to change, I gave fitting response to Angus's prose.

I held the wiper-washer unit on until the spray soaked the note and the blades rolled it into a hundred BB-size spitballs. When the last one rolled from view, I put a tape in the player and joined Hank Snow as he sang "I'm Moving On."

The Lake Como Nudist Resort was located in the Northwest corner of Hillsborough County, a once rural area saturated with small truck farms and sprawling citrus groves. The area was now urban, saturated with homes and shopping centers. It took nearly two hours to reach it from St. Petersburg Beach.

A neatly trimmed lawn of St. Augustine grass, banana plants heavy with fruit, and oval flowerbeds brimming with gardenias, roses, and sunflowers lined the club's long and narrow entry drive. Idling by this strip of scenery, I pictured myself, nude, mowing the lawn, or harvesting bananas. Maybe, but not likely.

I continued on until reaching a small frame building labeled as an office and sporting a welcome sign above the door. A lowered cross arm, much like ones used in long-term parking areas, barred further travel. Would the office employees be nude? Bracing for such a possibility, I parked and walked slowly to the entrance door.

My apprehension was for naught. The two middle-aged ladies staffing the office were dressed as casually as I'd be at a bargain table in the mall. I returned to Ridin' Hood with directions to Gwen's and a fistful of nudist literature: a listing of the club's ground rules; a pamphlet describing nude etiquette; a current copy of *The Bulletin*, AANR's official publication; and a Lake Como membership application.

Yep, I had the written stuff. The question was whether I had the right stuff, like in bare-nerve, to let it all hang out.

Gwen's residence was a white, singlewide mobile with wooden-lattice skirting, cross buck shutters, and scalloped eave trim the tone of Sahara sand. A screened porch, nearly hidden by a well-groomed flowerbed full of towering roses, ran the length of the entry side. She bounced from a chaise lounge as

I pulled in alongside her Honda Civic. When I reached the door, tote bag in hand, I was still grinning about her bumper sticker: "Put some color in your cheeks."

She was wearing white flip flops, a snug-fitting pair of olive walking shorts, a wrist watch with a golden stretch-band, and the gorgeous tan I'd thought came from a sun lamp.

"Come on in," she said. "Bathroom's down the hall. Change. I'll pack lunch."

The hall bathroom was only a tad larger than the closet-size one on my sloop, but it was brighter and much cleaner. Neater too. I stripped and studied my tan. Except for a couple of places that hadn't seen sunlight in a while, my tan looked as good as Gwen's. Should I advertise the disparity or disguise it? Simple choice. I slipped into my bikini. The top and the bottom.

When I returned to the porch, Gwen was standing at the door with a towel draped around her neck. Her shorts were on a glass-topped table surrounded by aluminum chairs with blue and white webbing. So was a file folder labeled, "Park."

She held a picnic basket in one hand and was balancing two cans of beer in the other. Both cans were nestled in insulated holders touting the Miami Dolphins' one-and-only perfect season. She handed one of the cans to me.

"Bud," she said. "I remembered your brand."

"Thanks, but you didn't have to get something special."

"I didn't. On my pay, I get it on sale, or I don't buy."

I understood. I'd been a coupon clipper most of my life.

She pushed the screen door open with her hip and nodded in the direction of the file folder. "We'll look through that later," she said. "Grab your towel. I want you to see my neighborhood."

On the way in, I'd seen her neighborhood. A lot of it. But it'd been from the safety of my car, behind its tinted glass, and with my surveying eyes hidden by mirrored sunglasses. Could I handle it face-to-face? There was only one way to find out. I slipped my sunglasses on, slung my towel over one shoulder, and hurried after her.

"The lakefront's this way," she said. "Before I show you anything else, I want to show you my play pretty."

I laughed. "Gwen, there was a chubby kid in my second-grade class. Leonard, I think. He wanted to show me *his* play pretty, but he wanted to see *mine* first. In your case, if you have something I *haven't* seen, I don't know where you're hiding it."

She blushed. "It's nothing like that. Honest. You'll see."

I dropped behind in single-file formation to avoid colliding with an elderly lady pedaling a three-wheeler. She was steering erratically, trying to quiet a pair of freshly groomed poodles frolicking in a wicker basket on the trike's handlebars. The poodles were wearing rhinestone collars. The cyclist was wearing a polka-dot bandanna. She and Gwen exchanged a "Good morning." I nodded. The poodles continued yapping.

Gwen swung onto a footpath angling obliquely to our left just as I regained my position at her side. The trail was lined with landscape timbers, covered with cypress mulch, and marked with an attractive, beige-and-blue sign shaped like a pointing hand. The sign said, "Beach."

Play pretty? *Hmm.*

"Now," she said, "I want to hear why you're dropping your investigating work."

When Gwen first met me, the day the drunken attorney killed the two boys in their anchored johnboat, I'd been captain of Dad's charter boat. When she saw me at Hangman's Key on Monday, I was no longer working as a captain, but I'd allowed her to believe I was. It was time to give her the real story.

When I'd poured it out, she said, "So you've never *really* wanted to be an investigator?"

We strolled past a squirrel engrossed in burying an acorn behind a landscape timber. I mimicked his chatter for a moment before answering Gwen's question. "An investigator? No way. In the years after Mom died, I worked alongside Dad in the bait shop or crewed as his little mate. Other girls had dolls and played house; I had my own skiff and played captain. Even so, my play was more than child's play; I played with the single-minded determination of becoming Dad's captain. I reached that goal shortly after I turned eighteen. That was the good part."

"And the bad part came last year—"

"Yeah," I said, "the bad part was one of the most stupid moments of my life. I have a hot temper and a fast mouth, and dumb-ass me let them screw up everything."

"I've been there a few times," she said. "But you've made up with your dad. That's good."

"It's good that I have another chance, one bigger than ever, but I still need to work on my temper. Dad says if I'd been born in the Old West with a gun as fast as my mouth, I would've been known as Karen the Kid."

She grinned. "With those sexy eyes of yours, I can see you as a flirtatious dance-hall girl or a notorious gunslinger's lover. I can't see you as a fast-draw killer."

I couldn't see myself as either, even with sexy eyes, which I didn't believe I had. "More like captain of a Mississippi River gambling boat," I said. "Anyway, my new job isn't really new, but this time it's special. I intend to hang on to it."

"You said the *Margaret Ellen* is a fifty-foot vessel. Surely you don't handle her alone."

"Better than I handle my car," I said, "but I never leave the dock alone with a charter party aboard."

"Oh, really? What's the difference?"

"With a charter party aboard, I not only have all the responsibilities I'd have while alone, I also have to be a multi-talented stewardess: make sandwiches, fetch beer, bait hooks, answer questions, bandage the occasional cut or scrape, and smile even when I'd like to scream. There's no way I can do it all without help. I have to have a mate, for safety and my sanity."

She raised an eyebrow and said, "Do you have one?"

This was a problem Dad and I hadn't discussed. Cecil was in no shape to crew. Patty was stepping out of the business as of the coming Monday. And Skip wasn't an option. "No," I said, "and I only have a week to come up with one."

She added a grin to the raised eyebrow and said, "Not if you'd consider hiring a burned-out TV journalist."

"Mate on a charter boat? You have to be kidding. Gwen, most women would kill to have your job. Besides, what do you know about boats?"

"Maybe more than you think." She stopped at the upper edge of the beach, spread her towel, and placed the picnic basket on it. "Come on," she said. "My play pretty is over here."

I dropped my towel alongside hers and sipped beer as I followed her down the beach. She stopped at a twelve-foot sailing dinghy the color of antler velvet. It was beached and lashed to a weathered cypress knee just above the lake's yellow-sand shore. The dinghy's name, written in crimson block lettering on either side of the bow, was an eye catcher: *Bob 'n' Bitch*. "Cute name," I said.

She placed her hands on her hips and grinned as she looked at the dinghy. "Yeah, my ex-husband, Bob, was a laugh a minute. He got the house, the car, the boat, and Holly, the younger woman. I got the dinghy and the old Honda.

If you're stumped over the other half of the name, don't hesitate to ask."

"I'm not that slow," I said, "but if I'd gone through what you just described, I'd be bitter. You don't seem to be."

"Oh, I was, at first, but I'm not anymore. The house, the car, and the boat all had huge payment books. Bob was a laugh, but I got the last one. He lost everything trying to keep Holly. Last year, he lost her too."

I caressed the dinghy's mahogany gunnel and said, "So, this vessel was the yacht tender to the boat you had?"

She nodded. "Yes, it was a lovely thirty-foot cabin cruiser. My dad had a thirty-six footer when I was still living at home. I learned to handle them both very well. I'll show you." She pointed at items on the dinghy as she ambled around it. "Bow, port, stern, starboard, detachable rudder, foldaway tiller, retractable centerboard, cat rigged, and, for ease of handling, a four-to-one purchase on the boom sheet." She looked at me and grinned. "And if you'd like to quiz me on the rules-of-the-road, ask away."

"After that recital," I said, "I'm sure you know them well. But what I'd like to know is why you'd drop a glamorous job to crew aboard a charter vessel."

"Glamorous? Yeah, I suppose it was, once upon a time." Then, staring into space, she added, "But I've learned the bitter reality since then."

"What reality?"

"These," she said, poking her thumbs at her breasts. "Large ones get attention. They don't insure respect."

"You mean sexual harassment?"

"Not like you're thinking," she said. "I mean women who reach the top in my profession fit a stereotype. Most of them are not blondes. The few who are blonde are petite."

I had a high school diploma, a captain's license, and a job I'd earned with brains and skill, not my bra size. In fact I'd never thought of breast size as a deterrent or an advantage in a woman's profession. Of course a lap dancer or porno queen might offer another point of view.

"Is your job in jeopardy?" I said.

"Not really. Even if it was, I have a degree in journalism and I've studied meteorology, so I can always get a job. The problem is, for the big break I keep hoping for at Channel Five, I don't fit the stereotype. If that wasn't bad enough, I'm also over thirty and a divorcee. When I talked with you on Hangman's Key, I'd have traded places with you in a minute."

The angry line of clouds I'd seen earlier blanketed the sun before we finished our lunch. Moments later a cool rush of wind swept across the small lake and the first drops began falling. We grabbed our things and ran, reaching her porch just ahead of the downpour.

CHAPTER 18

Each fall cold fronts slammed into Florida with a regularity dietitians could only dream of. A few of these fronts—like the one that raced through the Bay Area this past weekend—packed high wind and torrential rain. Most of them, though, were tame and quickly lost their identity, like the one that had caught us at the lake. They arrived with a little wind and a little rain and then, in a little while, they were gone.

In the time it took us to finish our cold cuts on rye, chips, and a second beer, the wind calmed and the rain slacked to a sprinkle. I changed back into my street clothes and stuffed my towel and bikini into my tote bag. When I returned to the porch, Gwen abandoned the mundane chitchat we'd exchanged over lunch.

"I take it," she said with a rising inflection, "you've forgotten the question I asked at the beach?"

"No," I said, "I was surprised by it, but I certainly haven't forgotten it."

"And?"

"Actually, Gwen, I've been giving it some thought."

Dad had made it very clear he wanted a captain and a partner he could count on. In taking on that combined responsibility I risked cheating him, and ultimately myself, if I settled for anything less than the best in my selection of a mate. This meant the person I chose, man or woman, *had* to be one I could count on. A bonus for me, of course, would be if that person were also one I was compatible with.

I'd considered Gwen for this position as we hurried back from the lake to her place. On the plus side, I enjoyed her company, and it appeared she had some nautical skills. On the downside, the question was whether those skills were sufficient to meet the demands of crewing as my mate. Another important reservation was whether she would collapse the first time we encountered rough seas. Amber, as I recalled, had talked a good one before we cast off.

"You didn't take me seriously. That's it. Right?"

"No," I said. "That's not it at all."

"Then what is?"

Honesty might've been the best policy, but in this case the truth was sure to cause some hurt feelings. And there was no easy way out. "Gwen, I've explained how much this job means to me. Actually, it's more than a job; it's the proverbial golden opportunity." With drawn face and clasped hands, she hung onto each word as I spoke. She was not going to enjoy the punch line. "I need a mate, Gwen, not a headache."

She jumped up, tipping her chair over backwards. "A headache? Jesus! You think I'd be a headache?"

Her fold-up chair collapsed when it smacked onto the concrete floor. "I'm sorry," I said, "that didn't come out anything like I meant it."

She stood close, listening quietly as I told her about Skip. "Gwen, he's not only a qualified mate, he's also my cousin. But there's no way in hell I'll work with him. We clash. Big time. More than once we've fought right to the threshold of mayhem." I tried for an apologetic smile before adding, "That's the kind of headache I meant."

"And you think—"

"Let me finish," I said. "On dry land I can walk away from Skip or kick his ass off the sea wall. When we're underway, I can't do either. In your case I know you can walk and chew gum at the same time. With two exceptions that's all the coordination and brains you'd need to qualify as my mate."

She placed her hands on her hips and squared her shoulders. "And those exceptions are?"

Myers had made his numerous points by wagging his finger. I tried it. "The big one is, you *do not* get seasick."

"No problem," she said. "I've been offshore many times and I have *never* been seasick."

"Then we're halfway there, *if* you're totally serious about the job. If not, now's the time to say so."

She turned and began pacing the porch, ducking beneath a spider plant in a hanging pot on her outbound leg and swinging wide around the two puddles forming where the rain was dripping through the aluminum roof panels on her way back. I unfolded her chair and placed it back on its legs. Three laps later she stopped before me wearing one of those cat-in-a-litter-box grins. "I have an idea," she said.

"If it brought on that grin, spit it out."

Imitating my finger wagging, she said, "You need a mate you can not only get along with, but also one who can do the job and won't let you down by getting seasick. Right?"

"That covers the high points," I said.

"Then allow me to prove I can handle the job?"

"Prove? How?"

"OJT," she said. "You know. On the job training."

Train someone in a week? Even if it were possible, it was the last thing I wanted to do. Still, it wouldn't hurt to listen to her idea. I held my tongue— no small job for me. "Go on," I said.

"I'll be working the late shift at the studio through the end of the year. I work ten nights on, and then I have five off. That means my days are free. Everyday. You said your charters start early and end in early afternoon. Try me for a week. No pay. Just show me what you want from a mate."

She paused, spread her open palms, and shrugged. "You do that, Seaweed, and I promise to give it all I have. If I don't cut it, you're no worse off than you are now. And I won't have burned a bridge; I'll still have my current job."

The woman belonged in sales. And, of course, I understood her concern about burning a bridge. To her offer, it was not only neat and fair, it also settled the question of how serious she was. Even so, I wanted to see her in action—especially her sea legs—before I left the dock with her *and* a charter party aboard. Taking her offer one step further might be the answer.

"When is your next five-day break?"

"It starts tomorrow," she said. "I don't have to go back until next Tuesday evening."

Tomorrow was Thursday. That wouldn't work for me. I wanted to spend the day doing maintenance on the *Margaret Ellen* and stowing my personal gear aboard.

"Okay," I said. "The *Margaret Ellen* is scheduled for dry dock Friday. Be at the bait shop by daylight Friday morning and we'll rehearse a charter as we take her to the yard." I finished by listing the items she'd need to bring with her.

"Thanks for the chance," she said. "I have all that stuff. In fact, my foul weather gear and deck shoes are brand-new."

"Fine. Oh, and sunglasses. Bring 'em. And when we finish, lunch is on me. Hope you like hoagies."

She was delighted. On Friday, if she worked out, I'd be delighted as well. The Big Tarpon Pass community was another matter. The area was a chartering Mecca with mostly all-male crews serving mostly all-male clients. In recent years a few male-female crews had popped up, and as far as I knew they'd done well. We'd be the first charter service with an all-female crew. I wondered how our customers would respond. I was betting we'd be a shoo-in. Skip's physique resembled a walking stick. Gwen's did not.

With that settled I reached for my tote bag. The trip to her place had taken two hours. The wet roads guaranteed my return-trip time would be no less. "I told Aunt Patty I'd pick her up at three," I said, "so I'd better start back no later than one."

Gwen looked at her watch and flashed a smug smile. "In that case," she said, "set your bag down. You still have fifteen minutes." She pushed our lunch scraps aside and reached for the photo file.

I scooted my chair closer and watched as she spread several photos in front of me. "I took these at the last charity ball," she said. "Sad to say, they're probably the last photos ever taken of Eva."

The last ones of her alive, I thought. Even so, they were undoubtedly more flattering than the ones the crime-scene unit would've taken of her after Angus and I left Hangman's Key.

She tapped a finger on an eight-by-ten photo of Eva. "This one," she said, "is the best of the bunch."

The charity ball had been held in the ballroom at the St. Petersburg Yacht Club. In the photo Eva was standing on stage holding an enormous plaque and smiling as if the photographer were the only other person in attendance.

"Wasn't she beautiful?" Gwen said. "Put that much makeup and jewelry on most women and they'd look gaudy. Not Eva. She was elegant."

My only other look at Eva had been when she appeared on TV several months before her death. Incredibly, she looked exactly as I remembered her. Even so I still believed her black evening gown was too daring, her makeup too thick, and her jewelry too lavish. But what did I know? I didn't own a gown, evening or otherwise; I didn't own jewelry, not counting my wristwatch; and I didn't wear makeup, except for Chap Stick. Eva's hairdo, however, was elegant.

"I remember her gown," I said. "She was wearing the same one when I saw her on TV."

"Actually," Gwen said, "except for the portions filmed at Eva's home, the TV special you saw later that month was filmed the night of the charity ball."

Hmm. I hadn't thought of that.

"Most of these faces should be familiar," she said, as she dealt a line of photos across the table. "Break out a camera and they crawl out of the

121

woodwork."

The faces might have been familiar to her, but I recognized only one. "That's Vivian, the mayor, right?"

"Yes, and I shouldn't lump her with the others. Vivian is okay." Gwen ran her finger down the line of photos. "This is Gladys, president of the Heart Fund; Phil, president of the city council; Steven, our congressman; and these seven darlings spearhead the Downtown Beautification Committee."

I tried to look impressed. Each individual in the various photos, male or female, was impeccably dressed. Big Tarpon Pass, located midway up the Pinellas peninsula, was a world removed from St. Petersburg. Our mayor, Captain Bill, wore a ball cap, T-shirt, shorts, deck shoes, and an unwavering smile. He's neat. My kind. Glancing at the other photos, I said, "Where's the photo of Reginald?"

She shuffled through the stack, bringing another glossy eight-by-ten to the top. "That's him," she said.

Reginald had the dark hair, handsome features, and go-to-hell mustache Errol Flynn was remembered for. The camera had caught him looking over his shoulder. He wasn't my type; however, he did look just right for Eva.

Gwen tapped her finger on the photo. "He had the damnedest ability to avoid the camera. You'll see him in several of the photos but never clearly."

She sat back as I flipped through the general crowd photos. Most of the faces in the photos were unfamiliar, but Reginald's shiny black hair or a piece of his Red Baron's scarf was visible in the background of several of them. One photo caught my attention. It featured a skeletal gentleman with brown hair and ferret eyes standing with his left arm around Eva and his right arm around a young, stunningly beautiful woman wearing little more than jewelry, makeup, and a provocative expression.

"That," Gwen said, pointing at the man in the photo, "is this area's biggest asshole: Stan Avery."

So far I couldn't remember a kind word spoken in association with Avery's name.

"I don't know how it happened," she said, "but Stan and Amber are a real number."

"In what way?"

"Like in the rumor they'll marry soon."

In my opinion Amber was a flake, but I couldn't see her with a jerk like Avery. Stranger things had happened. "Okay," I said, "but if he and Amber are such a number, who's the sexy twit he's with here?"

"She looks different with elegant clothes on, huh?"
I stared at Gwen and said, "What do you mean?"
"You took her fishing with you yesterday. Right?"
"This sexpot is Amber Brantley?"
"Of course."

CHAPTER 19

This unexpected revelation sent my just-eaten lunch tumbling like an Olympic gymnast. I tipped my head back and swallowed, trying to halt the foul tasting bile climbing my throat. Gwen grabbed the photo and pointed at the young woman standing with Eva and Stan Avery. "You mean this is *not* the Amber who called you?"

Shaking my head seemed safer than opening my mouth.

"I smell a story here!" she said.

She was right, at least about the smell. Something stank. The panic in my stomach eased, but to be on the safe side I swallowed once more before speaking. I took the photo from her hand and said, "Gwen, the Amber in this photo and the Amber I met are both female. Believe me, that's the *only* thing they have in common."

"I don't get it," Gwen said. "Why would whomever she is call you claiming to be Amber?"

Taking another long look at the woman in the photo, I said, "I have no idea."

What I did know—but couldn't divulge, much less try to explain—was that last Friday while impersonating Amber Brantley, the woman had flown out of Tampa International Airport under the further impersonation of Eva Park. She'd been in company with Reginald Wentworth, Eva's fiancé, and just hours earlier Eva Park had been murdered and her body dumped into the Gulf of Mexico. It was inconceivable to believe the woman calling herself Amber Brantley and the camera shy Reginald Wentworth weren't involved in Eva's death. So what was the woman's real reason for calling me Monday night? Again, I had no idea.

I pushed back from the table and stood. "I have to use your phone."

"This way," she said, leading the way to her wall phone in the kitchen.

"This," I said, waving the photo before handing it back to Gwen, "is going to shoot the shit out of Myers's scenario."

The man had given me three phone numbers along with explicit instructions concerning their use. Worry about getting fired for not following orders never entered my mind. I left a message on his home answering machine, another at the Sheriff's Office, and then dialed his beeper and punched in Gwen's number. She was still standing close at my side when I replaced the receiver.

Barely above a whisper, she asked, "What's going on, Seaweed?"

I didn't whisper as I hurried back to the porch. "When Myers calls tell him the woman we've believed to be Amber is a phony and that I'm trying to reach my boat ahead of schedule."

"Schedule? What schedule? What's going on?"

There was only one valid reason why I couldn't discuss the little I knew about the case with her: *time*. There wasn't enough. I snatched up my tote bag and pushed through the screen door. "Myers will fill you in," I said. "See ya Friday."

When I backed out of Gwen's drive and dropped Ridin' Hood's stick-shift into low, I felt the same wave of helplessness I'd felt at Hangman's Key after finding Eva's body. My racing back to *Skipjack's* radio to notify the authorities had not been a life-or-death necessity. Even so, I did it anyway. I was doing so again.

I zoomed out Como's drive with the wipers slashing at what little rain was still falling. A mile down US 41 the rain slacked to a mist. I drove on, an eye in the mirror and a foot in the carburetor. The clouds parted and the mist stopped soon after I flew across the Pinellas County line.

Despite heavy traffic, the still-wet roads, and my detour to pick up Aunt Patty, I screeched into the Buttonwood's entry drive at ten minutes of four.

Angus's yellow Eldorado, looking freshly washed and waxed, was in its penthouse-parking slot. A pair of mourning doves was pecking at a popcorn spill where the whore's MG had been parked. The beer can and drink glass were gone. I glanced around the parking lot. There wasn't an official-looking vehicle anywhere. Maybe like TV detectives, Myers drove an unmarked car.

During the time it had taken to drive from the bait shop to the Buttonwood, Aunt Patty and I swapped ideas about the woman who was passing herself off as Amber Brantley. Who was she? What was her motivation? We couldn't agree on those issues, but Aunt Patty probably came close when she said, "I bet she's a card-carrying member of that group who confess to crimes they didn't commit. In other words, she's nuts."

I couldn't mount an argument to the contrary because nothing the fake Amber had said or done made sense. That aside, I'd only thought of her as different, not nuts. But did it matter? When Aunt Patty set her mind, no one changed it. Knowing this I nodded my agreement and switched the discussion to Angus. He was unlikely to create a scene with both Patty and Myers present. We agreed on that. If it worked that way, our plan was simple: When the phone session with whatever-her-name-was ended, Patty would help me get underway and then return to the bait shop to help me dock. I loved a good plan.

After locking the Camaro, I handed the keys to Patty and led the way around the building. The sky had cleared; the light breeze had clocked to north; and, as usual after a frontal passage, the air was cooler and smelled fresher. A tight knot of mothers was at the far end of the patio watching their preschoolers splash in the kiddy pool. Neither they nor the elderly couple sprawled in matching lounge chairs paid us any attention as we passed and marched out onto the dock. With each step I fought the urge to turn and glance up at the penthouse.

Bonita and *Skipjack* were still wet from the recent rain, but they were both resting just as I'd left them. Myers was not in sight. "It's almost four," I said. "He was supposed to be here by now."

"Don't worry about it," Aunt Patty said. "You've kept your end of the deal. Anyway, the tide's slack. Let's get some of the lines aboard while we're waiting."

This was a good idea, as it would speed up my departure when business was done. "Go ahead and start," I said. "I'll open the hatches so we can hear the phone."

Aunt Patty brought the spring lines aboard and lashed them to stanchions along the toe rail. After opening the companionway and overhead hatches, I disconnected and stowed the TV, water, and electric lines. My answering machine wouldn't work without power, but my phone would. Wouldn't it? I checked it for a dial tone. Okay.

The top of the hour arrived.

No Myers.

No call.

At ten after four my sloop had only a bow and stern line holding her alongside the dock. Still no call or any sign of Myers. I started the two-cylinder diesel engine, watched the oil pressure needle climb into the green, and heard the water-injected exhaust start pumping okay. The engine was ready for duty. I set the throttle at eight hundred rpm, gave another glance at the instrument panel, and returned topside. Aunt Patty shrugged.

Twenty after four arrived without Myers or a peep out of the phone.

Something was wrong. I could feel it. Aunt Patty climbed onto the cabin top, sat with her back against the mast, and tipped her face up to the sun. I jumped to the dock.

"Don't kick anything!" she said.

I looked back at her grinning face. The woman was a mind reader. Not that it mattered. My toes were still too sore to kick anything substantial. I paced instead.

During my second trip across the dock and back, Patty stopped me with a wave of her hand. She pointed toward my phone-hookup box. "What's that hanging there?" she said.

Looking to where she was pointing, I saw a scrap of brown paper impaled on the exposed end of my phone's ground rod. The scrap looked like it'd been torn from a grocery bag. I lifted it from the rod and smoothed the ragged edges where it'd been pierced.

You can move the boat.

I got her.

M.

Got her? How? Where?

This morning I'd been a crucial element in Grim Lips' plan to snare his quarry. The "I got her" on his note was indication his plan had succeeded. Then, after my usefulness was history, he no longer considered me important enough to bother with an explanation.

I measured the succinct message against the large scrap of paper it was written on. It didn't take a professional eye to see there was ample room for him to have added another word—the one word I would've settled for: "Thanks."

I read the note to Aunt Patty before disconnecting the phone line and handing it aboard. "Just drop it down the forward hatch," I said.

She took the line and nodded at something behind me. I glanced over my shoulder. Angus was striding our way. "Get the bow line aboard!" I said. "I'll get the stern."

With my sloop free, Aunt Patty jumped to the dock and lumbered toward Angus. I stiff-armed the shift and throttle levers full forward and didn't look back until I was fifty-feet away. Patty was blocking the end of the dock, her feet spread and her arms akimbo. Angus waved both arms, screaming something over her shoulder, but I heard nothing above the pleasing rhythm of my diesel engine's *Ka-puut, Ka-puut, Ka-puut.*

CHAPTER 20

Under full power—with a clean bottom, no current, and a calm sea—
Bonita could make seven knots; now, with six month's worth of
barnacle growth clinging to her hull and *Skipjack* in tow, she could
make only five.

I made my way north, through the bascule spans at Corey Avenue and
Treasure Island, all the while wondering about the confrontation between
Angus and Aunt Patty. When I'd lost sight of them, they were still on the
dock standing toe-to-toe. Words were exchanged. To know Patty was to know
this. But how heated were those words? I wanted to know.

Also troubling were thoughts about the reception waiting for me at the
bait shop. Aunt Patty had said, "I'll handle your dad." If she'd done so in her
usual, efficient fashion, all would be well. If not, I was about to find out.

At Big Tarpon Pass, I turned out of the Intracoastal Waterway, swinging
wide around the channel marker, and began the last mile to the bait shop.
When the orange-and-blue, Cobia's Bait Tackle and Charter sign came into
view, I gave the helm over to my indefatigable autopilot and hauled in
Skipjack's bow close to the sloop's transom. Dad *and* Aunt Patty were waiting
on the catwalks when I came alongside. Both were smiling. I liked that.

Dad greeted me with a hug, a kiss on the cheek, and a scrub of his knuckles
on the top of my head. This was a good sign—the knuckle scrub. It didn't
necessarily mean he was happy with the world, but it did mean he wasn't
pissed with me. Aunt Patty just winked and led Dad back to the patio.

It was dusk before I had the Whaler and my sloop settled into their slips.
I gave all docking lines careful attention and then hooked up the power,
water, and TV. My phone wouldn't be operational until Friday, but I plugged
the line into the dock box anyway. With full-time employment only days
away, I wouldn't be day sailing anytime soon. The bright spot was that when
the *Margaret Ellen* came out of dry dock, I'd move aboard her. She was
cushy.

With things as tidy as I could make them, I turned off the lights in the
main salon and headed up the companionway. The night air spilling down

the hatch was cool and damp. For comfort control, my T-shirt wasn't going to cut it for long. When I turned around, what hadn't been noticeable with the lights on was glaringly obvious in the darkened interior. The light on my answering machine was blinking a one-two-three-pause rhythm. Why hadn't I noticed this before moving the boat? Easy answer. I'd unplugged the power cord before checking the answering machine.

I turned on the chart table light, punched the play button, and rounded up a long-sleeved shirt while the tape rewound. The first two calls were hang-ups; the third one had a voice—the voice of the woman calling herself Amber Brantley.

"Ah ... I know it's early, I just hoped you'd be there. Something's wrong. Real wrong. I'd better tell you, ah, I'll call back ... what? Cops!"

The last word was screamed. The voice was a woman's, but it wasn't the voice of the woman who'd placed the call. The tape ran until it reset. Nothing else.

Undoubtedly, then, Myers had traced one of her hang-up calls. Where had she been and what had he learned after arresting her? As much as I wanted to know, I had no intention of making his day by calling and asking. I dropped the overhead hatches, closed the companionway, and headed for the dock.

The heavy night air felt wet on my face. A glance out over the pass confirmed a lesson I'd learned in a junior high science class: When temperature and dew point shared the same number, fog was the offspring. Wispy pockets of it were forming over the warmer water of the pass and dimming the arched ribbon of clearance lights on the high-span bridge. The fog gave the white lights a harsh glare; it gave the yellow ones a soft halo.

On the plus side the damp air was saturated with delightful aromas drifting from Shanley's kitchen. This and the growling in my stomach reminded me it'd been seven hours since I'd eaten lunch with Gwen. Treating Dad to dinner would cure my hunger and also serve as a small thank you for his warm welcome when I'd returned home. I'd do it, but first I had to know what happened after I left the Buttonwood.

Dad and Cecil were near the smoker, sitting face-to-face with their feet propped up on the same milk crate. A third chair was empty. This meant I'd missed Aunt Patty. I'd have to call her at home or wait until the following morning to get the lowdown on her *discussion* with Angus. My inquisitive nature couldn't wait that long. I exchanged a wave with Dad and a wink with Cecil and headed for the phone inside the bait shop. I dialed Aunt Patty's number. In all likelihood Skip's nosing around Sheila meant his latest girlfriend had kicked him out. If so, he was probably back sponging at home. I hoped it would be Patty, not Skip, who answered the phone. It was.

"Sorry I missed you," I said. "I just finished up. What happened?"

Her words hissed like air escaping a punctured tire. "You wouldn't believe!"

I made compatible noises and repeated my question.

"I don't mean to butt into your private life, young lady, but you're best off being rid of that man."

I was learning nothing, at record speed, too. "What happened?" I asked again.

"That lunatic had the audacity to say he could explain everything. That's what happened."

"What'd he say?"

"Nothing worth repeating," she said. "I told him I didn't want to hear it."

"You left then?"

"I tried, but he blubbered after me all the way out to your car, begging me to make you listen to him."

"I don't want to listen to him," I said.

"That's what I told him, but I'll tell you this. The man can lie with a straight face."

"What do you mean?"

"The woman with him. He said it was his sister."

Angus had a sister named Angie, a brother named Albert, and parents with an obvious fetish for the letter "A." But who was I to talk. The Cobia lineage had an affinity for the letter "K." Dad's first name was Karl, mine was Karen, and had my sister lived she would've been named Karly. To Angus's siblings, one lived in Cleveland, the other in Tampa, but I wasn't sure which one lived where as I'd never met either of them. Even so, while I might accept and understand his drinking with his sister, I could never extend those limits to his fondling her. And the big no-no, of course, was his taking her to the penthouse as the aftermath of that fondling. "His sister? No way," I said.

"Well he doesn't give up easily." I heard more air escape. "He called twice while you were tying up."

I'd been around the block before meeting Angus, but in the time I dated him I never two-timed him, and I never lied to him. Until now I hadn't believed he had, either. After seeing his actions with a woman still filling my mind's eye, and hearing of his claim the woman was his sister, I now believed he'd done both.

Aunt Patty didn't wind down until she ran through it all again. When we finally hung up, I cussed my inquisitive nature for having called her at all. *Informed* was not always better than *blissfully ignorant.*

Dad called out when he saw me step out the rear door of the bait shop. "Bring us two more, baby, and grab one for yourself."

Cecil spread his arms, making an umpire's safe-at-home signal. "Not for me, Weed."

When others shortened my nickname, I got pissed; when Cecil did it, as he had forever, I smiled. He reached for his cane and struggled to his feet. "I got a lady waiting at home," he drawled. "She ain't gettin' any younger." He poked Dad in the ribs with the cane. "Trouble is, Cobia, we ain't either."

I gave Cecil a good-bye hug and watched as he ambled to his car. When he was on his way, I returned to the cooler. I'd have *one* beer with Dad before dinner. No more. To do otherwise on an empty stomach would guarantee a condition I wished to avoid: poop-faced.

I took the chair Cecil had used, moved it closer to the milk crate, and mimicked his sprawled position. I winked at Dad, my angelic-daughter one, and sipped my beer. I'd missed a year's worth of this because I let my damned fool temper build a fence between us. No more. Never again.

Dad never could wink worth a toot, but he had a smile as wide as the Gulf. He gave me one, and said, "It's good to have you home, baby." I watched the smile fade until he added, "Patty told me what happened."

"Angus? Myers? The note?"

"All of it," he said. "I'll leave Angus to your good judgment, since you're beginning to exercise some of it."

"Thank you."

Dad scratched at the back of his neck and said, "I agree with Patty about Myers and his note. The man owes you a truck-load of gratitude."

When the man couldn't even bring himself to say thank you? "Fat chance" I said.

He tipped the bottle to his lips, swallowed, wiped his mouth with his forearm, and burped with a tone rivaling the *Margaret Ellen's* exhaust. And I'd actually planned to take him *out* to dinner.

"Right now," he said, gliding his fingers over the label on the bottle as if it contained a message in Braille, "I want to hear about your new mate."

Hmm. Aunt Patty had told him everything. "I haven't committed to her yet," I said, before going on to explain how I planned to use the trip to the haul out yard as a trial run to test her nautical ability.

"Good idea," he said. "Put 'er through the paces. That'll show what she's made of."

I smiled as if the idea had been his from the beginning.

"What I don't understand," he said, "is why she wants to change jobs."

I tried to explain.

He listened, finished his beer, and stood. "Want another?" he said as he ambled to the cooler.

"No. I've barely touched this one."

After he'd fetched another beer and dropped back into his chair, he said, "This'll probably hurt your feelings, being a girl and all, but here goes."

I'd heard sermons beginning like this before. I waited.

"You," he said, tipping his bottle like an up-raised finger, "earned a respectable, top-of-the-ladder position using only your skill and your brains. No one gave you a head start because you're female, and you did it despite the fact most captains are male. I'm proud of you. What I don't like is a woman who uses her beauty to climb a job ladder and then gets her dander up when the men around her admire her body instead of bowing to her nonexistent skill and brains."

"My feelings aren't hurt," I said. "Besides, in most cases, you're right. In her case, though, I believe you're being a little too hard."

"Tell me why," he said, "and I'll cut 'er some slack."

I grinned. "This'll probably hurt your feelings, being a man and all, but here goes." When he returned the grin, I continued. "Dad, ask the average man in this world to describe a bimbo and his answer is going to be, 'A big-breasted blonde.' Gwen is that, to be sure, but she's also a very educated woman. She's earned every rung on her job ladder. The trouble is, being a big-breasted blonde in her line of work is like being that guy on TV. The one who says, 'I don't get no respect.'"

"Okay," he said, "there might be something to that."

"Actually, there's more to it," I said. "She's just lost a big home full of the latest amenities, a cabin cruiser, a new car, and a husband. What's worse, she lost them to a younger woman. Right now I believe she's searching for a life with something meaningful in it. Not money. Not glamour."

"In that case, forgive me. I was wrong. I hope she works out." He cleared his throat. "She certainly has the lungs for it."

"Dad!"

My admonishment fell on deaf ears. He glanced at his watch and jumped up. "Come on," he said. "I forgot about supper."

I hadn't forgotten it, but I wanted it to be my idea. "What supper?"

Again, deaf ears. I followed him to the cooler, where he set his empty on the bottom shelf and pulled a covered container from the top one. I stepped closer and peered at the contents as he pulled the lid back. Speckled trout filets? Knowing fishermen kept secrets better than the CIA, I should have saved my breath. I asked anyway. "Where'd you get 'em?"

"Beauties, ain't they? You're looking at supper."

"Supper? Dad, you've never cooked a meal in your life."

"Don't intend to start now," he said as he closed the cooler. "Let's go. We're eating with Steve and Roxie."

Steve held membership with the too-large group of Americans who returned from Viet Nam with fewer body parts than they left with. In his case it was his left arm—blown off at the shoulder. Roxie was his high school sweetheart and they married just months before he entered the Army. In her eyes he was still as whole today as he was when he quarterbacked the Tarpons at Bay Side High School.

And why not? Roxie was unique. She was old enough to be my mother, and easily twice my size, but when we were together we carried on like teens at a slumber party. If you knew her, you loved her. No exceptions.

Actually, I loved them both. That made the next two hours, despite eating long after I should've quit, more fun than I could remember having in a long while. And, because I could laugh, talk, and eavesdrop at the same time, I learned how Dad came by the speckled trout.

Unlike me, Dad doesn't kick things when he's mad. He goes fishing. This morning—after I'd slipped out without him—he collared Steve and they took one of the rental skiffs over to the grass flats off Dutchman Key. Fishing was great.

At ten, however, my jovial spirit vaporized when I looked up and saw Myers framed in the dining-room door. He looked around the patio, locked eyes with me, and crossed to my side of the table.

Roxie was not a beer lover. She loved white wine, and during the evening she'd had enough of it to float her a half-bubble beyond bubbly. She leaned back in her chair, pointed at Myers, closed her eyes, and went into her clairvoyant routine. "Tuesday afternoon," she said. "Corner table right over there. A woman. No, two women. One at each elbow. Gotcha. You were the steak hoagie and small draft."

If Myers was impressed with her memory or amused by her skit, he kept a tight rein on it. He ignored Roxie and swung his grim lips and expressionless eyes back to me. "I have to talk with you," he said. "Now. Alone."

Steve pushed his chair back. "I better check the kitchen."

"Oh well," Roxie said. "It was fun while it lasted." In slow motion she stood and began stacking dishes, all the while whistling "Dixie" through the gap in her lower teeth. She had an armload by the time she made it to "… look away, look away, Dixieland." She gave Dad and me a wink, scowled at Myers, and then ambled after Steve.

Dad tipped his chair against the patio railing and folded his arms across his chest.

Myers worked up one of his great squints and aimed it at Dad. "And who are you?"

"I'm her dad, sonny, and those folks," he said, nodding after Steve and Roxie, "are my friends." He reached out his right arm and stroked my hair. "This is her first night home in a while. I don't take kindly to you screwing it up."

"This is police business," Myers said.

I held my breath. Dad doesn't take intimidation well. In fact, he doesn't take it at all.

"And she's my business," Dad said. He patted my shoulder and stood. "You got three options, sonny: You can take a chair and talk; you can take the door you came through to go for reinforcements; or—"

"Or what?"

Dad's hands curled into fists as he nodded toward the patio railing. "Or you're about to get a swimming lesson."

Myers stared at Dad and then lowered his eyes to mine. I jumped up and swiped a mug and a chair from a nearby table. I pushed the mug into Myers's hands and pointed at the chair. "Sit and start over," I said. "The beer's a little warm but the hush puppies are out of this world."

Dad and Myers continued their stare-down.

I pushed between them and said, "Both of you sit or *I'll* take a swim!"

Myers blinked first. He sat. Dad followed. "Now," I said, "what's so important?"

Myers didn't use words to apologize, he just topped off Dad's mug and then filled his own. He sipped, wiped his mouth with the back of his hand, and said, "A major snafu."

CHAPTER 21

A major snafu? What in the world did Myers believe my life had been for the last three days? Euphoria? I'd found a body on Monday; Tuesday morning I met an impostor, who was probably a murderess as well; and then Tuesday evening I caught my lover red-handed with a barroom queen. Snafu, Detective Myers? Ask me about it.

And today hadn't started out a hell of a lot better. It had, however, smoothed somewhat after putting the Buttonwood in my wake. Since then, surrounded by family and friends, I managed to relax and have fun. Fun, that was, until Myers barged in like one of my worst dreams. Ironically, earlier in the evening, I'd laughed with Roxie about the message on her T-shirt. Now, it held real meaning: "Life's a bitch; then you die."

From the way his eyes had held mine when he said, "A major snafu," I was sure Myers expected me to ask, "What snafu?" He'd have a wait. The first lesson in mouth-control was to keep it shut. There *were* exceptions, however. I shifted my gaze to the stainless steel platter in the center of the table. The trout filets were a memory; two hush puppies remained. I scooped up one.

Then, like there hadn't been a full minute of silence since his revelation, he said, "You moved your boat."

This was another statement. I savored the hush puppy—still crisp and tangy with a scrumptious blend of onion and garlic—and made a mental note to ask Roxie about her recipe. When the man got around to asking a question, I'd answer it.

"I've tried calling you," he said. "Your line's out of order."

Maybe the man couldn't frame a question. I devoured the remaining fragment of hush puppy and used the grease-stained napkin clinging to my lap to dab my lips and wipe my fingers. Placing the crumpled napkin alongside my plate, I said, "My phone won't be reconnected until Friday. If you wanted to speak with me, you could've called the bait shop."

"It's not that," he said. "It's for our make-believe Amber."

I watched as he tightened his two-handed grip on his beer mug. His knuckles whitened. At Casey's he'd said, "Right now I wish I had my hands around her throat." I shuddered.

"If you haven't guessed by now," he said, "I missed her."

How could he have missed her? Especially since my recorder had picked up the announcement of the posse's arrival. I asked.

"We'd just installed the caller ID on your line," he said. "A call came in. I recognized the number as the payphone in the lobby of the Bamboo. I figured she was with Jean Hampton, so I requested a city unit to respond and hold her. When I got there, they were holding Hampton. She's not talking."

I thought of the three blinks on my answering machine. "It was a hang-up call, right?"

"Yes," he said, "but it didn't matter. Caller ID made it instantly."

I told him about the message and added, "The other voice must have been Jean Hampton's."

"No doubt," he said. "I'm hoping a night in jail will loosen her tongue."

The thought of a night in jail would certainly loosen mine.

"What's all this have to do with Karen?" Dad said.

"I might still need her help, Mr. Cobia. And, look, I'm sorry we got started on the wrong note."

I waved both hands in his face. "Whoa! I did my part, and all it got me was a kiss-off note written on a brown bag." Draping my arm over Dad's shoulder, I said, "Help's over. I'm home and I have a job, thank you."

Dad patted my hand and leaned forward, resting his forearms on the table. "What kind of help?" he said.

"Dad!"

"Let's hear him out."

"Thank you," Myers said, "but before I get into that, I'd better brief you on the latest."

I copied Dad's posture.

"First, the man who was using the name Reginald Wentworth was actually Sculley Kilgore."

I caught the shift to past tense and said, "Was? Like in—"

"Yes, I believe he's dead," Myers said. "I'm having his prints checked. I'll know for sure later tonight."

"How?" I said. "And where?"

"I told you I sent a copy of his photo to the Margate PD. I just got word from them. The photo matched a John Doe in their morgue. They fished his body out of a lagoon near Northeast Yacht last Saturday morning. Shot once in the head."

Myers had mentioned the Saturday morning business at Northeast, but it didn't jive with what he just said. "Then this Sculley couldn't have been the man at Northeast's place Saturday morning."

"No. Sculley was six-foot, two hundred pounds, and had dark hair. According to the assistant manager at Northeast, the man who showed on Saturday morning was tall, but he had a slight build, light hair, and weasel eyes."

Eva had been shot once in the head and then dumped into the Gulf. The similarity in the killing made me ask. "Was the wound the same? A forty-five caliber?"

Myers drummed his fingertips on the tabletop. "You got it."

"Well," I said, "with what's-her-name wanting me to find him, I can't believe she had anything to do with killing him. Do you?"

"No," he said, "not really."

"Neither do I," Dad said. "I saw her. If she packed a gun, it would be a twenty-five or a thirty-two, not a forty-five."

"That's my thinking, too," Myers said. "That and the fact she and Sculley split up in Atlanta."

The man was full of surprises. "How do you know that?" I asked.

"The doc and his wife I told you about, the ones who sat in row twenty-seven. The wife called me back. She said she'd just remembered the woman I'd asked about flew only as far as Atlanta. A man occupied her seat from there on to D.C."

Coincidence, or was this man the one who killed Sculley? "Did she give you a description of…"

"No, 'Just a man,' was all she was sure of."

"Bizarre," I said. "Sculley Kilgore, while impersonating Reginald Wentworth, left TPA at noon Friday and was found floating in a lagoon in New Jersey the next morning. The unknown woman with him had been impersonating Amber Brantley, but for the flight she pretended to be Eva Park. She turned around in Atlanta and called me at midnight on Monday to locate her missing accomplice." I paused for breath. "They have to be tied to Eva's death, but don't ask me how. I don't have a clue."

Myers sipped his beer and shook his head. "Sculley Kilgore had a long rap sheet. Served time on a number of occasions. But each time he was busted it was for the same thing: a con. And each time it involved a rich widow. Nothing violent. Ever."

"So his coming on to Eva was probably a con game gone bad?"

"I'd bet on it," he said. "Our fake Amber's a part of it, but there has to be someone else involved."

"In our scenario," I said, "the real Amber was a prime candidate."

Myers did his eyebrow wiggle. "*Was*, is right."

"What do you mean?"

"Yesterday, do you remember me saying Amber's attorney said she was in Europe?"

I remembered and said so.

"Surprise," he said. "She is. And believe me, I checked it seven ways. It's her. The real Amber Brantley. And she's been there for the last ten days."

"Did she know about Eva's death?"

"Yeah, Avery called her Monday. She'll be back tonight."

"Wait!" I remembered something Gwen had said when I was at her place. "According to Gwen, Amber and Stan Avery are a real number."

"A real number?"

"Like in sweethearts," Dad said.

I nodded agreement. "Weldon, at Global Insurance, told me it was Stan Avery who reworked the titling of Eva's worldly goods so everything would pass to Amber outside of probate. Not only that, Big Al told me Mack Avery covered his son's ass on something. A theft of funds from a client's escrow account, I believe."

Myers leaned forward. "Where're you headed with this?"

"Let's go back to our scenario discussion at Casey's," I said.

He nodded.

"As far as anyone knew," I said, "Eva and Reginald left the area last Friday. If her body hadn't been found, and we agreed it wasn't meant to be, it's unlikely the police would've ever dug deep enough to find out who Reginald really was. Right?"

"Probably," he said. "Go on."

"We're still in scenario mode," I said. "So let's say Eva's body is still in the Gulf when the man calling himself Reginald Wentworth is killed in New Jersey. Margate police find his body. At that moment he's a John Doe. Without your input, wouldn't they print him and eventually make an identification from his criminal file?"

"Sure. Happens all the time. So what?"

"I hoped it worked that way," I said. "So at that point, with positive ID made, the Margate Police Department could say with certainty Sculley Kilgore was deceased. Eva Park is just as dead, but no one knows it, and Reginald Wentworth, as such, never existed."

Myers shrugged. "What are you trying to point at?"

"Just this," I said. "The ones who now look to have the most to gain by Eva's death are Stan Avery and Amber Brantley. Just because she's been in Europe for ten days doesn't mean she couldn't be in on Eva's death. And think about the description Northeast's assistant manager gave you for the man who was there Saturday morning. The same morning Sculley's body was found nearby. In the photo I saw of Stan and Amber, he was slim, light brown hair, and ferret eyes. The man at Northeast said light hair and weasel eyes. Ferrets and weasels are both little animals. Just like Avery."

"I caught the similarity," he said. "And if he's in tight with Amber, it gives him one hell of a motive."

I rubbed my hands together. "You bet it does."

Myers did his eyebrow wiggle, again. "There's just one small problem."

"What kind of problem?"

"He has an alibi."

"You're kidding. Did you check?"

"Yeah," he said, "it was simple enough. Avery came down with the flu last Thursday. On Friday he didn't come into the office. He worked on a case file at home."

Cute story but my money was now on Avery as the killer. "Can he prove he was at home?" I said.

"His secretary backed up his story. On top of that she said he called her a few times during the day."

Not good enough. "He could make calls from anywhere," I said.

"I thought of that."

"And?"

Myers pulled a notepad from his shirt pocket and paged through it. "Madge, that's his secretary, said Avery's first call was to tell her he was going to see a doctor. When he returned home, he called her again. This time he told her he'd just taken some medication. He asked her not to call him because he was going to take a nap. Later, just before she left the office for the day, he called again and asked her to call him that evening."

"Why?"

"To wake him and remind him to take his next batch of medication. She called just after nine. He answered."

That wasn't fair. I wanted him to be the one. "Damn!" I said.

"Yeah," Myers said as he blew out breath and reached for his glass. "The time and distance take him out of the picture for Sculley's death."

I didn't want to turn loose. "That doesn't mean he isn't involved," I said. "He and Amber have the most to gain. And if they didn't do it personally, they could have hired someone."

"Don't sweat it," Myers said. "I'm not closing the door on any angle."

"And how about Karen?" Dad said.

Turning his attention to me, he said, "Our fake Amber can't know Sculley's dead. If she's still hot to find him, and she can't reach you by phone, she might show up. If she does, sit on her and call for help."

Sit on her? Sure. Count on it.

"This Sculley," Dad said. "How old a man was he?"

"About your age," Myers said.

"And the fake Amber?"

Myers glanced at me. "About Karen's age, I'd say. Why?"

"Just that if I were missing, I *know* my daughter would be looking for me."

Steve and Roxie returned to the table after Myers left. We tried to shrug off the interruption and recapture our earlier mood. Nothing doing. Roxie vowed our next dinner together would be a locked-door affair. Dad and I agreed before walking home. On the way he sort of promised to show me his hot spot for speckled trout off Dutchman Key.

At the rear door of the shop, Dad and I exchanged a goodnight hug. "Thanks for sticking up for me," I said. "And you were right about one thing."

"What's that, baby?"

"If you were missing," I said, "you could bet your last piece of cut bait I'd be looking for you."

My humor earned another hug and a knuckle scrub before we parted.

I hurried aboard my sloop, startling to flight a lone pelican roosting on the stern hatch cover. Just as well. If not, I would have had an unsightly mess to hose off the deck in the morning.

As tired as I was, sleep didn't come quickly. I stared at the clock in my berth as I considered Dad's speculation. What if the fake Amber were really the daughter of Sculley Kilgore? As I'd told Myers, her concern for Sculley was real. The difference in their ages, dismissing the possibility of an arrangement like the one I'd had with Angus, precluded a lover's kind of love; it didn't, however, preclude a daughter's kind of love.

One o'clock in the morning. Enough. I turned away from the clock, pulled the flannel comforter over my head, and began counting shrimp.

CHAPTER 22

In addition to shrimp, I also tallied stone crabs and rock bass from Tampa Bay to Key West before falling asleep. But needed rest didn't follow, only a nightmare. Rough hands picked me up and dropped me into a huge, open-top box. I ran, arms flailing, searching for an exit, as my tormentor calmly spiked a lid onto the box that held me.

Suddenly, the back of my left hand was on fire. I awoke, holding my throbbing hand. The glowing numerals on my travel alarm stared back at me from the foot of my berth. How had the clock gotten down there? I checked the time as I returned the clock to its shelf: three-oh-six a.m.

In previous dreams I'd scratched the berth's paneling, torn the sheets, and punched the pillow. This time I backhanded the clock, but it looked none the worse for wear. I opened and closed my hand. It was sore, but nothing felt broken. Best of all, I wasn't in the dark box that held center stage in my nightmare; I was safe in my berth, awake, sitting up, and fully aware of the pain in the back of my hand. This meant I wasn't still dreaming. Why, then, could I still hear the noise—a soft, intermittent tapping much like the hammering I'd heard in my dream?

Seeing anything through the condensation coating my berth's porthole was impossible. As quietly as possible, I released the latching knobs on the port and eased it open. Nothing but silence. Had I been wrong? No, the tapping resumed, sounding as if it were coming from the *Margaret Ellen*. Would a thief be so noisy? Not a sober one. Great. My phone was useless, but at least I wasn't helpless. I groped for my revolver beneath the edge of the mattress and crawled from the berth.

After creeping through the main salon and then to the top of the companionway stairs, I slid the hatch back. The tapping resumed, this time accompanied by some whispering. Despite the low tone, I recognized the voice as belonging to the fake Amber, who was now aboard the *Margaret Ellen* and standing at the locked door to the pilothouse. I stood, just enough for my head to be seen, and said, "What in the hell are you doing?"

She spun around. "I thought you—"

"Get off the boat. Now!"

"Okay, sure," she said, "but I have to talk to you."

Now what? Even if she'd voluntarily lie down so I could sit on her, I had no phone with which to call for help. Of course I could march her to the bait shop, awaken Dad, and have him call. The problem was, I was nude. Two hours at Gwen's place had not erased all my inhibitions. I opened the companionway and said, "Come over here."

After placing the pistol under a cushion on the chart table seat, I hurried into jeans and T-shirt and then turned on every light from the berth to the main salon area. When she came aboard I led her to the dinette seat and returned to the chart table, a move that put me between her and the only escape route. Maybe that wasn't such a great idea.

She perched at the edge of the seat, knees touching and both hands clutching her humongous purse. Until my thoughts were sorted, beating around the bush seemed the best way to start. I was still sorting when she spoke.

"I've been trying to call you, but your phone's not working."

Now what? Tell her the phone wasn't connected? No way. "I turned it off to get some sleep," I said. "Besides, you were supposed to give me a number where I could reach you."

Her hand darted into the mouth of her purse; my hand flew to the gun at my side. Her draw was faster. "There's your money," she said, tossing a stack of bills onto the table. "I need the ring back."

Now what? Myers had the ring, not me. Before I could think of a delaying tactic, she continued.

"Have you found him yet?"

"I know where he is," I said.

She fired a high-five with both hands and then slapped her knees. "I knew you could do it! Where is he?"

I couldn't return the ring or accept the cash, so I went on offense, comforted by the reassuring lump beneath the cushion at my side, "I'll get to that in a moment," I said. "First, let's drop the bullshit."

Her smile vanished. "What do you mean?"

"For openers, you're not Amber Brantley, and last Friday you left TPA with Sculley Kilgore, the man calling himself Reginald Wentworth."

"How did you—"

After meeting Myers, and despite myself, I'd practiced his squint. My quality was shy of primetime, but I gave it my best shot. "Never mind," I said. "Who are you, and what's the scam you two were working?"

"Where is he?"

"After you fess up."

She jumped to her feet. I pulled the pistol.

Clutching the purse to her breast, she said, "You wouldn't shoot me."

Of course not, but I had to play it through. "Why not?" I said. "There's a warrant out for your arrest. Sit."

Her shoulders sagged as she sat back at the edge of the dinette and placed the purse between her feet. "There's no need for the gun," she said.

The soft tone returned to her voice, but with only the toes of her running shoes touching the floor, she looked like a coiled spring. "Who are you?"

Silence.

I nodded at the phone and said, "How 'bout we let Detective Myers sort it out."

"No. Please. Don't call him. I'm Betty. Sculley's my father.

As usual, Dad had been right. Now that I was dressed I could slip on some shoes and march her to a phone. Or I could keep her talking and call after I'd learned more. I decided to try talking first. The woman-to-woman thing, as Myers had called it. "Betty, this doesn't look good for you or your dad. Eva's dead and your dad's involvement with her was a scam of some kind."

"He didn't kill her."

"I don't believe you did either, Betty, but the police don't share my view."

"They can't think—"

"Of course they can," I said. "Didn't your dad know he'd get nothing from Eva's death, even if he married her?"

She nodded. "No one was supposed to get killed. He was paid to get close to Eva and propose marriage. That's all."

"That can't be all, Betty. You and your dad left Friday pretending to be Eva Park and Reginald Wentworth. What was that all about?"

"I know that looks bad," she said, "but you have to believe me. Dad didn't kill Eva."

"Tell me about Friday."

"It was all supposed to be over on Friday," she said. "All we had to do was fly out under the other names and it was done."

"What was the payoff?"

She patted the purse on her lap. "The jewelry," she said. "That's why I have to have the ring back."

144

That meant she still thought it was real. "Why did you split up with your dad in Atlanta?"

Her eyes narrowed. "You've learned a lot, haven't you."

It wasn't a question. "Well?"

"Dad didn't trust the son-of-a-bitch."

"Who do you mean?"

"I don't know who he really is," she said. "I never saw him before we met at the airport Friday morning. He gave Dad the jewelry and two tickets. We were supposed to fly as far as Washington D.C. Our part would end when we got there."

"Why didn't you go all the way to Washington?"

"I just told you, Dad didn't trust him. Just before we boarded, Dad pretended to pass the jewelry to me and said he had to go to the men's room. He didn't like the thought of us and the jewelry and the man being together. Dad stashed the jewelry in a locker and gave me the key."

"This man went with you?"

"Yes, but on the way Dad was still worried. In Atlanta I ducked away when they boarded the Washington flight. He wanted me to get back to Tampa, pick up the jewelry, and hide at a friend's place until he called."

"That would be your friend, Jean Hampton. Right?"

"Yes, but he hasn't called, and I can't go back to Jean's. The cops know about her."

She was also in jail, but I didn't mention the fact. "Where are you staying?"

"A place Jean told me about. It doesn't matter where, just tell me where he is."

"I think I should do that with the police present," I said.

"I don't care anymore. Just tell me. I'll help the police. I promise. You can have the jewelry. I just want him back."

And I wanted the name of the other person, but she wasn't apt to spit it out unless I shook her up. There were two bombs in my arsenal. I dropped the first one. "Betty, they say it takes a con to take another con."

"What's that supposed to mean?"

"The pouch of jewelry you have," I said. "It's fake."

She gasped. For one split second I saw the same look on her face as I'd seen on Angus's at the Buttonwood's elevator. "No! It can't be fake!"

"You've been conned, Betty. Now tell me who this other man is."

"No! No! No! No way." She hugged her purse. "They can't be fake. No. Not after all he did."

"Betty, give me the name. Please."

She jumped to her feet. "Oh, no. I'm going to kill the pea-eyed son-of-a-bitch."

I leaped into her path and stiff-armed her back to the table. "Sit. There's more to this."

Perspiration covered her forehead, and fear danced in her eyes, but she backed down into the same position and set her purse between her feet. In recent hours I'd heard three terms: ferret-eyed, weasel-eyed, and pea-eyed. Alibi or not, I was sure the other man was Stan Avery. But what in the world would he have in common with the likes of Sculley Kilgore? "Betty, I think the other man's name is Stan Avery."

If the name triggered recognition, it didn't register in her expression.

"I don't know his name," she said, "but I know where to find him."

"We're going to let the police handle him." I fished for words. Easy words, ones that would soften the blast my next bomb was sure to cause. I couldn't snag a one. Telling her, then, as Myers had told me seemed to be the only way.

"Betty, your father and this other man would have reached New Jersey Friday evening. The next morning a man who identified himself as Reginald Wentworth showed up at Northeast to make arrangements for the delivery of the new yacht."

"So he's okay!"

"Whoa," I said. "That man wasn't your father, but his description fits the man your father was with."

"I don't understand."

"Betty, that same morning a body was found in a lagoon near Northeast. Tests will tell for sure, but at this point it looks like the man was ... your father."

Her head dropped to her knees. I stood, thinking she was crying. I'd made two steps toward her when she sprang to her feet, swinging her purse like a two-fisted uppercut.

I saw the huge bulk coming, but I couldn't dodge it. The purse caught the tip of my chin and started me stumbling backwards. If that was all she had, I could handle her. That was the last thought I had before my head cracked into the bulkhead.

CHAPTER 23

When I opened my eyes, Dad was kneeling at my side, cradling the back of my head; the rest of my body was sprawled at the base of the companionway steps. I closed and then reopened my eyes several times before focus returned, allowing me to see my toes as toes, not a stubby row of asparagus shoots.

Dad pulled one hand away from my head, refolded the handkerchief in his palm, and returned it to my epicenter of pain. I grimaced, but the pain was only part of the reason why. Dad had a drawer full of handkerchiefs. None of them was red.

The spot where he was holding the compress throbbed with each beat of my heart. This was understandable, but why the painful throb in my chest? I looked at my T-shirt and saw a curlicue tread mark centered over my left breast. Had Betty used me as a starting block in her race up the companionway? Or had she simply stomped me for being the messenger bearing bad news? Continuing to stare at my breast, I wondered if there would be any swelling—enough, perhaps, to gain a cup size out of the ordeal. In spite of the pain, the thought triggered a laugh.

Dad tightened his grip on my head. "What's so funny?"

Being a man and all, trying to explain my thought to him would be hopeless. Instead, I said, "Private joke."

"Well there ain't one damned thing here to be laughing at. The crazy bitch could've killed you."

"You saw her?"

"Got another handkerchief?"

Yeah, I had a few, but it took a moment to remember where I kept them. "Ah, portside, top drawer, under the berth."

"Hold this," he said. "I'm gunna clean that cut."

I held the sticky handkerchief, as he ordered, but with far less pressure against the wound than he'd used. My right arm tired, so I switched to the left one. Bad move. A wave of dizziness swept in, pausing a moment before ebbing like waves playing upon a beach. Slowly, then, I began moving my head side to side and then back and forth. I was still doing so when I spotted strands of my hair hanging from the fire extinguisher handle. The extinguisher was mounted to the bulkhead alongside the companionway for ready access in case of fire. So far I was the only thing it had put out.

I crawled to my feet and was sitting at the chart table when Dad returned with a wet handkerchief. After some dabbing and fussing, he asked about my vision.

"Foggy at first," I said. "Dizzy once." I did some head moves and then flexed my shoulders. "Seems fine now."

"Good. And the bleeding's stopped. You'll live, baby, but ...."

When he didn't finish his thought, I repeated my earlier question.

"See her? Yeah. Something woke me. When I finally got my butt out of bed and looked out I saw your lights on. Thought I'd better check. She was flying across the patio when I came out the rear door."

I told Dad what I'd learned before getting smacked. Struggling to my feet, I said, "I better call Myers."

Dad helped me reach the catwalk; then, with his arm around my waist, he guided me to the bait shop. I felt like an injured player being helped from the playing field.

The large-face clock on the wall behind the cash register said four-fifteen. Dad came by the clock when the vessel he'd served aboard, *Skipjack*, had been decommissioned. Every small vessel he'd owned since carried the same name; every larger one carried Mom's.

I asked him once, when I was still pretty young, why he did that. That is, naming something small, like the Whaler, after something big like the *Skipjack* and naming something big, like the *Margaret Ellen*, after something small like Mom. He just scrubbed his knuckles on the top of my head and said, "You'll figure it out one day."

Dad started a pot of coffee; I headed for the phone in his office. Calling Myers at home was my intention, but his card and home number were still aboard my sloop. No such problem for obtaining the number of the Pinellas County Sheriff's Office, however. That number, along with other emergency numbers, was on a dog-eared card taped to the wall near the phone.

I made the call, gave a brief rundown of what'd happened, and told the dispatcher Myers would want the information immediately. I gave the bait shop's number for call back before hanging up.

The aroma of fresh-brewed coffee drifted into the room. I started backtracking it, but before I cleared the hall, Dad spun me around and headed me for the bathroom where he insisted on swabbing my cut with iodine. With that done he then made me promise to get a tetanus shot. No problem. I just didn't promise when. Myers called before I finished my first cup.

He listened without interrupting and then blew me away with his first question.

"How bad are you hurt?"

Compassion? From Grim Lips? "Nothing's broken," I said. "Just sore in a wide variety of places." I didn't mention all the places.

After additional words of concern, he added, "How about your gun?"

The question took my breath away. My stomach knotted. The pistol had been in my hand when she swung at me. It had not been there when I woke. I looked at Dad, knowing the answer before I asked.

"I didn't see it when I got there," Dad said.

Thinking about where I'd been standing when she hit me, I said, "Maybe it slid under the companionway steps."

Dad started for the rear door of the bait shop. "I'll check."

I told Myers I'd have an answer on my pistol in a minute, and then mentioned Betty's comment on where she'd been staying.

"Great. So Jean Hampton knows where Betty's been hiding. I'll lean on her."

"Fine," I said, "but I think you'll find Betty quicker by keeping an eye on Avery."

He was quiet a moment. I could still hear my own pulse, and my breast ached, but the throbbing at the back of my head had eased. When he didn't speak, I added, "Maybe you ought to lean on his secretary, too. She lied. He's the one. I can feel it."

"Whoa," he said. "If this mystery man is Avery, seems to me Betty'd know his name. Especially so if she knows where to find him."

"Not necessarily. Remember, her dad worked the scam; she just filled a seat on the plane. Could be she only heard her dad mention a meeting spot."

"Maybe."

"And," I said, "she called him pea-eyed."

"I see pea-eyed sons-of-bitches every day."

"Yes, but the same description is coming from separate sources."

"A lawyer screwing somebody I can buy. This is murder."

"In my book, murdered for money *is* the ultimate screwing."

He muttered something I didn't catch as Dad came in shaking his head. "My pistol's gone," I said.

He asked me to describe it. I did and also promised to dig out the serial number and call it in.

After finishing with Myers, I returned to my sloop, doffed my T-shirt, and examined my breast. I saw evidence of bruising, but if it were swelling, it was taking its sweet time. In exaggerated slow motion, I performed a few upper-body stretches and then put the shirt back on. Movement was painful, but I reminded myself that pain afflicted only the living. Considering the alternative, I was happy to pay my dues.

I added socks and a long-sleeve shirt to my apparel and then fished an elastic headband from my underwear drawer before returning to the shop. With Dad's help I fashioned a small pad for my wound and positioned the headband to hold it in place.

Daylight was still two hours away, but returning to sleep was out of the question. Dad suggested breakfast at Shanley's was a fitting way to kill time until the coming of dawn's early light. I agreed.

In the time it took me to finish an order of Roxie's cinnamon raisin toast and a cup of coffee, Dad polished off a double order of scrambled eggs, four sausage links, a mound of grits, an order of wheat toast, and a tall glass of orange juice. We discussed the details of Betty's visit while we ate.

"We can get another pistol," he said. "At least she didn't try it out before she left."

Yes, stomped beat being shot. "Amen," I said. Silently, I said another amen because she ran from Dad rather than raise the pistol against him.

Roxie paused at the table long enough to top off our coffee and to pick up our empty plates. Despite the pre-dawn chill, her face and arms were gleaming with perspiration. She was wearing her usual knee-length black skirt, hugging her enormous hips tighter than wet hugs water, and a black T-shirt with the message "Scuba divers do it deeper." Roxie didn't notice my wound, and to avoid an outpouring of her mothering, I didn't mention it. Dad picked up his cup, leaned back, and began relating his thoughts on the upcoming run of king mackerel.

"Once the run starts," he said, "you'll be on the water every day. Might be weeks before you have a day off."

The thought of a steady paycheck brought a smile. "I can handle it," I said.

"I know you can, but I don't want you to burn out. Here's what I have in mind."

I sipped and listened.

"When the kings fizzle, drop back to five trips a week. I'll help with the bookings, but let's avoid back-to-back overnighters. When you lose a day to weather, use it to keep up with maintenance. And *this* is the big thing. One day a week, whether you like it or not, park the *Margaret Ellen* and get away from here. Do something else, something you enjoy. You need to do that. Believe me, I know."

What were the things I'd done on my days off during the three years I captained the *Margaret Ellen*? Sailing, water skiing, or beachcombing. Work or play, then, I was drawn to the water. Regardless, I knew what Dad was getting at. We'd work it out. What we hadn't worked out was the partnership thing. How did he plan for me to earn a piece of the business? We had time. I asked.

"Earn?" He dismissed the word with a chuckle and a wave of his hand. "You're all I have, baby. If I dropped dead now, it'd be yours anyway."

"Dad! Don't talk like that."

He blew across the lip of his cup, sipped, and then said, "Just statin' facts, baby. Until then, here's what we'll do. I've already set up a separate bank account. All charter money goes into it. You'll pay standard wages to your mate. And you'll draw the standard percent for yourself. Bait, fuel, overhead, and maintenance expenses come out of the account. You'll pay the phone bill for your sloop out of your pocket; I'll cover your electric and water costs along with the shop's bills. In a few months we'll have a comfortable cushion in the account. That's when we'll start splitting the surplus right down the middle. Just like fifty-fifty partners are supposed to do."

By the time he finished spelling out his thoughts on our new partnership, I was squirming in my seat. If I still had any pain, I couldn't feel it. All I could feel was that night-before-Christmas tingle I used to get as a child.

"Well? What do you think?" he said.

I jumped from my chair, tore around the table, and threw both arms around him. "What do I think?" I kissed his cheek. "You've got a partner, partner."

He pulled me onto the chair at his side. "Good."

Anxiety welled in me as I watched his eyebrows and hairline try to touch, the old sign meaning what followed would be serious.

He brushed my hair back over my shoulder and said, "Baby, the feeling you're feeling right now is special. There's nothing like it. But I don't want it to get you hurt."

Hurt? I studied his eyes. His expression. No clue. "What do you mean?"

"The special feeling that goes hand-in-hand with this boat business." He tightened his hug around my shoulders with one arm and gestured toward the pass with the other. "The special feeling that starts when you look out over the water. It builds as you step aboard your vessel and start the engines. It builds higher as you feel the power pulsing below deck. Then it peaks as you cast off and get underway."

My arms tingled. Those were the exact things I felt every time I got underway. I'd never told Dad, because I never dreamed he'd experienced them too.

"You're on a high," he said. "You ride it as you swing into the channel and head under the high span. But when you enter the Gulf, the rules change. You're a guest out there. Sometimes you're welcome. Sometimes you're not."

He paused and hugged me with both arms. His eyes filled. Choking more than speaking, he added, "Fifteen years, seven months, and four days ago, the Gulf killed your mother."

CHAPTER 24

Dawn was stirring, giving birth to a new day, as we ambled back to the bait shop. The hibiscus hedge lining Charter Drive from Gulf Boulevard to the ICW drooped beneath a night's accumulation of moisture. At sunrise the hedge would dry and perk; the pre-dawn shadows, now ominous shades of gray, would transition to a spray of color. Gulls and pelicans would leave their roosts and take to the air as they soared and searched. As with each sunrise, the pass would come alive. But would Dad?

I hugged his waist as we walked, but he didn't speak. He wouldn't, I knew, until he'd put Mom back to rest. To this day he still blamed the Gulf for taking her. I never did.

A month or so before Mom died, I'd earned a year's perfect-attendance award at Sunday school. During that year I learned that God created all we could see and hear and touch and taste and smell. Having grown up on the water, I could easily apply each of these senses to the Gulf—yet the Gulf was only one of God's creations. Why would I blame Mom's death on something He created? I didn't. Instead, I took my anger to the top. I blamed God. This was no longer the case, but I still wanted to know why He allowed some to live and some to die.

Dad unlocked the shop and propped the front door open with a conch shell. With a parting hug, I left him with his thoughts and skirted around the building toward the *Margaret Ellen*. Sometimes Dad would snap out of his mood in a few minutes; sometimes it took days. I loved him dearly for still loving her, but if he hadn't shifted back to normal by early afternoon, I'd drag him down to Capt'n Pete's Raw Bar on Pass-A-Grille. We'd start with a tray of oysters on the half shell, move on to a bowl of boiled shrimp, and share a pitcher of draft to wash it all down.

Pete's is a throwback to an earlier time, a time Dad calls, "A better time." Knowing this, I would use Pete's, if necessary, to bring Dad around. You see, you can be down, or you can be at Pete's; you cannot be down at Pete's.

I boarded, strolled forward to the pilothouse, and started both engines. My first charter as Dad's new partner was six days away. On four of those days the *Margaret Ellen* would be in the haul out yard. This meant I had today and next Tuesday in which to make her shipshape, move my gear aboard, and to complete a number of maintenance items. When I eased her from the dock on Wednesday, I wanted her to be more than just another charter boat. I wanted her to be the "Pride of the Pass."

When the engines were up to operating temperature, I shut them down and headed for the engine room below the aft deck. I worked by rote—draining oil, changing filters, wiping spills—all the while thinking of the events since Monday afternoon when Angus and I discovered Eva's body. In actual time less than seventy-two hours had lapsed since our discovery; in mental time it seemed like years.

Part of the reason was Angus, of course. But, mad as I'd been, my anger quickly ebbed. Had it done so because I never really loved him? No. That wasn't true. In fact, despite a few of his annoying habits, I'd loved him with increasing intensity since our first meeting. Maybe, because of our age difference, I'd always known what we had wouldn't work for the long haul. Regardless, thinking about it started Roxie's cinnamon toast tumbling in my stomach. Shifting my thoughts to Myers helped, but not much.

Why was he having a problem believing Stan Avery was involved? If greed plus opportunity equaled motive, Stan Avery fit the equation. And it wouldn't be the first time he'd dipped into a client's purse. I couldn't prove anything, but, despite the alibi he gave Myers, I believed he was involved.

It was after one when I completed my below-deck chores. I wiped up, stowed my toolbox, and replaced the hatch covers. Both engines now had fresh oil and filters; both fuel lines, primary and bypass, had clean filters; and both propeller shaft stuffing boxes were repacked and adjusted. When her bottom work was complete, the *Margaret Ellen* would be ready for duty.

Dad trusted my mechanical ability, but I couldn't remember a time when he'd failed to put in an appearance while I was doing engine work. "Just takin' a peek," was his usual comment. But that hadn't happened today. During the morning Patty climbed aboard to shoot the breeze while I worked, and Cecil came as far as the catwalk to offer advice on bleeding air from the fuel filters before I tightened the last fitting. Even Skip showed up and chatted for a moment before recalling he was supposed to be ignoring me. But Dad had not. In fact, I hadn't heard or seen him since starting work at daylight.

Aunt Patty lumbered up the boarding ramp as I was washing up. She paused at the transom gate to catch her breath and to crush out her cigarette. Before she stepped aboard, she lit another. "Your dad's still lower'n a possum's pouch," she said as she shuffled across the deck. "What brought it on this time?"

I told her.

"Figured it was something like that," she said as she dropped into one of the deck chairs and motioned for me to take a seat. Not wanting to dirty a chair with my oil-stained jeans, I perched on the corner of the bait well and finished drying my hands.

"I can't add much to what you already know about your dad," she said. "He's a fine man, and I don't think one ever lived who loved a woman more than he loved your mother. Used to be when he'd get down like this he was grieving for her."

The hair on my neck bristled. "Used to be? What in the world do you mean by that?"

"I mean I don't believe that's it anymore. There's someone else—"

I threw the towel to the deck and jumped to my feet. "How can you say that? There's never been anyone else since Mom! He'll always love her. No matter what. I know he will."

She sat, hands folded on her lap, staring down the flame in my eyes. Aunt Patty was unflappable. I blinked first. She nodded at the bait well. I sat. She leaned closer. "Seaweed, honey, that someone else is you."

"Me?" What are you talking—"

"Hear me out," she said before I could go on. We waited as a delta wing fighter—flying low, engine whining—swept in from the Gulf, headed for the Air Force base south of Tampa. When she could make her words heard above the fleeting aircraft, she continued. "Seaweed, your dad has the strength of two men." She stared out over the pass and then slowly turned her gaze to the Gulf. "But that night, out there, it wasn't enough to save your mother. Now you're about to venture there. I think what's eating him up is knowing his strength can't protect you any more than it did your mother."

"That doesn't make sense." I rapped my knuckles on the bulkhead. "You know I ran this vessel all over the Gulf for three years before our tiff. Why would he feel differently about me now?"

"That's easy," she said. "When your mother was alive, she was his wife, but she was also his partner *and* his best friend. When you captained before, you were his teenaged daughter. Now you're not only a woman, you're also his new partner, and, whether he'd admit it to the world or not, you're *also* his best friend." She took my hands in hers. "Honey, your dad isn't afraid of anything on two feet, but down deep where he can't reach or fight, he's scared of losing you."

Despite the midday heat, I shivered. My throat constricted, strangling speech and breath. I jerked my hands from hers and raced to the bow.

A pair of gulls, gliding the sea breeze above a Cal 39 motoring toward the Gulf, swooped closer anticipating an offering. When none was forthcoming, they shrieked their disdain and resumed patrol over the swift-ebbing waters of the pass. Patty, with unusual discreetness, left me to myself for several minutes before easing to my side.

I dabbed my eyes with the tail of my T-shirt and choked out my question. "Why couldn't he tell me?"

She hugged my waist and led me back to the aft deck. "Like most men, your dad isn't good at explaining his emotions."

"So what am I supposed to do?"

She leaned against the gunnel and crossed her arms beneath her bosom. "Same thing women have been doing for centuries: be close. I don't mean to lean on him; I mean asking him for advice and opinions and help even when you don't need it."

"Isn't that being a little—"

"Yes, it is," she said with an all-knowing wink I'd never seen her use before. "You know a woman needs to be needed. A man does too. More so if the man is a daddy and the woman is his daughter."

"You make it sound like a recipe."

"Maybe it is," she said, "but the really smart women know it works. Keep it in mind." She pushed away from the gunnel and brushed her hands together. "Right now, though, we need to snap him out of his mood."

I told her my idea.

"Pete's? Hmm. Good thinking. I've had lunch, so if you can get him to go, I'll watch the shop."

Before I could thank her, we heard the barrel-chested rumble of Dad's laughter. What made the sound especially pleasing was the tone mixed with it. I was hearing gaiety. Genuine gaiety.

Aunt Patty nudged my side. "Sounds like your trip'll be fun instead of therapy."

I nodded agreement and skipped down the boarding ramp. At the sea wall, I spun around and waited for her to catch up. "Come on," I said, "let's see what miracle turned the tide."

We spotted the reason for Dad's jovial mood before we reached the patio. It wasn't a miracle; it was Gwen, hanging on Dad's arm, punctuating whatever he was saying with oohs and aahs. That he was back in the here-and-now was pleasing. The jealousy I felt was not. Aunt Patty and I exchanged glances. If my face looked as flushed as I imagined, she didn't say so, but she did ask, "Who's the moon-struck calf?"

I told her as we crossed the patio. We were nearly to the back door before Dad looked up, smiling with an intensity I hadn't seen in too long. "Here she is now," he said.

Gwen and Aunt Patty exchanged a "Pleased to meet you," and then Gwen answered my question before I could ask it. "I know it's Thursday, not Friday," she said, "but I wanted to make a test run. I was just telling your dad I hate being late for work."

Dad's beaming face said Gwen had made a favorable first impression. He was still grinning like a kid with a toy store credit card when he said, "I think you've made a good pick for a mate, baby."

I wanted to say I'd know more about that after trying her out, but I didn't get a chance. Dad glanced at his watch and added, "It's been a while since breakfast, so why don't you two grab some lunch?"

"Can't you join us?" Gwen asked.

Dad's shoulders drooped as he nodded toward the side of the patio. "Cecil and I got a little somethin' we're working on right now," he said, "but tell you what. You hang around till sundown and I'll treat you to one of my home cooking specials."

I bit my cheeks, trying to keep from laughing. It didn't work. "Dad, you can smoke fish and boil shrimp. Which is it going to be?"

He winked at Gwen. "Shows what she knows," he said. "Sundown, Gwen. Right here."

She'd learn the hard way. I headed for my sloop to exchange my oil stained T-shirt for a halter and my jeans for walking shorts. Dad's mood reversal erased any need to fight the gauntlet of tourist traffic to lunch at Capt'n Pete's.

CHAPTER 25

Gwen and Dad were still linked arm-in-arm when I returned to the patio. After invoking a timeout in their mutual mesmerism, I led Gwen to my favorite patio table overlooking the pass at Shanley's. Was the knot in my stomach related to Dad's obvious enchantment of Gwen? Odds were that it was.

Before dawn the temperature had been a cool and damp sixty-five degrees; now the temperature was in the eighties, but comfortably so because of the southwest breeze sweeping over the chilly waters of the pass. This was fine for now, but a southwest wind was not one to ignore, as it was tantamount to a new frontal system working closer to Florida's West Coast. When the breeze strengthened, clocked to west, and picked up the aroma of sweet spring water, I'd pay closer attention. The high, streaky cirrus and the hazy, rust-colored scud on the horizon indicated I'd be doing just that within twenty-four hours.

Lou Ann, Steve and Roxie's daughter, glided to our table as we took our seats. She's my age, with her father's height and curly, cinnamon hair, plus her mother's sense of humor, dimples, and flawless complexion. Like me, she hasn't married. Unlike me, she needed a computer database for tracking her horde of suitors.

I ordered—and endorsed the same to Gwen—but instead of a draft, I asked for a Pepsi. My reasoning was if Gwen was planning to stay for Dad's sundown surprise, we had enough afternoon left for lunch and a little boating. Dad appeared ready to accept Gwen as my mate without seeing her in action. I was not.

She listened to my raving about Roxie's steak-and-onion hoagie, but despite licking her lips, she asked for a light salad, no dressing, and a glass of water. After Lou Ann delivered our food and drink, I asked why.

She dropped her shoulders and snapped the elastic waistband of her tan shorts. "This," she said. "I've put on two pounds." Before I could pooh-pooh her worry, she added, "When I put on a pound, the camera sees two. Worse, my boss sees four. And who are you to talk anyway?" She tapped her little finger against my drink glass. "Hot afternoon and you're drinking Pepsi instead of a beer?"

I'd been behind the wheel of Ridin' Hood and *Skipjack* after having a couple, but I'd done so only once with the *Margaret Ellen*. The act led to my tiff with Dad. It was a mistake I'd never forget. It was also one I'd never repeat. "Simple," I said, cocking a thumb toward the open Gulf. "We're going for a spin after lunch." I tipped my glass in salute. "As much as I'd like a beer right now, I can't afford to set a bad example."

"We're talking my check-out ride. Right?"

"Let's call it my peace-of-mind ride. Either way, I have to know you can cut it."

"I think you'll be surprised," she said. "If not, I'd still like to hang around and see what your dad has planned for later."

Seemed fair enough to me.

She was still picking at her salad when I finished my hoagie. I scooped up what was left of my drink, pushed back from the table, and began watching a fool on a jet ski engrossed in a nautical version of Kamikaze. He was jumping the wake of a red-and-white Bayliner screaming toward the Gulf when Gwen gave forth with one of those clearing-the-throat noises that translate to, "Excuse me." I abandoned the jet skier, confident he could handle his self-destruction unobserved, and turned back to the table. "What is it?" I said.

"A confession," she said, wringing her hands like a revival evangelist. "I actually had two reasons for coming over today."

I'd suspected as much. Even so, I offered a naive reply. "I've got it! Besides seeing how long the drive would take, you wanted to spend the day in my charming company."

"That too," she said, drawing looping lines with a fingertip through the condensation rings on top of the driftwood table. "Truth is, I also wanted to know what was going on with the woman pretending to be Amber."

"What did Myers tell you?"

"Nothing. Nada. Not one damned thing." She abandoned her artwork and sat stiffly in her chair. "On top of that, the arrogant asshole won't return my calls."

"If you're off for five days," I said, "what do you care?"

"Reporter's curiosity. More so after talking with your dad. He told me about last evening and the episode earlier this morning." She leaned forward and grimaced. "How's your head?"

I'd forgotten about it until she asked. I touched at the pad still hidden by my headband. No pain. I pressed harder. Touchy, but nothing I couldn't handle.

"Fine," I said, "no problem."

"What do you think it all means?"

I studied her a moment before replying. I'd promised Myers to keep a lid on what he'd shared about the case. On the flip side, Dad was aware of everything I knew, but he'd made no promise of silence. "Before answering that," I said, "tell me how much Dad told you."

"Still protecting Myers, huh?"

"I call it keeping my word."

"Sorry," she said. "That was a dumb thing to say. I try to keep my word, too. And I told Myers I wouldn't air anything without his approval. That still goes."

"Good. So what'd Dad tell you?"

"Everything he knew about the case, I think." She ticked off items with her fingers as she spoke. "The woman calling herself Amber is really named Betty. She's the daughter of Sculley Kilgore, a con man who was also impersonating Reginald Wentworth but who may now be as dead as Eva Park. Did I miss anything?"

"You said Dad told you about Betty's visit this morning. Did he mention her taking my pistol?"

"Yes," she said, "including the fact she didn't try to use it on either of you."

What a switch. After breakfast Dad had been solemn and silent; after Gwen's arrival he switched to motor mouth. In that mode, as I well knew, there were only two who could out-talk him: Roxie, and Captain Pete's bilingual parrot, Salty.

"Okay," I said. "You know as much about the case as I do, so there's no harm in discussing my thoughts about it. Where do you want to start?"

She pushed her salad bowl aside, scooped up her fork, and began waving it like a symphony conductor's baton. "Eva!" she said. "Eva's the key. If she was killed in the commission of a burglary, I can't believe the killer would've taken the time and trouble to dump her body in the Gulf."

Those were my thoughts as well. I said so and added, "Eva was the key, no doubt about that, but I think her death was set up months ago."

"How? Who? Why?"

"Stan Avery," I said. "With one small exception, I can paint you a scene that'll show him as the killer."

"You're kidding." Her body snapped forward. "What's the exception?"

I explained about the phone calls between Avery and his secretary. "So my small exception is, he has an alibi."

She smirked. "Way to go, Seaweed. My alibi for JFK's death was I hadn't been born yet."

"I think I'm a little closer than that," I said.

"But why Stan Avery? Most people who know him agree he's a worthless turd, but a killer? Hmm. I don't know. Why do you think so?"

"Dad's theory."

"Your dad's a neat guy." She wiggled in her seat. "What's this theory of his?"

I leaned back and sipped at my drink, buying a moment before answering. Since Mom's death, there'd been few lady friends in Dad's life. Even so, with each of them I'd felt a tad of jealousy, including his latest, Cynthia. Nothing overwhelming, just the feeling they were stealing his time, time that rightfully belonged to me.

With Gwen I wasn't feeling a tad of jealousy; I was feeling a welling of it. And I knew why. Ironically, the difference in age between Dad and Gwen was the same as that between Angus and me. It was premature, ridiculous actually, but I was sitting there staring into my glass and picturing her as my stepmother. It was doing nothing to help settle my lunch.

"You all right?" Gwen said.

I leaned back to the table and set my glass aside. *Call her Mom? No way. Never.* "Sure," I said. "Just a stupid daydream."

"I do that sometimes. So tell me about this theory."

"Nothing profound," I said. "Let's use the *Margaret Ellen* as an example. Yesterday her engines ran fine. But let's say tomorrow one of them has an oil pressure problem. What happened in between? Simple. This morning I changed oil and filters on both engines. Dad would say to look over the last work I did on them. The principle works with other examples as well. The last tinkering: That's where you'll usually find the problem."

"I like that," she said, "but what does it have to do with Avery?"

"Just this. I think if we look at Eva's life the same way, it'll give us the answer."

"Some tinkering or a change involving Stan Avery, you mean?"

"Yes," I said, "and I think what we're looking for will be obvious if we start where Eva and Christine came into their inheritance."

"How could that be? Stan was just a kid back then."

"True, but you can't see a change if you don't know what went before it."

"Okay," she said. "Eva and Christine have each inherited twenty-five-million dollars. Now what?"

"At the time of receiving their inheritance Mack Avery was their family's attorney and financial advisor. At this point he began working for Eva and Christine as well. Year after year Eva's net worth increased. Christine, on the other hand, pissed money away as fast as she got her hands on it."

"Yes, they were opposites. Everyone knew that."

"Hold on," I said. "Five years ago, when Christine was killed along with Eva's husband, Eva's net worth was four times greater than the amount she'd inherited. That, despite being a philanthropist. On the other hand Christine's net worth wasn't worth a nickel more than ever."

"That wasn't Mack Avery's fault."

"No," I said, "and had it not been for the provision in Christine's trust barring her from touching the principal amount, I doubt she would've had *any* money left at the time of her death."

"So Christine's death is our change?"

"It was a minor change," I said, "but it's not the one we want. After Christine's death, Eva became administrator of Christine's trust. Eva put Amber on an allowance, and with Mack Avery's help, Christine's trust principal began to grow for the first time. Then a year ago Mack retired. His son, Stan, began managing Eva's financial affairs."

"Ah, ha," she said. "That's the change. Right?"

"You bet. For twenty-five years, with Mack Avery as her financial advisor, Eva prospered. A year after Stan entered the picture, he's sucking up to Amber and Eva's dead."

"Shit, Seaweed, we're talking the biggest story of my career. 'Prominent Attorney Kills Philanthropist.'"

Except—"

"Yeah," she said as she slumped back in her seat. "Except he has an alibi."

CHAPTER 26

Gwen continued to slouch in her chair, biting her lower lip and staring at the rings of condensation she had doodled in minutes before. Then her eyes widened, her mouth opened slightly, and the tip of her tongue started making laps around her lips. I waited and watched, thinking she was about to speak. She didn't. Instead, she picked up her fork. This time she didn't brandish it, she held it between her thumb and first finger and began a gentle, rhythmic tapping against the side of her water glass. Until she missed a beat, it sounded liked a drum solo of Johnny Cash's "Folsom Prison Blues."

My thoughts shifted to our after-lunch agenda, mulling the numerous items I'd have to cover to insure her proficiency. If Gwen had picked up some boating skills during her time aboard the thirty and thirty-six footers she'd mentioned, her checkout would run smoothly and I would soon know she had what it took to handle the job. The downside was that once she knew what the job entailed, she might not want it. My next option wasn't a pleasant thought, either. That is, there were several experienced mates in the area, but each, as I well knew, was unemployed for good reason. Gwen, despite her infatuation for Dad, remained my best bet.

"Perry Mason!" Gwen shouted.

Gwen's booming exclamation was loud enough to have been heard from Gulf Boulevard. I snapped my attention back to her. She was no longer slouching; she was perched at the edge of her chair, upright as a fireplug on a street corner.

"I know how he did it, Seaweed. I saw the same thing on one of the summer reruns of Perry Mason."

"Saw what?"

Now that she'd grabbed the attention of the other diners on the patio, she leaned closer and whispered. "It was a lowlife attorney like Avery. You just knew he was the killer, but he had a perfect alibi. It was a two-hour show, and I chewed my nails the whole time thinking he was going to get away with it. Then, at the last minute, Perry figured out how he did it."

I scooted to the edge of my chair, glancing at her nails as I did so. They were short, like mine, but they were also well groomed. Maybe she had a tendency to exaggerate. "Care to share," I said.

"It was the phone calls that reminded me." She took a full-fist grip on her fork and began waving it in time with her words. "During the day on Friday, Avery called his secretary. She didn't call him until that evening. Right?"

"That's what Myers said."

"So let's try this," she said. "His first call to her, the one telling her he was going to see a doctor, was probably made from his home. Then, making credit-card calls so he could direct dial, he called her from the airport just before he left. In that one he told her not to call him because he was going to take a nap. Then he called her from Atlanta just before she'd be closing up the office. In that one he asked her to call him later that evening." She dropped the fork and rubbed her hands together. "What do you think?"

"Sounds great," I said, "but how could she call him when he wasn't home?"

"Simple. It's how Perry caught the scumbag attorney. Before Avery left here, all he had to have was a number where he could take her call Friday evening. After he told her not to call him, he set his home phone for call forwarding. At nine-thirty, when she did call, the phone rang wherever he was in New Jersey. He answered. How could she have known or have even suspected he wasn't right there at home where she'd dialed?"

"Call forwarding has been around a while," I said. "Don't you think Myers has checked that out?"

She stuck out her tongue and made an obscene noise as she jumped to her feet. "Myers? You've got to be kidding. I know someone at the phone company who'll check it out."

I thought it took a court order to get someone's phone records. At least it did on one of the TV shows I'd watched recently. She was gone before I could mention it.

Ten minutes passed and she hadn't returned. I paid the check, left a tip for Lou Ann, and headed for the front door. Gwen was still on the phone. I stepped outside.

A high-level haze covered the sky, dimming the sun's brilliance but doing little to ease its heat. The breeze, now at about twelve knots, had clocked a few degrees past west. The front was closer. My early morning run to the haul-out yard was shaping up to be a wet and blustery one.

I turned at the sound of the screen door screeching open and banging shut. Gwen stomped toward me, kicking at the pinecones littering the oyster-shell walk. "After all I've done for that little twit you'd think she could return one simple favor!"

I gave her my previous thought about phone records.

"That's what Collette said."

"So why are you pissed at her?"

"Why? The police have Avery's records, but I know Collette saw 'em first. She knows what I want; she just won't tell me."

"She's just doing her job," I said. "Besides you can't leak anything even if she did tell you."

"That's not the point. She owes me."

Starting for the bait shop, I said, "Forget it. If the police have Avery's phone records, that means they're interested in him. That's good enough for me. For now we have other business to tend to."

She marched along at my side, muttering and swinging her arms like a majorette. *Hmm. She had a temper and she kicked. That gave us two things in common. Three, if I counted Dad.*

We'd just passed Danny's when she stopped and spun to face me. "Piss on Collette. There's something else that'll show he's the one."

"A confession would be nice," I said.

Gwen raised one eyebrow and said, "Or finding out Avery knew Kilgore before Kilgore began calling himself Reginald Wentworth."

Believing what I did about the case, I was sure he had. I said as much, and asked, "But how do you propose to prove it?"

She placed her hands on her hips, shifted her weight to one foot, and began tapping the toes of the other. "Avery's a lawyer. Kilgore was a con man. What's the most likely reason for them to have met?"

"A legal proceeding, I suppose."

"Exactly. And if they did so in the last few years, I can find out with an electronic data search."

I'd heard of such things but didn't possess a clue about how to go about it. "You know how to do that?"

"Well, not exactly," she said, "but I know someone who does."

I tried not to smirk. "That's what you thought about Collette."

"This is different." She eased her shoulders back. "Brian has an incentive for helping. He's my assistant at the station."

Brian? Hmm. "You want to call him?"

"You bet. Then I'm ready to qualify for my new job."

On the road to becoming a licensed charter captain, I'd had to know more than how to start an engine and read a compass. Much more. A mate, on the other hand, did not. Still, a knowledgeable mate, or one willing to learn, was a blessing to any captain. With that in mind, I approached Gwen's checkout with three goals: Before we left the dock, I wanted to determine the extent of her boating skills and her willingness to learn more. Then I wanted to test her sea legs under actual job conditions.

I began with a familiarization of the *Margaret Ellen*, which included emphasis on the location and proper use of all safety and emergency gear, and ended with a hands-on lesson of the marine VHF radio, including the use of the weather, boat-to-boat, and emergency channels. The *Margaret Ellen* carried two marine radios. The primary radio was used for all the purposes I'd pointed out but normally stayed tuned to channel six-eight, the channel Dad monitored at the bait shop; the other one stayed tuned to channel sixteen, the official calling and emergency channel. In the days ahead, as time allowed, I'd introduce her to the single sideband radio and encourage her to study for an amateur radio operator's license so she might use the ham radio as well.

After our two-hour session of discussion and demonstration, I asked a few questions. She had the answers, which told me she hadn't just nodded her way through it all for my benefit; she'd absorbed it. With the accomplishment of my first two goals, and two hours of daylight left in our overcast afternoon, we headed offshore to address the third.

Under settled weather, with the breeze out of the northeast where it belongs this time of year, the Gulf hosts ideal boating conditions. With the approach of a front, as was now the case, the wind clocks into the west and boating conditions deteriorate. First on the scene is a long-fetch swell, followed by a chop. Then breaking seas. I take the first two as going with the job. With the third the *Margaret Ellen* stays tucked in her berth, and I curl up with a good book.

Long before reaching the sea buoy, we encountered the swell I'd been expecting; the size of it, however, was something I didn't understand. In my estimation a three-foot sea was more than should've been running before a mediocre front. I shared this view with Gwen and then cocked a thumb at the radio. "See what NOAA has to say."

Without hesitation she punched through the weather channels and then returned to the one with the strongest signal.

" … the low pressure area now stationary in the central Gulf has sustained winds of thirty knots and is expected to begin moving east by 0600 Eastern Standard Time on Friday. All marine interests along the Gulf Coast between Ft. Myers and Cedar Keys should stay tuned for further developments."

The Atlantic Hurricane Season would officially end in a few weeks, but someone, it seemed, had failed to notify Mother Nature to tone it down. I switched the radio back to channel six-eight and said, "Okay, the sooner we get this over with, the sooner we can head for home."

She beamed. "And check out your dad's sundown surprise."

"That too," I said, with a feeling I didn't really feel.

It was a dirty trick, but I couldn't think of a better way to test Gwen's sea legs. I turned, putting the sea on the starboard beam, and pulled the speed back until the *Margaret Ellen* was rolling gunnel to gunnel. Satisfied we were getting maximum roll, I set the autopilot and led her to the aft deck.

Like I'd done in the past, I planned to run three types of charter trips: half day, full day, and an occasional twenty-four hour, dawn-to-dawn one. Wednesday's booking was a half-day trip, so I started my demonstration with the requirements for it by running through the duties we would actually perform if we'd had that party of six aboard. Thirty minutes later I'd learned all I set out to learn. I'd also had enough. She was still on her feet and still at my side. I achieved my goals like a good half-inning in baseball: three up, three down.

"That's it," I said. "Checkout's over. Stow the rods. I'll set course for home."

"Well, how'd I do?"

"We'll discuss the exam after I grade your papers." I grinned at the question filling her eyes, hugged her waist, and stepped into the pilothouse. I heard Dad's voice before I reached the helm.

Before giving attention to the radio, I disengaged the autopilot, spun the wheel to put the stern to the wind, and pushed the throttles forward until we were smooth stepping over the swells. When the sea buoy was in sight, I grabbed the mike.

"Cobia base, the *Margaret Ellen*, go ahead."

"Been calling for twenty minutes, baby, ya got trouble?"

"Negative. Just finished the checkout. We're headed in. ETA thirty minutes, over."

"How'd she do?"

"Great," I said. "She's got the job…if she wants it." Pausing a moment, I wondered if Dad's inquiry about Gwen was the purpose of his call. No way to know without asking. "So that's why you called?"

"No, it's Gwen's friend, Brian. The guy called. Said he'd found a match for her search. That make any sense?"

"You bet," I said, glancing back at the aft deck. Gwen was still busy stowing equipment. She wouldn't like it, but there was no other choice. "Ah, Dad, on my last trip out here I asked you to make a phone call for me. Remember?"

"Our party pooper, right?"

"Roger that," I said. "Call him again. He needs Brian's info. Immediately."

As I signed off with Dad, Gwen entered the pilothouse. There were two things to tell her. The question was which one to start with. Her inquiry settled it. "Exam results in yet?"

Fighting to keep a smile off my face, I turned to Gwen and said, "As a matter of fact, yes. Take the helm a moment." I pointed to our next marker a mile ahead. "If you know the rules of the road, you know to keep that one to starboard."

She saluted and took the wheel, a wide grin covering her face.

While she was occupied, I removed a pair of dark-blue ball caps from the hanging locker. Both had gold stitching saying, "*The Margaret Ellen.*" One was labeled, "Captain." I put it on and moved back to the helm. I handed the other cap to Gwen, the one that said, "Mate."

She grabbed me in a bear hug and began dancing in a circle. We quickly drifted off course. Breaking free of her grasp, I pointed at the helm and reminded her we were doing eighteen knots.

"Aye, aye, ma'am."

She tightened her grip on the wheel, stared straight ahead, and didn't speak as I told her about Dad's call. Her response wasn't unexpected, but it wouldn't do.

"Gwen, I want you aboard as my mate, but it's your call."

"You don't understand. This is a big story."

"No," I said, "It's something you don't understand."

"Like what?"

"Like I entered your big story before you did. Since then, I've been in the newspapers and on TV. I couldn't have bought greater publicity, but when Dad made his offer, it was decision time: charter or continue investigating. My choice was easy."

"So you're saying—"

"Yes, that's exactly what I'm saying. You can do this, or you can go back to what you've been doing. Give me your answer by the time we dock."

CHAPTER 27

G wen snatched the cap off her head, spun from the helm, and stomped out of the pilothouse. I took the wheel and watched as she marched forward as far as the bowsprit would allow. With her feet straddling the anchor, she snapped into a parade rest, hands clutching her cap, and facing the shoreline now creeping into view. She seemed oblivious to the flying spray or to her own hair whipping in the wind like a tattered flag.

Twenty minutes later Dad's fuel dock was off the port bow and she was still locked in the same position. Turning out of the channel, I slowed the engines to an idle and made for the *Margaret Ellen's* slip. We'd reached the moment of truth. She had to put her ass in gear, or I'd have to hit the air horns to summon Dad's help with docking. Then, as if reading my mind, she smoothed her hair, put on her cap, and began shaking out the docking lines and rigging the fenders. She was in position and ready with the boat hook when we reached the slip. Berthing and tying up went as smoothly as each element I'd put her through in the previous three hours. She was good. Damned good. But would she stay?

I shut down the engines and electronics and led her through the after-docking chore of washing down the decks. Still in silence, we reconnected the electric cord and the water line and made a final inspection of the docking lines.

"That's it," I said. At the catwalk's junction with the sea wall, I sat facing the pass and patted the space beside me. "Have a seat and tell me how it's going to be."

She scuffed her feet across the planking as she ambled toward me, but she didn't sit at my side; she settled onto the catwalk before me and wiggled into a cross-legged position. "Don't worry, Seaweed, I haven't changed my mind. If you still want me, I want the job."

Those were the words I wanted to hear. Even so, her tone worried me. She looked worried, too. "Of course I want you," I said, "but is there something else on your mind? Something I should know?"

"Should know? No, but I'd like you to understand." For the first time since we'd sat, she lifted her eyes to mine. "When I started with Channel

Five, it was with the dream of earning an anchor position. Years passed, but it never happened. Then, six months ago, a slot opened. Not a top one, just late news and weekend anchor. A position I'd been promised. Instead, the studio brought in Pam Meckler from Ocala. The next day I wrote my letter of resignation."

"But you didn't—"

"Turn it in? No. I was working a big story, the one on Medicare fraud. I did a good job. Thought I'd at least get a pat on the back. It didn't happen. Last week I was in the dumps. I pulled out my letter, but, again, I didn't turn it in. Then on Monday you found Eva's body. Now I'm in a position to be covering the story of the year."

"Gwen, story or no story, we couldn't keep Brian's discovery a secret."

"I know that."

"Then I don't understand what you're getting at."

"I'll tell you," she said, "but I need your help."

I could have waited and given her time to explain, but I didn't like the direction we were heading. I raised my hand. "Gwen, you asked me to give you a chance. I have. Our first trip is next Wednesday. If you want this, you have to quit the other."

"My contract requires a two-week notice."

"I have no problem with that. You said you'd be working nights, so for the next two weeks I won't book anything but half-day trips. If you need help beyond that, I can't promise a thing."

"No!" she said. "That's perfect."

"What's perfect?"

She leaned closer and took my hands. "I'll turn in my resignation tomorrow. That'll put me out of there in two weeks. You have my word. In the meanwhile I'd like to work the story. Eva's story. Nothing would please me more than to hand in the story of the year and then walk out. It's silly, and I know it's an ego thing, but that's the way I'd like to leave. You know, put my nose in the air and give them one of those frankly-my-dear things." She released my hands and gave me a weak smile. "It won't happen that way, but I'd like to try."

Myers would've called it the woman-to-woman thing, but I understood. I told her so and stood, pulling her to her feet. "Now," I said, "unless you're really worried about your waistline, I'd like to treat my new mate to a beer."

The evening was midway into that delightful span between sundown and full dark when we settled into a pair of lounge chairs at the edge of the patio.

The heat of the day was gone, and it wasn't yet cool enough to need a long-sleeved shirt. Best of all, the breeze sweeping the patio was sufficient to keep the mosquitoes at bay without driving us away as well.

Considering her commitment to crew with me, I wanted to know how she planned to stay on top of her potential story-of-the-year. When I fetched our second beer from the cooler, I asked. She brightened as she began explaining.

"I already have the edge," she said.

"How so?"

"For openers, I have the only film taken of the scene at Hangman's Key. I have my interview with you and Angus out there, and I have all the info you and your dad gave me here. I have—"

"Orders not to leak any of it," I said.

"Yes, but let me explain. I also think I've guessed correctly about Avery's use of call forwarding. And now Brian's uncovered some connection between Avery and Kilgore."

That statement triggered a thought. "I thought you'd want to call Brian," I said.

"I do, but I didn't want to be rude about sharing my first beer with my new boss."

"Big deal," I said. "You know where the phone's at when you want it." I made a circle in the air with one finger. "Okay, you've rounded up a wad of info, but you can't divulge it. Now what?"

She pushed her beer aside and rubbed her hands together. "I'll handle the story the same way the media does celebrity obituaries."

"Which is?"

"You don't wait for the final curtain to write the review. I'll do the same, putting a story together with what I know and filling in with what I think. When the case wraps up, I'll make adjustments as necessary. That way, even if the other stations are in at the end, I'll have my story first."

"If it happens in the next two weeks," I said.

"Yeah. If." She stood and said, "Right now I'd like to call Brian."

While we'd talked I'd noticed Dad and Cecil fussing over a large pot on the gas grill. I also noticed a nearby table covered with a lace-edged tablecloth and a place setting for four. A pair of hurricane candles nestled deep within glass globes—one red and one green—sat at either end of the table. I couldn't remember seeing the candles or the tablecloth in years. Surely Gwen's presence hadn't inspired Dad to dig them out.

Gwen was still inside the bait shop when Cecil called out, "Good night."

I rushed over to give him a hug and then walked with him to his car. When Cecil was safely on his way, I turned back to the patio. Dad gave another look at his party setup, swung by the cooler for a beer, and then dropped into Gwen's chair. "Where'd she go?" he said.

I returned to my seat and said, "She's calling Brian."

"Good. While we got a moment, there's somethin' I want to ask you."

"Fire away," I said.

He stood and reached for my hand. "Let's do it on the *Margaret Ellen*. I want your mother to hear this too."

I shivered, nearly spilling my beer. "Mom!"

"I'll explain," he said.

We ambled across the patio in silence, reaching the *Margaret Ellen's* aft deck just as the floodlights on the fuel dock came on. Their master of on-and-off, a light-sensing gadget half the size of a tennis ball, had declared official darkness. At dawn the little sucker would reverse its decision.

Dad dropped into his favorite deck chair; I took the one alongside him. A number of times over the years—usually late at night, and long after I should've been asleep—I'd heard him talking to Mom from that very chair. He saw me one evening, watching from the shadows, but he'd never offered to explain. And I'd never been able to ask.

He laid his arm along the back of my chair, stroking my shoulder with his fingertips. The only sounds breaking the evening silence were the hum of traffic crossing the high span and the tail swishing of mullet working around the pilings beneath the catwalk.

"I think it's time I did something," he said, "but I wanted you to know first." He cocked a thumb toward the patio and added, "You noticed the table?"

Oh, yes, I'd noticed all right, but mentioning my thoughts about it didn't seem like a great idea. I nodded instead.

"Cynthia's coming over tonight." He pulled a small box from his shirt pocket and placed it in my hand. "I'd like to give this to her."

CHAPTER 28

There was no need to open the black velvet box to know what it contained. As he'd said, "It was time." And Cynthia was right for him. In my heart I knew this. Even so, there'd been countless times over the years when I'd thought of this moment. A few times, knowing Dad needed to put Mom to rest and get on with his life, I looked forward to the occasion; most times, though, I dreaded the day when it would finally happen.

While slowly lifting the lid on the tiny box, I prepared to give an enthusiastic ooh or an aah or maybe a sharp intake of breath to seal his belief in my pleasure. No faking was needed. The engagement ring was a lovely gold band engraved with lines, flowing and swirling like an ancient language. The single-diamond setting, however, was in vogue and head-turning gorgeous. Dad had made a lovely choice, and I was sure Cynthia would be thrilled.

I closed the lid, pressed the box back into his hand, and launched into self-admonishment for my earlier thoughts and fears concerning him and Gwen. How could I have been so dense? Long before I was half done with my mental butt kicking, he asked, "What do you think?"

Summoning the maturity to say the words he wanted to hear came easier than I'd expected. "You should do it, Dad." I kissed his cheek and added, "It's time, and if I may speak for Mom, I believe she'd want you to do it, too."

In the minutes before Cynthia arrived, we discussed his plans for the evening. The wine before a candlelight dinner met my approval. So did the menu: lobster boiled by Dad; trimmings supplied by Roxie. It was how he planned to present the ring that triggered my argument. "Wine her and dine her, Dad, but don't you dare bring out the ring until you're alone with her. Years from now she'll remember every detail about tonight. Gwen and I have no business being a part of it." I pinched his cheek for emphasis. "After dinner you two disappear. Promise?"

He ruffled my hair and stood. "Here she is now."

"Dad!"

"All right already, I promise."

I hung back to allow him a few moments alone with Cynthia. He didn't get ten seconds with her before Gwen danced out the rear door of the bait shop. Dad made gestures of introduction and then pointed my way. After exchanging a handshake with Cynthia and a hug with Dad, Gwen sprinted across the patio, ran up the boarding ramp, and dropped into Dad's chair. "It's over, Seaweed, it's over."

"What's over?"

"Avery!" she said. "He's the one!"

"What are you talking about?"

"Myers. Called. Talkin' with Brian. The connection—"

"Whoa," I said. "Slow down, catch your breath, and start over."

She jumped up and began making laps around the aft deck. With her hands on her hips and her chest heaving, she looked like a marathon runner who'd just crossed the finish line. She made three laps before dropping back into her chair. "Whew. Okay, I'm ready."

"Then start at the beginning," I said.

"Brian came through," she said. "He found a link between Stan Avery and Sculley Kilgore. It's weak, but it's enough to prove they'd met before Sculley arrived on the scene pretending to be Reginald Wentworth."

"A court case?"

"You bet. Two years ago. Kilgore was on trial, a swindle case involving a West Palm Beach widow. It wasn't Stan's case, but he had a role assisting Kilgore's attorney."

"That's good enough for me," I said. "What about Myers?"

"Well, I'd just hung up with Brian when the phone rang. It was Myers. He'll be here in a few minutes."

I couldn't imagine why. I asked.

"Something to do with your gun. Said he'd explain when he got here. But get this. Whatever's happened isn't public knowledge yet. I get the exclusive." She squeezed my hand and added, "Can you believe it? Grim Lips kept his word!"

I'd believe that when it happened. "And the 'it's-over' business you mentioned. What's that about?"

"There's a warrant for Stan and Amber's arrest," she said. "When they're nabbed, it's over."

I doubted that. After his first-degree-murder conviction and subsequent death sentence, Ted Bundy circumvented justice for over a dozen years. How much longer would he have avoided justice if he'd also been a lawyer? No

174

matter. Myers was due any minute, and I wasn't about to let him screw up another evening, especially not this one. I told Gwen about Dad's plans and said, "Wait out front and head off Myers. Take him to Shanley's. I'll be there as soon as I can get Dad alone and explain what's going on."

"Got it," was all I heard before she raced down the boarding ramp and across the patio. Her previous excitement about an evening with Dad was lost in her current excitement for a story. If she maintained the same level of enthusiasm for chartering, I'd be one happy captain. I picked up our empty beer bottles and headed for the patio.

The overcast was darker, with heavier cloud fragments racing in at treetop level from the northwest. The breeze, now laced with the scent of rain, was also stronger, yet the hurricane candles, true to their reputation, were holding their own. A NOAA weather update wasn't needed to know the low-pressure system was tracking our way. I loved storms, but not on weekends, at funerals, or parties—especially an engagement party.

I spent an anxious twenty minutes talking and sipping a glass of wine with Dad and Cynthia, half expecting Myers to barge in at any moment. While Cynthia was at the bait tank inspecting the live lobsters, I briefed Dad on the latest. When she returned, I wished them a memorable evening and made what I hoped was a graceful exit.

Gwen and Myers were sitting face to face over a pitcher of draft at a booth in Shanley's dining room. It wasn't my favorite location, but it was out of the wind. I ordered onion rings and a Pepsi before crossing the room and sliding into the booth next to Gwen and her interview equipment. Knowing Myers wasn't long on greetings, I didn't expect one, nor did I bother with one. I gave him a nod and fired a question. "You found my gun?"

I was right-on about the greeting, but in gentlemanly fashion he topped off Gwen's glass before he said, "You could say that."

I glanced at Gwen. She shrugged.

He placed her glass on a coaster, nudged it across the table, and turned to me. "First, as I've explained to Gwen, nothing I say tonight leaves your lips before noon tomorrow. After that you can shout it from the top of the Skyway Bridge."

"What's so special about noon?" I said.

He sipped his beer and ran his tongue across his lips. "Because that's as long as I can keep a lid on Betty Kilgore's death."

Gwen and I snapped upright like puppets back for a curtain call. Her mouth was open, but I spoke first. "Death! How in the hell can she be dead?"

"With your gun," he said. "There was also a clumsy attempt to make it look like suicide."

Even knowing his meaning, I asked anyway. "Make it look? Like in—"

"Yeah," he said. "She was murdered."

Hours earlier Betty had expressed intent to murder the one she believed had killed her father. Instead, she was now another victim. "Where was she?" I said. "And when did it happen?"

"I'll tell you what I can in a moment," he said.

"Whoa!" I offered an angelic smile. "You said it was my gun. You can't think … and even if you did, Dad'll tell ya I was here all day."

"Relax," he said. "The only reason I called was to tell you that your part in this mess was over."

"I'm very happy you've accepted that. So what about my gun?"

"It'll be a while," he said, "but you'll get it back. Anyway, when I realized I was speaking with Gwen instead of you, I decided to come over."

Gwen pushed her glass aside, placed a notebook on the table, and began fiddling with the settings on her tape recorder. I looked from her equipment to him and said, "So this is about your promise on Hangman's Key?"

He raised his glass like a convention speaker about to propose a toast. "She's kept her part of our deal," he said. "I'm ready to keep mine."

So I'd been wrong about Myers. As Gwen pumped him for information, I polished off the order of onion rings and a second glass of Pepsi. I was delighted to learn none of the information she'd dug up on Stan Avery was actually news to Myers. Through channels he referred to only as *sources*, Myers said he'd learned of Stan Avery's brief link with Sculley Kilgore and of Stan's use of call forwarding to support an alibi. Myers would always remain a certifiable Grim Lips in my book, but I liked knowing he was also a proficient one.

What I didn't like, however, was the thought that came to mind as I listened to his summation of the case. That is, his take contained too many items that were alleged or circumstantial. And those items, as I knew from watching TV detective dramas, were the exact items defense lawyers used to get their clients off the hook. My wish was for Eva's murderer to pay the full price for his deed, not to escape on a technicality.

Betty's murder promised to be different. Myers had learned her whereabouts after leaning on Jean Hampton. In the telling, however, he failed to share his definition of "leaning." Even so, Betty's killer found her first. If there was a bright spot to be found in this, it was that the killer had botched the job. Myers wasn't willing to discuss the details, but he hinted at *hard evidence* and an eyewitness, both of which pointed at Stan Avery.

Gwen placed a new tape in her recorder and flipped back to the beginning of her notes. "I'll read back the highlights," she said. "Jump in if I've got something wrong."

Myers nodded, scooped up his beer, and slumped in the corner of the booth.

"It won't have anything to do with what you've told me," she said, "but I want to start my story with Eva's background and touch on the highlights of her community involvement. From there I'll move to the discovery of her body and then present the events leading to the arrest warrants for Stan and Amber."

"Hold it," Myers said. "Good detective work takes a careful look at background. Spot any change in what has been the norm and lock in on it. That's where you'll turn up the key. In this case it was Stan Avery entering the picture after his dad's retirement."

Gwen looked at me and grinned. "Like the oil pressure example you used."

"Works for Dad," I said.

"A turning point," she said. "Good slant. Okay. Stan Avery's dip into a client's funds is a matter of record. I'll use it to establish character. Two years ago he met Sculley Kilgore, which at the time was a benign encounter. A year later the malignancy started when Stan replaced his father as manager of Eva's financial affairs and Sculley turned up as Reginald Wentworth to woo Eva. It was also about that time when Stan began his romantic move on Amber."

She paused and looked at Myers.

"What's the problem?" he said.

"The problem is, from that point forward I'm out of facts. All I have is your scenario."

"I think I have it nailed," he said.

As I recalled, he'd said much the same about two previous scenarios. I kept it to myself.

She continued her deadpan expression.

"Look," he said, "I can't cut you in on the hard evidence. That'll come out at the trial."

"Fine," she said, "but I have a choice of roads after Stan makes the scene. Did he recruit Sculley for a simple con on Eva? One he'd share in financially? Or was he going for it all right from the start?"

"I think it started simply enough," Myers said, "but it just got out of hand. Maybe Eva caught on, or Stan was afraid she was about to. Something like that."

Gwen poked a finger at her notes. "For my time frame, that would be just before Eva was supposed to have left with her fake Reginald to pick up the yacht?"

"Right," he said. "And to stay with the thought of a simple con for a moment, maybe Sculley's target was only Eva's jewelry. That fits his MO."

"And her real set of jewelry is still missing?" Gwen said.

"No sign of it."

I butted in. "How about the imitation set Betty was carrying."

"We found her monster purse with her body. No jewelry."

"Okay," Gwen said. "For reasons we don't know, Stan killed Eva, dumped her body in the Gulf, and staged a burglary at her home. He then managed to get Sculley and his daughter to fly out as Eva Park and Reginald Wentworth. He went along to kill them both. Had he done so the bodies would've been identified as Sculley and Betty Kilgore, just two murder victims with no obvious connection to Eva. As far as the world was concerned, she disappeared with the non-existent Reginald Wentworth." She leaned back in the booth and added, "Damn! Stan would've been home free if Eva's body hadn't turned up and Betty hadn't cut loose in Atlanta."

"If!" Myers said as he did his eyebrow wiggle. "The thing is, even the smart ones trip on the little ifs."

"Well I have another one," I said. "If Amber was in Europe during all the action, why the warrant on her?"

"Simple," Myers said. "Considering her romantic link with Stan, I'd be a fool not to believe she had some part in this. In fact, her trip to Paris may have been to set up a safe haven."

"How would that help if they're in Paris and the money's here?"

"That's the cute part," he said. "Most of the money isn't here. Other than a few million in real estate, Eva had the bulk of her wealth in world-market securities. Stan now controls the strings. He can pull them from anywhere in the world."

"All but a few million!" I said. "Crap! You make it sound like loose change under a sofa cushion."

"Compared with the total, it is," he said.

"Jeez. A few ... okay, how about the yacht?"

"En route, as far as I know. We'll impound it when it arrives, but my feeling is the yacht was never more than a smoke screen. The Coast Guard is listening for radio traffic. If they hear something, they'll alert us."

"Whoa," I said. "That might not be good enough. Most oceangoing vessels are also equipped with side band radios."

"What's that?"

"You've probably heard them called ship-to-shore. The point is if Avery had a similar radio, he could've stayed in touch with the yacht since it left. In fact, he wouldn't need a radio. He could've contacted the yacht by phone using the high-seas operator. Either way, the Coast Guard wouldn't have heard the calls. Stan could've already set up a meeting spot. In fact he could be on the way to South America right now for all we know."

"I don't think so," Myers said. "Betty was killed this morning."

The idea still sounded good to me. "So why don't I hear an optimistic tone? You really think they've fled the area in another way. Right?"

"That's my feeling," he said. "Stan keeps a Mooney 21 at Albert Whitted airport, but it won't do him any good. We're watching it. We're also trying to locate their cars. Both are missing."

Debbie, the dining room waitress, approached my side and whispered, "Your dad just called. Said he was about to disappear." She frowned and added, "Also said you'd know what he meant."

Gwen and Myers hashed out a final understanding. He would hold a news conference at noon the following day. While reporters from the other stations attended, Gwen's story would be airing on Channel Five's midday news.

Knowing Dad's evening was safe from ruin, I invited Myers to return to the bait shop with us for leftovers. He declined the offer but did pick up our tab before leaving. I shot the breeze with Debbie while Gwen used Shanley's wall phone to call in her story. That done, we walked back to the bait shop.

Over a lobster tail and a bowl of salad, I told Gwen I didn't expect her to return the following morning to help me move the *Margaret Ellen* to the haul out yard. She had a suggestion: Allow her to bunk aboard my sloop, and she'd be happy to tag along and use the opportunity for more learning. It seemed like a deal to me. The breeze was thick with moisture and steady at twenty knots. Gusts were touching thirty. I gave the docking lines a close look before we turned in.

CHAPTER 29

The noise started with a single tap—then another, and another, building to a deafening staccato. I jerked upright from a deep and dreamless sleep, nearly knocking myself out when my head slammed into the cabin top.

How in the world could my head have hit the cabin top? And why did my body feel as if it were a discarded mass sitting in a debris-filled ditch? Simple answer: My sloop was tilted twenty degrees to starboard. And it had happened before.

Hello frontal system.

My berth behind the bait shop was aligned north to south. It was also the westernmost of the three slips, making my floating home's port side vulnerable to every storm system sweeping in off the Gulf. With this one, if I'd been the primary target, the hit was a bull's-eye.

The hail pounding the hatch just inches from my aching head sounded like dueling jackhammers. Above that roar the wind shrieked through the standing rigging, the halyards whipped the aluminum mast, and the docking lines groaned in protest.

I clicked on the light. The articles that'd been on my portside shelf were now the lumps beneath my flannel comforter and me. I groped for the bulkhead-mounted VHF, flipped the power switch, and spun the dial to the weather channel. It appeared the radio was the only item in my berth that was still where it belonged.

" … a tidal surge estimated at two feet above normal will accompany this severe line of thunderstorms. Nautical interests along the West Coast of Florida between Cedar Keys and Cape Romano should expect gusty winds, heavy rain, lightning strikes, and the possibility of hail. This line will move ashore at 0500—"

A switch to channel sixteen produced dead silence. No radio traffic. The same system hitting the area during daylight hours would've triggered a spate of distress calls. I searched for my alarm clock. *0430? The man just said* ….

I clawed my way out of the berth and then nearly tumbled into the hanging locker while grabbing for my foul-weather jacket. Why bother putting it on?

The hip-length slicker would do little to hide my nakedness, and at 0430, in the midst of a hailstorm, who cared? With the hood pulled tightly about my face, I reeled up the companionway.

In the glow of lights from Dad's fuel dock I could see the thundering wall of hail sweeping east down the channel. An icy rain, driven by at least forty-knot gusts, stung my face and legs. I crept across the cockpit and knelt at the stanchion gate, timing several surges of the boat before leaping to the catwalk. My portside lines were singing under the strain of the wind and the current hissing past the hull. After first easing the bow line, I then duckwalked to the stern to ease its line. Better, but before I could give attention to the spring lines, the wind died and the rain slowed to a sprinkle.

The first line of the system was past. More squall lines would sweep through before the sky cleared and the wind clocked to north, but the worst was over. Should I readjust the lines? Nah. *Bonita* was riding easy. Later, when it was warm and dry, would be soon enough.

Gwen, of course, slept through it all. After drying off and dressing, I woke her and then headed to the bait shop to start a pot of coffee. Silly me. If I'd ever been up and about before Dad, I couldn't recall the occurrence. This morning, early as it was, was no exception. He was not only up, he was on his second cup when I hurried through the rear door. His wide grin and warm hug said more than words about his evening with Cynthia. I asked anyway. If a wedding was in the offing, I needed to know. That is, I didn't own a dress.

Dad was still hedging about having set a wedding date when Gwen joined us. I winked at Dad, turned her around, and herded her out the door. What Dad had to say was personal, and I wanted to hear it privately.

At six a.m., after a toast and coffee breakfast at Shanley's, Gwen and I had the *Margaret Ellen* moving east up Big Tarpon Pass Channel. Our run to the haul out yard wouldn't take an hour, and all of it, thankfully, would be through the protected waters of the Intracoastal Waterway, which even in a big blow were usually passable. The Gulf, by contrast, had faces ranging from tranquil to downright angry. At the moment it no doubt was wearing a hostile one. I was glad we didn't have to face it.

A squall, with zero visibility for a minute or so, caught us while turning south into the ICW. I slowed, watching the depth sounder to stay in the deeper water. Gwen, without prompting, dialed in the weather channel. The recorded message from NOAA called for diminishing squalls until noon followed by rapid clearing. The wind would clock to north and drop below fifteen knots. Gulf seas now running five to seven feet would subside to five or less by midnight. Inland waters would remain choppy for another twenty-four hours.

Choppy seas I could handle. Five to seven foot ones? Not if I could avoid it.

Nearing the Buttonwood, my gaze took in the penthouse, the dung streaks below the parapet, and then the empty slip that had been mine for most of the last year. When my eyes swept the rest of the dock area, I saw the reason for my departure.

Angus was kneeling in *Mud Flats*, bailing rainwater over the stern with a scoop made from a plastic milk jug. Alongside him the catwalk was heaped with the assorted crap he normally kept in the boat. Was he just cleaning out this ancient craft? No. He was about to get underway for Hangman's Key.

Storms were a natural high for beachcombers, but with the sea still running as it was, I thought he was pushing his luck to try it in a flat-bottomed boat. Maybe a V-hull like *Skipjack* .... He looked up when he caught the sound of the *Margaret Ellen's* engines. I turned my eyes back to the channel but not before I saw recognition in his. My right hand flew to the throttles, yet instead of slamming them wide open, I gritted my teeth and continued holding a no-wake speed like a mature and responsible member of the boating community.

Gwen looked from Angus to me and back to him. "Hey, isn't that—"

"Hush!" I said.

"I'm sorry—"

"No! The radio. Listen."

I didn't mean to snap at her, but the *Fifth Amendment* had just made a call to the Coast Guard.

"This is Coast Guard group St. Petersburg, go ahead."

"Roger, St. Pete. I've just entered Tampa Bay by way of Southwest Channel. Be advised that bell buoy three is off station. Copy?"

"*Fifth Amendment*, Coast Guard group St. Petersburg. Copy bell buoy three off station in Southwest Channel. Coast Guard group St. Petersburg, clear."

During the exchange of transmissions I'd watched the signal-strength meter on the VHF. Coast Guard group St. Petersburg was a solid seven. The *Fifth Amendment* was pegging the needle. He was close.

Gwen fished a chart from the chart drawer, spread it on the console, and pointed out our position. "If he just passed where buoy three should've been, we can get to the main ship channel first." She gave me a wicked grin. "We should go look, huh?"

"You bet." I shoved the throttles forward and cocked a thumb behind us.

"You'll find a pair of binoculars under the pilot berth. Grab 'em and start panning the horizon."

We were still in a no-wake zone, and I usually played by the rules, but there were exceptions. Besides, once the *Margaret Ellen* was on step, her wake was minimal. Certainly less than the current chop pounding the adjacent seawalls lining the channel.

While Gwen searched for the binoculars, I tried some crystal balling.

After entering Tampa Bay by way of Southwest Channel, and bound for St. Petersburg, any vessel the size of the *Fifth Amendment* would pick up the main ship channel and then proceed under the high span of the Sunshine Skyway Bridge. We were closer to that span than the *Fifth Amendment* would be if the captain had promptly reported the missing buoy. But what if he'd delayed making his report? Simple. He would've already passed ahead of us.

If possible, I wanted to see the vessel, but would there be any great loss if I didn't? That is, the Coast Guard was supposed to notify the Pinellas County Sheriff's Office of any radio traffic from the *Fifth Amendment*. The two had just concluded an exchange, so if the Coast Guard radioman at St. Petersburg were as sharp as I wanted to believe, he would be on the phone with the sheriff's office right now.

But what if he wasn't?

"Got 'em," Gwen said, "and guess who got underway just after we passed the Buttonwood?"

I watched engine gauges and channel markers while explaining about the good beachcombing after a storm. The story was one I could've related on Monday at Hangman's Key. I hadn't bothered.

"So you think that's why he's right behind us?" she said.

I pondered her question. There was no way Angus could've known we would pass when we did. Therefore, he wasn't really following us. We'd had a storm. Now it was over. He was headed for Hangman's Key. Beachcombing. Nothing else.

And whether I liked it or not, his route to Hangman's Key would follow our wake until we entered Tampa Bay. At that point we'd take up a heading for the haul out yard; he'd take up a heading for Hangman's Key. But even if he didn't alter course, and was really trying to follow us, I had nothing to worry about. With the current conditions nothing with a flat bottom would keep up with the *Margaret Ellen*, certainly not *Mud Flats*.

Suddenly, the haze lifted. Gwen raised the binoculars and swept the bay from the Skyway Bridge to a point on our side of Southwest Channel.

"Nothing," she said. "Not even a pelican." She lowered the glasses and turned to me. "What now?"

Good question. The *Fifth Amendment's* radio signal had been strong, meaning he'd been close. Now he was gone. I could accept that or chase his invisible wake up the bay. And do what when we caught up? "I'm not sure," I said.

She tapped a finger on the VHF. "Shouldn't we call someone?"

Now she was reading my mind. The *Fifth Amendment* was arriving on schedule, but if something clandestine were afoot, the captain would never have called the Coast Guard to report a missing buoy. Still, as much as I knew we should call the sheriff, as a backup to the call the Coast Guard should've made, I was reluctant to use the radio. We heard him; he, or anyone else with a VHF radio, would hear us. And we'd promised our silence, on all aspects of the case, at least until noon.

"Well?" she said.

I explained my worry about using the marine radio. "But, you're right. There's a phone near the big fishing pier on Mullet Key. We'll pass on what we know to the sheriff and then we're out of it."

She pulled a quarter from her pocket, flipped it, caught it, and returned it to her pocket.

"What was that all about?" I said.

"While we're at a phone, I'll call the station."

I gave her a mother-to-naughty-daughter look.

She faked a pout. "I know," she said. "Info not to be released until noon."

At marker seven, I swung around the last spoil bank lining the channel and took up a west-southwest heading, running close along Mullet Key's Southern shoreline. With the frontal winds now out of the north-northwest, the water was calmer than the ditch had been.

Just before we entered another squall line, I spotted a huge freighter anchored offshore. This was smart, waiting for better visibility before entering the bay and trying to thread a small city through the gap beneath the new Skyway Bridge. New because in nineteen eighty a Tampa Bay pilot had tried to bring in a vessel under similar conditions. He failed, destroying one of the original spans and killing thirty-five people in the process.

When we passed out of the squall line, I took the binoculars and had her take the wheel while I glassed in the direction of Southwest Channel. There was still no boat traffic. I swung my attention to the fishing pier. No fishermen were in sight, but two vessels were tied alongside. One was a blue-and-white runabout. The other was a humongous yacht. I snatched the throttles back to an idle.

"What's wrong?" she said.

Handing her the glasses and taking the wheel, I said, "I think we've found the *Fifth Amendment*."

CHAPTER 30

Mullet Key had several fishing piers of various shapes and sizes. The one we were approaching on the Tampa Bay side was the largest and T-shaped as well. On most days the pier's length and breadth were crowded with fishermen, hoping to hook a big one, and swarms of tourists armed with cameras, elbowing for a closer shot of the action. Today was not typical. Except for the yacht and the runabout, the pier was deserted. Funny. Tourists were a fair-weather bunch, but I'd never thought fishermen would wash out because of a little storm.

"I can't see the yacht's name," Gwen said. "The runabout's in the way."

That had also been my problem. We'd have to get closer. I nudged the throttles, bringing the engines up to fifteen hundred rpm. "Keep watching," I said, "and sing out as soon as you see a name."

A commercial vessel, such as the *Margaret Ellen*, was required to display its name on the stern as well as both sides of the bow. A documented pleasure vessel was only required to display its name on the stern. A registered pleasure vessel, on the other hand, was under no requirement to display a name at all, only its current decal and registration number. In this case seeing only numbers on the vessel ahead would tell us nothing without a check with the Florida Department of Motor Vehicles. We needed to see a name, if the vessel displayed one. I eased closer.

"Nothing yet," she said.

If this were the *Fifth Amendment*, why had it stopped at the fishing pier? And how about the runabout? It was too large to have been towed from Northeast, certainly not through last night's storm. Trusting my reasoning, this meant the smaller vessel belonged to some fishermen and had no connection with the yacht. But, if so, where were these fishermen? "See anything yet?" I said.

"Nothing. Other than a few seagulls, the pier's clean."

"How about aboard either of the vessels?"

"Ah, there's something or someone aboard the runabout. I don't see anyone aboard the yacht." She lowered the glasses and turned to me. "What gives?"

I wondered the same thing. The problem was my thoughts ranged from ho-hum to ones causing me to shiver. From a hundred yards out I was certain the yacht was a Hatteras, but from our angle of approach, there was no way to determine its length. To know for sure we had to get closer.

"Okay," I said, "here's what we'll do. Get a bow and stern line ready and rig the starboard fenders. I'll pull alongside this end of the pier and stop well behind the runabout. You handle the bow line; I'll take the stern. When we have her snubbed, we'll amble down the dock, turn, and head for the phone. Call the sheriff first, then Dad, and then the Coast Guard. I'll watch. We get that far, you can jolly well call the station."

Docking went smoothly. So much so that an observer would have believed Gwen and I'd teamed together for ages. My previous years as captain would've been more fun if only Skip and I could've worked together as well. It rarely happened.

The *Margaret Ellen* pitched and rolled alongside the pier, but she didn't bump or scrape her topside. With the wind against her starboard hull and the fenders in place as added insurance, I figured she'd behave herself for the few minutes we'd be gone.

I straightened up and adjusted the hood of my rain gear, getting in a glance at the runabout and the yacht as I did. From close range it was easy to see the object Gwen had spotted aboard the runabout. The object was a someone, and from the size it was probably a kid. But where was Dad? No one else was in sight.

"Okay," I whispered, "let's go. Stay on my right and keep your head down. I'll peek at the transom when we pass. Then, straight to the phone."

The runabout was equipped with twin inboard/outboard engines. And while there was nothing unusual in this, the number of antennas planted on the stern was. I'd never seen so many on such a small vessel. Why so many radios? And why were the engines idling? The kid didn't look our way as we passed.

When we reached the gap between the runabout and the yacht, I glanced to my left. *Fifth Amendment.* "Bingo," I said. "Keep moving."

The yacht's boarding gate was centered at the end of the dock, a point we had to pass before turning and heading for shore. A voice called out Gwen's name as we started our turn. Before I could say, "Don't look," she did. When she sucked in breath, I looked as well.

Stan was at the yacht's boarding gate. He pulled a pistol from under his rain slicker. My gut tumbled. Dad had a pistol just like it: a military issue .45 automatic. Stan raised the pistol and aimed at Gwen. I pushed her as he fired.

She flew off the pier and into the water. Had he hit her? Did it matter? In full foul-weather gear she didn't have much chance against drowning. And neither did I if I jumped in behind her. Stan swung the pistol toward me as I charged him.

I drove my shoulder into him at belt level, propelling him back across the deck and into the main salon. Confidence surged in me as I felt his body give before my strength. We crashed to the floor. This was no time for scratching and pulling hair. I cocked a fist and sent a blow into his face. Blood spurted from his nose. In a blur I saw the pistol in his right hand arcing toward my head. I felt it slam against my left temple and then heard the thundering roar as the pistol fired.

An article on death by firing squad was running through my mind when I woke. The author had written that death was instantaneous and the condemned suffered no pain. I'd always wanted to believe that, maybe for the sake of the condemned, or maybe for my own, as I had a very low threshold for pain. Now I knew the article was bullshit. I'd been shot and the pain felt like I was doing overtime in hell.

The engines were screaming at full-throttle, and the vessel was pounding in heavy seas, bouncing my body on the sole carpeting with each slam of the hull. Had the carpet always been red, or was I seeing my own blood? Where was the vessel headed? I rolled my face. The helm was in the blurry distance. No one was at the wheel. Where was Avery?

A violent pitch sent me sliding closer to the helm. I heard cavitations as the twin propellers cleared the water. She was in trouble. So was I if I didn't do something.

I reached for my temple but felt only loose flesh. Bile raced up my throat. I retched then stared at the carpet until the sickness faded. A gagging taste remained in my mouth. I tried to stand. The next slam of the bow pitched me forward onto my hands and knees.

The helm was now a body length away. *Don't stand. Crawl. Closer now.* I clutched the wheel, using it as a crutch, and pulled myself to my knees. My legs wouldn't straighten. They were too weak. I sat back on my heels. *Breathe deep. Rest. Now try again.*

Sitting as I was I could feel the vessel plowing and hear the propeller cavitations. Why was she running bow down? I studied the breaker panel alongside the helm. All the pump circuits were off. The bastard had opened the seacocks. We were sinking. *Get up or go down. Got to try.*

I wedged myself between the helm and captain's chair and wiggled to my feet. A wave of dizziness swept me. I dropped into the seat, hanging on to the wheel for balance until the spell of lightheadedness passed. *Okay. Better. Now figure it out.*

The vessel was in trouble. I could hear it and feel it. But all I had to do was head for shore or find a sandbar, anything so I could run her aground and prevent her from sinking. But which way should I turn? The compass was spinning wildly. I tugged at the wheel. It wouldn't move. Was it stuck? No. The autopilot was engaged and I didn't have the strength to override it. Where was the control? I searched the console. Nothing was familiar. I looked up. All I could see was a rusty, red wall. I wiped blood from my eyes. Nothing changed. The wall was still there. Then, there was nothing.

CHAPTER 31

S ome stuff," as Dad once said, "stays etched in your memory."
This was one of those times, as I didn't have to open my eyes to
know I was in a hospital. It had been ten years since that single,
overnight stay, but I'd never forgotten the impersonal sounds or the pungent
scents of birth and death and the diverse odors residing between the extremes
of each.

For me that overnighter was at the Bayfront Medical Center almost
immediately after Dad discovered the problem I'd been hiding for days. The
tip-off was his little Miss Motor Mouth had fallen silent. Off we went to the
family doctor.

After looking down my throat with the aid of a chunk of wood resembling
a Popsicle stick, Dr West said, "This young lady needs her tonsils out."

By this time my throat was too sore for me to speak, but I could do a
fantastic no-no shake of my head. Not that it mattered. Dad took me into
Bayfront early the next morning and had me back home the following
afternoon. If he left my side, except during the operation or trips to the
bathroom, I was never aware of it.

Was I at Bayfront again? There was no way to know, as nothing in the
room provided a clue. Did I really care where I was, or how I gotten there,
for that matter? No! That I was still among the living, not crab bait at the
bottom of the Gulf as Eva had been, was all that mattered.

I was alone in a small room with an acoustic-tile ceiling heavily dotted
with recessed-lighting panels. All were glowing with the intensity of noonday
sun. The oyster-white walls, above a mahogany wainscoting, gleamed like
lawn frost. The floor was imitation tile, the one-foot square variety heavily
flecked with slivers of gray and gold. Wal-Mart, in Sunshine Mall, had a
floor just like it.

A small cubicle occupied one corner of the room. Through the partially
open door, I saw a vanity with a mirror above it. This was probably the
bathroom. The thought triggered a new ache. The hall door was wider than a
johnboat and was held open with a stainless-steel foot wearing a worn crutch
tip. Foot traffic traipsed by the door at odd intervals—singles, pairs, and a

herd at times.

A raised table on hard-rubber wheels was parked to one side of the bed. Some items on its polished metal top looked benign; others did not. A pair of plastic-bottomed chairs, both with chrome legs, were positioned like lost children in the center of the room. One chair held a newspaper; the other a magazine with half its cover missing.

The head of my bed was inclined slightly, and except for my arms I was covered to my neck with a sheet starched beyond the flexibility of plywood. I wiggled my toes, rolled my feet, and then lifted my knees. From the waist down I was whole with all parts working. Had I left it there and not lifted the sheet, I'd have been spared the sight of the catheter plumbing. Yuk. To make matters worse my thirty-second checkout left me feeling as if I'd just completed an hour-long aerobics session.

Tired is okay, I reminded myself. Dead is not.

With that part of my inspection complete, I inspected my arms. The good part was they were both still there. The bad part was both were bandaged above and below the elbows. The more bad part was the flesh not covered by bandages was discolored, streaked in shades from rotting tangerine to the black-and-blue of rotting grapes. And there was additional bruising around the needle inserted into the back of my hand.

Bruises, even rotten-looking ones, were okay. Funerals sucked.

My eyes were fine and I was breathing okay. My head, however, felt like it'd been used as a stand-in for the piece of luggage they use in that TV commercial, the one where they demonstrate a suitcase's durability by heaving it off the top of a high-rise apartment building. At least my head was still in one piece, unlike the *other brand* of luggage they toss from the top of the same building.

Yeah. Hurt was okay. Smashed to bits was a bitch.

The sober thought, however, was wondering what condition my head was really in. That is, if it hadn't all been a bad dream, I remembered the bullet wound at my temple. I also remembered the wound being large enough to swallow my index finger when I tried a damage-assessment probe. That just before I retched. I was about to risk another check, and probable retch, when I heard the out-of-this-world, wonderful sound of Dad's voice. A moment later he and a slender young man wearing doctor garb stepped into the room.

"Ah! Awake." This revelation was from the doctor as he took a stethoscope from his shirt pocket.

I opened my mouth, but nothing happened. I nodded instead.

"Can't speak?" These words from the doctor again, as he quickly stepped to the side of the bed.

I made another attempt to speak, but my mouth felt drier than butterless popcorn. My eyes cut from Dad to the pitcher of water on the table alongside my bed.

He sprang into action. "She wants water," Dad said. "Outta the way." He pushed by the doctor, poured a glassful from a stainless steel pitcher, equipped the glass with one of those dogleg straws, and held it to my mouth.

God! I loved him.

Two sips fattened my tongue. Most of the third dribbled down my chin. I licked my lips and managed to make words with my next attempt. "Gwen?" I said. "Stan shot her. Is she …?"

Dad brushed his eyes with the backs of his hands. "No," he said. "She's fine. You're both going to be fine. Let the doc do his thing, baby, then we'll talk."

Running away was not an option, so I let the doc do his thing—mostly looks and probes of my arms, chest, face, and head, followed by an eye examination under the beam of a weenie-size flashlight. After ten minutes of such, punctuated with little coughs and throat clearing I read as "good" and "not good," he scurried from the room with a, "Five minutes, Mr. Cobia."

Dad grabbed a chair, the one with the newspaper, and brought it close alongside the bed. He sat with a sigh that would've blown out birthday-cake candles at fifty feet. "It's not good to do this to your dad, baby."

I tried to smile, but my cheeks felt stiff as cardboard. Maybe it was because of the way my head was wrapped. "Sorry," I whispered.

The doctor had dismissed worry about the minor wounds to my arms and chest. "Scrapes and nicks," he called them. None required stitching. The catheter and IV would be removed shortly. My head wound was another matter. I'd asked "How serious?" but the doctor was evasive—downright noncommittal, actually. Dad would've asked the same question. He wouldn't have accepted the same answer. I clutched the water glass and stared into his eyes. "My head, Dad. Tell me. How bad?"

He tried for a grin. "Would you believe you wrecked your hairdo?"

"Dad! You know I haven't had a hairdo since senior prom. How bad?"

The partial grin faded. "The bullet tore up some flesh above your ear," he said. "Took a few stitches to close it up."

I could handle stitches. "Having a hard head paid off for once, huh?"

"Yeah," he said, "but … "

My gut tightened. "But what?"

"Nothing now, baby. Your hair'll grow back and hide the scar, but it could've been more than a mild concussion. If the gun barrel had been tipped a fraction more, the bullet would've hit your skull. The result could've been memory loss, maybe even a coma, or …."

Thankfully, he didn't add "death." I didn't either.

My head felt like something the Marlins had used for batting practice, but my memory was fine up to the moment I tackled Avery. After that, events were fuzzy. I told Dad the story as I remembered it. "I may have woken up after that, or maybe it was just a dream."

"What do you remember?"

"Lots of stuff, but it's all kind of stupid. The yacht was pounding through rough seas, but the bow was dipping much too low. You know, plowing, as if she were taking on water. I thought of the pumps. The breaker panel was near the helm. The circuits feeding the pumps were off, but I couldn't reach them. We were going down if I didn't beach her first. I crawled up the helm. Then I didn't know which way to turn. All I could see was a rusty, red wall. I wiped blood from my eyes but the wall was still there. Now I'm here." I tried to shrug. My shoulders wouldn't buy it. "Dumb, huh?"

"Your memory's just fine." This time Dad didn't brush away the tears. "Baby, that rusty wall was an anchored freighter. You broadsided it."

An anchored freighter? Yeah, the good guy waiting for better conditions before entering the bay. But how had the yacht managed to hit it?

Dad glanced at his watch. "I'd better hurry," he said. "My five minutes are up."

"I don't care. Don't go. Not yet. Gwen? Tell me the truth, Dad. Is she—"

"Just like I said. Your shove probably saved her life. The bullet missed, but, dressed as she was, she might have drowned if Angus hadn't been right behind you. He saw her go in and was able to fish her out."

Dad paused while I sucked up more moisture. "Then what?" I said.

"Well by the time he had her aboard *Mud Flats*, the yacht was under way. Gwen gave Angus the rundown on what was happening and while he gave chase, she called the Coast Guard on his VHF."

"Dad, how could he chase in those seas?"

"Right then I don't imagine he could see 'em. He knew Gwen should've been dead, and he was convinced you were. He wanted Stan's ass. They were chasing but losing ground when they saw the runabout pull away from the yacht and start south across the bay. The yacht continued tracking west, out the ship channel and into the Gulf. Angus knew he'd never catch it, so the ballsy fool rammed the runabout."

"Rammed it! Jesus! Is he hurt?"

Dad nodded and said, "Yeah, he's banged up a bit. Broke his left arm in two places. Collarbone. Some ribs. Punctured a lung. His room's down the hall."

In the past Dad had never hid his dislike of Angus. Now I was hearing a tone of admiration as Dad detailed Angus's efforts. "What happened to Stan and Amber?" I said.

"Stan didn't make it. Sliced in half by the impact. They recovered part of him. One of the props, probably *Mud Flats*', chewed Amber from her knees to her face. She'll live but she won't be pretty. Gwen was thrown clear. A Coast Guard chopper was picking them up when the yacht slammed into the freighter."

"But how? You said the yacht headed into the open Gulf. I remember seeing the freighter. It was anchored close in."

"A piece of luck," Dad said. "From the moment Stan and Amber left the yacht, it began a slow turn to starboard. Made a full circle. If he'd set the autopilot …."

I remembered my moments at the helm, trying to turn the wheel. "No," I said, "it was lucky he did set it." I told Dad that Myers had mentioned the bad autopilot on the *Fifth Amendment* when he asked me what a sea trial was. Stan had not risked the time to replace it. Had he done so, the yacht would've continued tracking into the Gulf until she went down. The pump switches were off and she was riding bow low in the water. I hadn't dreamed that. It happened. That meant the bastard had opened the seacocks and aimed me for a watery grave before jumping ship.

"How about the *Margaret Ellen*?" I said. "We only had the fenders and two lines on her."

"Boat yard crew picked her up. Not a scratch."

"And the delivery captain?"

An enormous woman wearing a nurses' uniform entered the room and said, "Time's up, Mr. Cobia"

Dad stood and reached for my hand.

I looked from him to the sunbeam slanting through the window. It had inched toward the bed since I woke. I didn't need an almanac to know my window faced west and it was now afternoon. But what time? My watch, along with everything else I'd been wearing, was gone. I asked.

"It's two, baby. But it's Saturday afternoon. You've been unconscious for over thirty hours."

CHAPTER 32

A nd unconscious, as I soon learned, was where I was headed again. The behemoth disguised as a nurse sailed through the pulse, temperature, and blood pressure routine and then handed me some pills and a glass of water.

I held both, staring at her.

"I'm bigger than you," she said.

Valid point. I took the pills, followed by a ride on the bedpan after she'd removed the catheter and IV. Then, I was *out*.

When I woke the room was dark except for the glow spilling from the cubicle I knew was a bathroom. Until now it was also a room I couldn't have used because of my hookup to the auxiliary plumbing. Now I was free and I had to go, but I'd be damned before doing another pan job. After easing the nurse's call button aside, I inched my legs from beneath the covers. With both hands locked to the bed frame, I stood. Bright stars floated across my vision. When the dizzy feeling passed, I whispered, "You can do this."

Despite some upper-body stiffness and the feeling my head was still a time zone behind the rest of me, the stroll to the bathroom went well. The crying jag erupted when I looked at myself in the wall mirror. I knew my head was bandaged, but no one had bothered to tell me about the black eyes and assorted bruises on my face and neck.

My cry started with the soft tears of self-pity, cranked up to full-blown wails, and wound down with a number of why-me sobs. Then, anger set in. I wet a washcloth and dabbed at my face and eyes. "You're alive," I said to the horrid-looking me in the mirror. "You *will* heal." In thought, I again reminded myself that the worst bruise was better than the best funeral.

The cool dampness of the cloth felt refreshing against my face. I leaned against the wall, eyes closed, letting my mind's eye see myself healed. When I removed the cloth and looked into the mirror, the bruises looked darker. I flung the washcloth into the basin and shuffled to the hall door.

The corridor to the left was empty, just more rooms until it dead-ended at a pair of doors marked, "Emergency Exit." To the right was a nurse's station, which seemed to be centered at the junction of four hallways. Better to thwart escape, no doubt. On the soffit above the four-sided counter, a large-face clock read, three fifty-five a.m. Female voices, in a soft, conversational tone, were the only sounds. I wanted to seek them out, but my reward for doing so would probably be another fistful of pills.

At the moment I looked dumpier than a mudslide, but I was awake and alert. I wanted to stay that way.

The newspaper was still on one of the chairs. I lugged it to the bed and clicked on the lamp. My face looked back at me from the front page. Funny. I hadn't been half-bad looking before I was shot and my body hurled against a tanker's hull. I crawled into bed, figuring I'd pushed my freedom far enough for a first outing.

My photo was one of five covering half the front page under the giant-print headline: Killers-Hero-Heroines. The photos were positioned, left-to-right, just above their appropriate caption: Stan Avery, Amber Brantley, Angus Loman, Gwen O'Dell, and me, Karen Cobia. I didn't feel slighted for being last in the gruesome lineup. Hell, I didn't want to be there at all.

Before I could get into the lead article, a nurse stepped into the room. This gal was my size. Friendly too. After taking my pulse, blood pressure, and temperature, she was gone. No pills. She didn't even think it strange that I was reading the paper at four in the morning.

At six, when she returned for another round of checks, I was still holding the paper. Dad had neglected telling me a few things.

Most of the coverage was old news. Separate articles detailed Eva's background and the social realm she'd traveled in. Another outlined the sordid lives of Sculley and Betty Kilgore. One asked how a prominent attorney and a beautiful socialite could've steered their lives to such an end.

"Greed," was my answer.

An article titled "Body Count" answered my question about the yacht's delivery captain. He and his mate had been shot to death. Both bodies were found in the yacht's master stateroom. The final tally, then, stood at six: Eva, Sculley, Betty, a delivery captain, his mate, and Stan. The article's slant seemed to begrudge its final line: "Amber Brantley, Angus Loman, and Karen Cobia are expected to recover."

The *St. Petersburg Times* gave Gwen credit for much of the coverage, but it was a horn-tooting statement by her station manager that knotted my gut. Gwen was the station's star reporter; her coverage was story-of-the-year material; and she was a shoo-in for the next anchor position. I tossed the paper to the floor.

Daylight filled the room an hour before my next round of checks at eight a.m. At nine the same doctor I'd met the day before put me through another look-and-probe examination. This time the ordeal was accompanied by fewer coughs and throat clearing. I took this as good news. It was. Sort of. He didn't give me an answer as to when I could go home, but he did grant bathroom privileges before leaving the room.

Breakfast arrived. The quality was more than I expected, and normally I would've packed it all away and asked for extra juice and coffee. Not now. Nothing looked appetizing. I picked through a bowl of mixed fruit, arranging apple slices as walls for a miniature house and using orange and pineapple wedges for a roof. A delicate cube of papaya served as a chimney. I licked my fingers. Later, I ate the little house, closed my eyes, and drifted into thought. At some point I fell asleep.

When I woke, Dad was sitting next to the bed holding the newspaper I'd thrown on the floor. Sunshine was touching the windowsill. That meant it was afternoon. It also meant I'd slept a week's worth of sleep in the previous forty-eight hours. I worked the button raising the head of the bed. "What time is it?"

"Almost one," Dad said. "How're you doing?"

"Fine!" I said. "Just hot damned fine!"

"Sounds otherwise. What is it?"

I pointed at the paper on his lap. "The Princess of Channel Five. That's what. You know I have a charter Wednesday. I have to get out of here and find a new mate."

"No," he said, leaning forward and patting my hand. "Right now the only thing you have to do is sit still and listen."

I'd always read Dad as easily as roadside billboards. The current message was clear: "Do as I say." I nodded.

"First," he said, "you don't need to find a new mate. Yesterday's paper had a statement from Gwen's boss. Today's has a statement from her. In very few words she suggested an appropriate slot for him to stick his anchor."

Dad set the newspaper aside, scooped ice into a glass, topped it with orange juice, and nestled it into my hands.

I sipped.

"Next," he said, "our doctor will be here at ten in the morning. That means you'll be here, too. Barring a setback in your condition, I think he'll let me take you home after his exam. But until he says you're healed, and I mean completely healed, you will *not* be at the helm of the *Margaret Ellen*."

"Dad!"

"Don't argue. Patty will stay and help for as long as it takes for you to get better. She and Cecil will run the shop. Gwen and I'll handle the charters."

"How about Skip?" I said.

"Wonder of wonders. It took a year, but the Air Force finally accepted the kid. He leaves Wednesday for basic training."

Regardless of branch of service, I knew basic training meant taking orders. Skip? Never happen. "And Cynthia?"

"We're on hold," he said. "You come first. She has to accept that."

Has to accept it?

He stood and sorted through the stack of newspapers on the cart at the side of the bed. What he handed me was the A-section of the *Times*. "You and Gwen didn't make today's headlines, but you're both on the front page again."

"Where're you going?"

"Take care of the paperwork," he said. "I don't want any last-minute surprises. I'll be back. In the meanwhile, the waiting room's full of folks screaming to see you."

"Full? Who?"

"Right now it's Patty, Skip, Cecil, Roxie, and Gwen. Myers swung through. Said he'd be back for evening visiting hours. You feel up to seeing them?"

"I can handle it," I said.

"Even Skip?"

That I'd come so close to never seeing any of them again made it easy to say, "Even Skip."

I opened the paper but didn't have time to read a word before the flood of beautiful faces filled my room. This bunch was not playing by the one-visitor-at-a-time rule. With Aunt Patty *and* Roxie in the pack, I didn't see anyone— even my nemesis, the behemoth nurse—putting up a challenge.

Other than the fact I was flat on my back, I felt like a hostess in a greeting line.

Skip stepped forward first. He held my hand for a long moment and then kissed my cheek. I wished him the best of luck in the Air Force, and also reminded him we all took orders until we were qualified to give them.

The tears in Aunt Patty's eyes triggered a new flood of my own. I thanked her for staying on to help Dad.

Cecil, with cane in hand and a single bandage covering his knee, stated that any dime-store captain could hit an anchored freighter. "But," he added, rapping his cane against the bed rail for emphasis, "hitting a speeding runabout with a worm-eaten mullet boat, that's seamanship." I promised to let him help hone my boating skills.

Roxie delivered three hugs—one each from her, Steve, and Lou Ann. Then with a wink and dimpled grin, she slipped me a grease-stained bag of fried onion rings. A certificate attached to the bag entitled the bearer, me, to a lifetime supply of Shanley's famous steak-and-onion hoagies. The woman made a big mistake.

Gwen waited until the others filed out of the room before approaching the bed.

In a matter of minutes on Friday morning, we'd each cheated death. In her case the bullet that missed her could just as well have killed her; my shove, saving her from a bullet, could have caused her drowning; or she could've been killed like Stan or horribly mutilated like Amber when Angus rammed the runabout.

In my case the bullet that wounded could also have killed. And without the quick action of the freighter's crew, I would've gone down with the *Fifth Amendment*.

We didn't boo-hoo as we talked. For me, that crying would come later, when my mind finally accepted the reality of my near-death. I expected it would for her as well.

"The rotten thing is," she said, "if the delivery captain hadn't radioed the Coast Guard about the missing buoy, Stan would've pulled it off."

"Where'd you come up with that idea?"

"Myers," she said.

"Another scenario, no doubt."

"No. He got it from Amber. She's talking like a pull-string doll. And dumping all the blame on Stan, of course."

"What about the buoy?" I said.

"I'll get to that, but get this. Stan stayed in radio contact with the yacht from the moment it left Northeast."

"So I was right about the sideband radio."

"Yeah," she said, "there was one aboard the runabout. Remember the antennae farm on the stern?"

I remembered.

"Stan asked the delivery captain to stop at the fishing pier under the pretense of wanting to ride along for the balance of the trip into the St. Petersburg Marina. He then killed the captain and mate. Next he was going to put a number of his and Amber's personal effects aboard. You know, stuff that would float and be found. Once he had the yacht headed for the open Gulf, he'd turn off the pumps and open the seacocks. He and Amber would get into the runabout and send a distress message to the Coast Guard saying the yacht was going down. While rescue attention was centered on the yacht, he and Amber would head for his plane and fly out of the country."

I shook my head. "No, that wouldn't work. Myers said they were watching Stan's plane."

"Yes, but Stan anticipated that. Myers's stakeout has been watching the wrong plane. A few weeks ago Stan moved his plane to a strip near the bay in Manatee County and sub-leased his hanger. That's why Stan was headed south across the bay when Angus hit him."

"The call to the Coast Guard about the buoy was no big deal then. Stan could still have made his plan work, but we dropped in."

"Exactly," she said. "Unfortunately, even with the binoculars I couldn't see him behind the yacht's tinted glass, but he could see us approaching. He recognized me when we started for the phone."

I didn't want to relive what happened next. "So with Stan dead," I said, "Amber can whitewash her involvement and walk. That it?"

"No way. She was in the runabout. And she followed in it while Stan aimed the yacht for the Gulf. Angus and I saw her pick up Stan after he jumped off the stern of the yacht. She wasn't an unwilling captive. She was a willing accomplice."

"But Amber didn't actually kill anyone."

"Maybe. Myers has a scenario—"

"Enough! I never want to hear another of his scenarios. What's done is done. As far as I'm concerned, my boat accident investigation business went down with the *Fifth Amendment*. All I want is to be back at the helm of the *Margaret Ellen*. And when I am, I want us to work at being the best damned charter crew out of Big Tarpon Pass. Maybe the entire West Coast of Florida."

"We'll do it," she said, giving me a high-five. "But right now I need a favor."

"What is it?"

"Well, after I told my boss where to stick his anchor slot, he told me where to shove my two-week notice."

"He wouldn't accept it?"

"Just the opposite. He told me to turn in my gear and hit the bricks."

"So what's the favor?" I said.

"I'm going to start work with your dad on Wednesday. I know it'll be crowded, but until I can find a place close by, could I bunk aboard your sloop?"

"Of course," I said. "And don't worry about crowded. You'll have the sloop all to yourself. Dad set up my old bedroom. I'll be under his eye in the bait shop."

"Thanks. Ah, there's something else."

"Name it," I said.

"It's not a favor, exactly, it concerns Angus."

"Oh?"

"You told me what happened ... that night, but there's something you don't know."

"You've talked with him?"

"Yes," she said. "But this came from his sister, Angie. She was with him that night."

"Did you ask the bitch how long she'd been carrying on an incestuous relationship with her brother?"

"It wasn't that way, Seaweed."

"Gwen, I was there. I know what I saw."

"Yes," she said, "but you didn't understand what it meant. It took guts for Angie to tell me about it. Please listen. After that, if you still want to be mad at him, at least you'll know the truth. Okay?"

"I can hardly wait."

Gwen scooted her chair closer. "Angie admits being the black sheep of the family. And quite frankly, after talking with her, she's not a person I'd want as a friend. She's an alcoholic and she's never worked at anything except exotic dancing."

How about whoring? I wanted to ask.

"She's been married and divorced four times. Two kids by her last husband."

"Where's your violin?" That I did ask.

"You're going to hear this, Seaweed."

"Yeah, like I have a choice."

"She's not proud of herself, but she loves Angus. And not in the way you think. For years he's begged her to fly right. She never tried. When he came into the lotto money, he tried to buy things right for her."

"Buy? What do you mean?"

"Angus bought her a new home and toys of all kinds for the kids. Paid for a private school. Gave her money. Enough so she didn't have to work at all, but she has this thing about dancing. She won't quit. You've seen her face, her body. She'd never make Hollywood even if she were a good dancer, which she admits she's not. And that's the rub. That's what set up what you saw."

"I saw him fondling her."

"Not exactly fondling. She told me that at the club where she works the women with the largest breasts get the largest tips. She wanted breast implants. Angus tried to talk her out of it, but when she wouldn't give up on the idea, he paid for the operation."

"So his playing with them was payback. That it?"

"No. She was teasing him when you saw them, telling him they felt just like the real thing. She dared him to touch them. You know he did so, but Angie told me he didn't want to."

"Great!" I said. "Then he's turned on and they make a trip to the penthouse."

"Not even close. Angie lives in Tampa, near the club where she works. The father of her kids lives in Pinellas Park. She visited Angus that day for two reasons. The first was to thank him for paying for her breast implants. The second was to ask Angus to lean on her ex-husband. The guy was a year behind in child support. He's now caught up."

"That doesn't explain the trip to the penthouse," I said.

"To pick up her kids. Angus paid a baby-sitter to watch them while they visited the ex-husband."

"Gwen, I also know they were together at the Rudder Bar. Did she happen to explain that crap?"

"As a matter of fact, yes. Angie said Angus wanted to see Gambino."

"The bartender?"

"Yes, Angus told her you two were having a fish and hush puppy dinner the following evening. Gambino makes your favorite hot sauce. Angus stopped to pick up some."

CHAPTER 33

Myers entered my room a full hour after evening visiting hours ended. Power of the shield, I figured. He had a few questions.

He: "Were you underway Friday morning for any reason other than to move the *Margaret Ellen* to the haul-out yard?"

I: "No."

He: "Did you have knowledge of the *Fifth Amendment's* position prior to hearing the radio transmission between the delivery captain and the Coast Guard?"

I: "No."

He: "You then proceeded to the fishing pier for the purpose of notifying authorities of what you'd overheard?"

I: "Yes."

He: "Did you see anyone else aboard the yacht before tackling Stan?"

I: "No."

He: "Did you see the bodies of the delivery captain and his mate after you were aboard?"

I: "No."

Myers tucked his notepad into his shirt pocket. "That jives with Gwen's statement up to the time she hit the water the first time." He smiled, the best looking one I'd ever seen cross his face, "I'm glad you're both among the living."

"We came close to not being," I said.

He pulled one of the chairs to the side of the bed and sat. I took this as meaning the official part of his visit was over. "For you," he said, "maybe closer than you know."

"What do you mean?"

"A .45 automatic has an eight-round capacity if you load seven in the magazine and then drop another into the chamber. Add up the shots: One each for Eva, Sculley, and the miss on Gwen; then two each for the captain and mate. You were hit with the eighth round. The pistol was empty or he might have finished you off instead of believing you'd go down with the yacht."

"How comforting. Gwen said you thought Amber might be in on some of the killing."

"Proving it might be a problem."

"No witnesses. Right?"

"That too, but what has me thinking she did is this: Eva, Sculley, and Betty were all killed by one shot to the head. The shot that missed Gwen was aimed at her head, and that's also where you were hit. But the captain and mate were each shot twice in the chest. The difference makes me think a different finger pulled the trigger."

Dead was dead, was the way I saw it. "Good luck proving it," I said. "How about Eva's jewelry? Did any of the pieces turn up?"

"Amber said two pouches of jewelry were aboard the runabout. We didn't find them in the wreckage or on either piece of Stan's body."

I winced. Dad had mentioned pieces.

"My guess," he said, "is they're somewhere out there on the bay bottom."

Myers departed at ten p.m., just moments before my night nurse arrived to interrogate my vital signs. She returned at midnight, at two, and again at four. Another nurse, one I hadn't seen before, performed the now-familiar tasks at six. Sometime between midnight and two, I may have dozed.

I ambled to the bathroom and washed my face. The massive shiner below my left eye was as dark as ever, but it'd lost some of its puffiness. The other bruises, although still visible, had lost size as well.

In self-admonishment, I'd told myself, you *will* heal. Now I whispered, "You *are* healing." I winked at the better looking me in the mirror and returned to bed.

Dawn was softening the stark shadows outside the window. I was thankful to be alive, to be sharing the birth of a new day, but I was also anxious about what would happen in the hours ahead. The same worry had kept me awake most of the night.

What I'd refused to worry about, though, was my return to the helm of the *Margaret Ellen*. It would happen. Tears and self pity wouldn't make it happen sooner.

Dad and Cynthia was another item weighing heavy in my thoughts. I hated to believe what had happened to me could have caused a problem between them. Maybe it was his sudden switch of time and attention from her to me. If so, I could identify with her jealousy, but I also knew that right now Dad was being Dad, as I'd always known him. I hoped she understood.

The biggest reason for my sleepless night, however, was Angus. He wasn't guilty of what I'd thought. For this I owed him an apology. The trouble was, an apology wouldn't right what had been going wrong even before finding Eva's body. In fact, could anything make it right?

I heard a whirring sound in the hall. The noise stopped at my door. It was Angus sitting in a motorized wheelchair. His left arm, from wrist to shoulder, was in a cast and held at an awkward-looking angle with a grotesque wire arrangement. His upper body was wrapped from chest to naval. I saw an inch of suntanned flesh before the rest of his body disappeared into pajama bottoms. Black stubble covered his face but not his wickedly handsome smile. This wasn't going to be easy.

"May I come in?" he said.

I opened my mouth but only managed to nod.

He parked alongside the bed. Before he could speak, I touched a finger to his lips and said, "Me first."

He took my hand and held it against his cheek. "You don't have to say anything."

"I have to say I'm sorry."

At ten, when Dad, Cynthia, and Dr. Baker entered the room, Angus and I were still holding hands. We'd been renegotiating.

EPILOGUE

At 0500 Wednesday morning, I joined Dad, Gwen, and Cecil for breakfast at Shanley's. Later, as dawn was breaking over the pass, I watched the *Margaret Ellen* get underway. I didn't move until she was out of sight. The pain-wrapped knot in my gut hurt worse than the residual pain of my injuries. When would I be at her helm? Dr. Baker said a week. Ten days at the outside.

I spent most of the morning moping around the bait shop, pacing the patio, and bottom fishing for catfish from the sea wall. Before noon I'd had enough and headed for *Skipjack*. Her tanks were full. I started the engine and tossed off her lines.

When reaching the lee side of Hangman's Key, I slowed *Skipjack* to an idle, shivering, despite the midday heat. I'd anchored here only ten days ago. Or had it been a lifetime?

Off to my right a dozen runabouts were scattered over the grass flats, their occupants laughing and drinking and plugging for speckled trout. Beyond them in the main ship channel, *Miss Texaco* was bound for her unloading berth at Port Tampa. I watched until she made the final course change before sliding under the Sunshine Skyway Bridge and entering Tampa Bay.

At the north end of the island I picked up deeper water and turned west toward the Gulf, paralleling the same route Angus and I'd walked hand-in-hand that horrible Monday just over a week ago. Ahead, lazy surf spilled over a sandbar created by the last storm. The next storm would wipe the bar away, but for now access to the Gulf by way of Hangman's Key Channel was impossible.

At the Gulf side of the island, I turned south, keeping to the deeper water close behind the sandbar and avoiding the second curl of surf washing up on the white sand beach. Except for a pair of gulls and scattered patches of seaweed drying in the sun, the beach was deserted.

I idled on, praying the sandbar would close with the beach and prevent me from reaching the spot morbid curiosity had compelled me to return to. The sun danced on the wave tops and burned at my body, but the sandbar continued.

Once abreast of the *spot*, my eyes swung to the beach, searching for a sign. The golden patches of sea oats clinging to life among the endless dunes and the cone-heavy tops of the towering Australian pines were swaying to the rhythmic pulse of the onshore breeze, but all trace of the death we'd found here was gone. Washed clean by wind and water. I felt better about that, as I hit the throttle and headed for Big Tarpon Pass.

At four, Cynthia and I'd shop for her wedding dress. At seven, and until thrown out, I'd visit Angus. We'd agreed to bury the past and try again, starting with a new *first* date after his recovery. No beachcombing this time, just a dive trip.

There'd been a bag of jewelry worth three million dollars aboard Stan's runabout when it went down. Angus remembered the exact spot.

Printed in the United States
20473LVS00008B/52